. . . something with the air lamps, which seemed to dim strangely; and a sound in Bet's ears, like a roaring of wind. Magic, she thought, starting to her feet, seeing Eia staring at her oddly, seeing Delan seem to fly across the room, wings spread, all expression blanked out of ids face, seeing the Lan's wine cup float into the air and land, slowly, spewing wine onto the priceless carpet. And Delan, grasping Eia and throwing id physically aside, throwing idreself on top of idre, spreading ids bright, bright wings to cover id, like a parent protecting a young child from the cold wind. And the Lan, a horrible, hoarse scream gutting out of his mouth, twisting in a weird dance across the delicate designs of the carpet, screaming and screaming, clawing mindlessly at his body, as if he wanted to jerk out his very bones.

His bones were on fire. How strange, thought Bet, how very strange. And she could see a thin thread of fire, which ran from the Lan, through the ceiling, and into the sky. How strange, thought Bet, that she could see through the ceiling like that. And where did the thread go? She tried to follow it, but she could not fly without her Wing. So she started across the room toward the Lan instead, who continued his maddened, screaming dance, past his shocked and paralyzed advisors, past the servant who had frozen with the cakes sliding slowly off the tray and onto the floor. If she could cut the thread, she thought. . . .

In a spray of guts and hot blood and fried flesh and shattered bone, the Lan's body exploded.

LAURIE J. MARKS
in DAW Books:

THE CHILDREN OF TRIAD

ARA'S FIELD

LAURIE J. MARKS

DAW BOOKS, INC.
DONALD A. WOLLHEIM, FOUNDER
375 Hudson Street, New York, NY 10014

ELIZABETH R. WOLLHEIM
SHEILA E. GILBERT
PUBLISHERS

First Printing, May 1991

1 2 3 4 5 6 7 8 9

DAW TRADEMARK REGISTERED
U.S. PAT. OFF. AND FOREIGN COUNTRIES
——MARCA REGISTRADA,
HECHO EN U.S.A.

PRINTED IN THE U.S.A.

Prologue

Many-bodied, many-voiced, the Mer herd sang one endless, never repeating, never ending song. They sang of all they loved, and of all they remembered; of mating, birth and death, of journeys and seasons, of sea caves and underwater volcanoes, of light and dark. They sang of the sun and the moons dancing beyond the liquid surface of their world. They sang of ships they had seen, of encounters with other herds, of more rare encounters with the other thinking people who inhabit the larger Universe. The Mers sang of what they knew. They did not ask what more there was to learn.

They were one people, one mind, born out of the primordial darkness of the earth's beginning, swimming through time as if it were water: unchanging, unforgetting, and in their own way immortal. They were the people of the sea, as ancient as the water in which they swam.

In the autumn, the changing currents shifted in their blood, and they followed the ocean southward, until they came at last to a warm, shallow sea rimmed with golden and red coral and blooming with plants and fish and the many small creatures which scuttled or crept across the ocean floor. In the spring, the currents shifted again, washing the warm sea in a bath of cold northern water, shriveling the plants and sending the creatures into hibernating shells. The Mers followed the currents north again, to a shoreline of honed, rocky shelves, there to bear their young and feast all summer long on caricha and the sweet northern flatleaf seaweed.

So they traveled, autumn to spring and spring to autumn, for thousands of years, until, one summer, something in the water began to itch at their skins. A tickling, burning, sour-tasting element had tainted the rich salt water which supported and sustained them. With each passing day, as the herd grazed along the coastline, they became increasingly distressed by the fetor of the pollution. It scoured across their memories like water across sand, dusting away the accumulation of centuries. At last, they remembered an old, important memory which had been stored carefully away and passed from generation to generation.

Once, many generations in the past, the same herd had encountered the same foul taint in the water. They could not reach their winter home without swimming through the contamination. That winter, all except a handful of their number, including all of the calves, died. Other herds, which had once shared their migration route with them, disappeared entirely, with not one of their members surviving.

In the world above the surface of the sea, strange fires burned. Sometimes, bodies of the strange peoples who lived above the water plummeted into the sea, and sank like stone. The beautiful, alien voices which had sung within the Mers' awareness fell gradually silent. Even the Mers, their population devastated, for many generations sang no more.

We must swim away, decided the herd of Mers. We must alter our migration route, and swim far out from shore in deep water. The journey will be hard on the calves, and we will have to dive deeply in order to find food to eat. But the water will not be poisoned there, and the herd will survive.

The herd will survive . . . but the world will once again fall silent.

This new possibility distressed the herd deeply, for the rich, alien songs and thoughts of the upper world's residents profoundly enriched the lives of the sea people. They milled in the shallow water of the warm shore, too distracted and distraught to graze on cari-cha or even to suckle their young. Within the sea of their single mind, thoughts gathered and darted like fish at the changing of the tide. They were just a Mer herd: a single mind flowing with the tides of the sea. Was it possible that their decision could affect the welfare of the world?

What shall we do? they asked themself. What can we do? they replied in a chorus. But, in time, their thoughts coalesced into a single idea. In a swirling tangle of lithe bodies, they began to swim away from shore, toward the safety of deep water.

All except for one.

They left her first with their bodies. She had never in her life been separated from the twisting, sleek, warm presence of a hundred Mers, and the discomfort was hard to bear. But when the herd had swum far out of her sight and her hearing, they abruptly cut her out of their gestalt, as coldly and determinedly as a surgeon amputating a limb. She hung in the warm embrace of the water, seeing for the first time through only her eyes, swimming for the first time with only her body, thinking for the first time with only her mind.

She uttered a cry of terrible fear. But her herd paid her no heed, and swam silently out to sea.

Chapter 1

On a platform overhanging an abyss, Ysbet ib Canilton crouched, trembling, clutching with both hands the platform's slender edge. The Wing harnessed to her back, a frail contraption of hollow pipe and stretched astil, shuddered with each breath of wind. At eye level, the violet peaks of remote, glacier-capped mountains blazed in the light of the afternoon sun. Below, deep, knife-edged fissures gaped in the mountainside. Huge chunks of glass, shattered loose and tossed aside by the elements, lay in tumbled heaps, bristling with needle-thin shards, nearly invisible in the bright light.

This whole deadly jumble, partially obscured from Bet's view by the angled walls of the cluttered Aeyrie town built on the mountain's peak, swept to the valley far below, where other, more modest dangers awaited her. There the chasm of the Panicblood River slashed across the valley. There the turning windmills fed water to the series of artificial lakes in which caricha was farmed, and there a multitude of chunks, shards, and powdered bits of glass ground loose from the very foundations of the earth and obscured by the lush sucker plants of summer littered the valley floor.

If I were to die, Bet reflected, I could do so in a whole multitude of ways.

During her five-year sojourn at Ula t'Cwa, Bet had overcome even the last vestiges of her natural horror of heights. Sometimes as often as two or three times a day, she had been required to mount or descend the long, railless spiral staircase which ascended up the hollow interior of the glass mountain. Nowhere in the Ula could she turn her head without looking out an unshuttered window, where yawned a vast chasm of sky and abyss. The terrible, swooping plunge of an Aeyrie diving through the air, shouting ecstatically as ids wings filled with wind, had become a commonplace sight to her, no longer cause for either fear or wonder.

But today, beyond any doubt, in spite of the long, repeated trials which had taken her at last to a flight platform at the very top of the mountain, she felt afraid.

It was the Aeyries who had decided that it was time for a Walker to fly. They had come to her, carrying cunning models in their hands, all puffed up by their recent success with the baggage kites. The whole world had opened up before them because of this invention, which made it possible at last for Aeyries to carry supplies in the air with them. "Why not a Walker?" they said to Bet.

"Why not an unwinged Aeyrie?" she replied. They told her a dozen reasons why not. Very young l'shils would lack the necessary coordination and judgment, and older l'shils would be weighed down too much by stored up body fat. The Aeyries who had been crippled in flight accidents could scarcely be expected to have the courage.

"But you," they said, examining her in that odd, calculating way of the Aeyries, "you are not fat, and you are very strong. And your hand-eye coordination . . ." They waved their expressive, long-fingered hands in exaggerated gestures of wonder until Bet told them they looked like bugs, and kicked them out the door.

But they came back, and eventually she had to agree to try it. Either that, or admit to being afraid— not of heights or open spaces—but of trusting so much in Aeyrie ingenuity. And how could she admit even this little, when she was already a stranger among them?

Except, perhaps, to Laril.

Crowded among others on a streamered balcony,

Laril watched her, with only the slight fluffing of ids shoulder fur and a sharp shine of the eye betraying ids anxiety. Ids summer coat of silver fur had burned almost white in the hot sun, and id glowed in the dim window like a ghost or a slender flame, ids tightly folded wings hooding ids shaggy head with the white of clouds. The other Aeyries whose winged and furred bodies filled the balcony seemed vague and faded, in Bet's eye little more than ghosts or shadows.

She had lived a third of her life among Aeyries. Over the years, she had become able to perceive them first as intelligent, complex people, and only second as creatures completely alien to her. But sometimes their strangeness still shocked her: their hermaphroditism, their wings, their frail, hollow-boned, furred bodies, their inexplicable passion for the wasteland of glass in which they slowly declined toward their final extinction. That she had been the lover of one of these beings for five years sometimes seemed the height of ridiculousness. But, at other times she understood how only passion could truly bridge the gulf which separated their peoples.

Someone twitched at Ysbet's Wing, checking for one last time the many, painstakingly crafted joints and grommets and attachments. Long ago, in the Forgotten Times, the Aeyrie people had commonly used kites like this one. But the means of manufacturing the lightweight, marvelously strong metal with which the kite's framework was constructed, had been lost, destroyed, or forgotten. Only recently had the metal finally been reinvented by the t'Cwa inventors and alchemists, to be followed within a matter of days by the first successful flight of a baggage kite. But three more years had passed before Arman the inventor thought to challenge Bet to climb to this flight platform.

Since she lacked fur to insulate her against the wind's chill, they had dressed her in a suit of quilted astil. They had created for her a padded metal helmet with an eye shield of thin-sliced blue glass—this as a substitute for the nictitating membrane which she also lacked. When she slid the shield down over her eyes, as she did now, it muted the dazzling brightness of the day into dim shades of blue and gray.

"Ysbet, are you ready?"

Her mouth felt too dry to speak. She signaled to Arman, and ids sweet tenor began the countdown. *I must be mad,* she thought. *I truly must be mad.* The spectators' murmur fell silent. The dozen flyers, each of whom was linked to Bet by a long rope, walked out to the edge of their respective platforms, ready to spread their wings. Two Aeyries could lift a third from the ground and carry id in the air for a short distance. One alone could launch a baggage kite and keep it in the air indefinitely. But a full dozen would be accompanying Ysbet. They had practiced this flight repeatedly, harnessing a stuffed mannikin in the place which Bet occupied now. "Nothing will go wrong," Arman had assured Bet. "I know that Laril would kill me if I overlooked anything."

The inventor's chant neared its end: "Ons, font, elant . . ."

Bet tore her steadying hand loose from its deathgrip on the edge of the flight platform, and grasped the stirrups with which she supposedly could turn the kite. With sheer willpower, she forced her thigh muscles to contract. "Jump!" cried Arman. She pushed herself forward in an insane leap no Walker had ever been meant to take. The astil crackled as the wind gusted it taut. The harness pinched Bet's torso and thighs as she tossed her weight into its embrace. The mountainside's broken glass leapt at her. Bet could not even move her hands to cover her mouth as she screamed.

With a soft jolt and a sickening drop in her stomach, the wind took hold, and the mountainside swooped gracefully away. A cacaphony of whoops and hollers came faintly to Bet's ears.

The familiar landscape of the valley, covered with the velvet softness of ast, and crisscrossed with a network of footpaths, swept past. Even viewed from above, the random jumble of rooftops, skylights, and wind-banners of the Aeyrie town still made no architectural sense to her. The triangular, maned faces which crowded the windows and balconies blurred into a mob of alien strangers. Now the often-repaired water towers and their companion windmills which crowded the peak of the mountain came into sight.

Arman dropped suddenly into Bet's view, and shouted incomprehensible words through ids cupped hands. Then, id signaled ids query: *Are you all right?*

Bet nodded.

Arman grinned suddenly, like a child. Ids hands swooped through the air: *You're flying!*

A cloud of onfrits, all bright eyes and flickering wings, engulfed her, then swooped away. Arman gestured that id wanted Bet to try turning on her own.

The wing swooped obediently as Bet directed: left, right, and left again. But there would be no aerial acrobatics for her—no swoops or twirls or hair-raising dives. No amount of Aeyrie technology could give her the sensing hairs with which to distinguish every motion of the air so perfectly that she would be able to accurately use the hundreds of h'ldat words which describe the wind. Nor could the Aeyries have somehow gifted her with s'oleil, the combination of trust and passion by which the air becomes known to them. Bet turned the Wing in the air, but she would never truly fly.

In fact, without a dozen pairs of Aeyrie wings buoying her up, the surface of the earth rapidly drew closer. The stretched astil snapped as the pressure changed—she had dropped out of the influence of the h'mara. Arman, who throughout the maneuvers had hovered nearby, swooped a hand upward. They would lift her again, this time in search of a h'lana, a river wind. They wanted to determine whether the strong wind could carry Bet a far distance without the support of the Aeyries, and how well the Wing would hold up. It was this test which would decide whether the Wing was a useful tool, or merely an inventor's toy. Bet nodded her agreement, and Arman climbed out of sight.

She was thirty years old, by Walker standards well

into maturity. The rebel Aeyrie mage, Raulyn, had stolen her youth from her soon after she first realized that she had the gift of what the Walkers call sorcerous talent. The weird, dark mysteries of magical powders, and spells woven like lace, had not appealed to Bet. Instead, she had longed for power as she imagined the Aeyries practiced it: the direct, unmanipulated power which comes from within. Raulyn had promised to teach her, and had eaten her alive instead. For seven years, an angry but broken slave, she had served idre, until, with Laril's help, she had killed idre.

She thought that with Laril she would be happy at last. But she missed her own kind: plodding, pragmatic, and, above all, predictable, she missed them. From time to time a daring Walker or two had come to the Ula to study at the University, but even these pioneers had been tongue-tied before Bet. Perhaps she seemed more alien to them than did the Aeyries themselves.

But Bet herself could scarcely communicate with the Triad Walkers, with whom she should have had much in common. Her bitterness made her seem a stranger at Triad, where they were all idealists, people who believed that by living in a cooperative community with members of the other races, they were somehow changing the world. Bet could not count herself among them.

She missed her own kind; but there was no one in the world like her.

The h'lana swept them up into its current. The ground suddenly began to slide away so quickly that Bet's dizziness, which had been lulled by the uneventfulness of her flight, reemerged, though accompanied by a strange, wonderful exultation. No Walker had ever traveled so sweetly, so silently, so effortlessly across the face of the earth. No Walker had ever seen these folded canyons, these brilliant rivers, across which no foot traveler could ever pass.

It was over too soon. Some of the Aeyries had to

come at her from below, snagging the astil cords that she trailed behind her, and with their weight and their wings pulled her free of the h'lana, and then turned her slowly, to oppose the wind. Arman had warned Bet that this maneuver, should it prove necessary, would be the most dangerous. This warning seemed quaintly obsolete now—if something did go wrong, what could Bet possibly do about it?

Flying against the wind now, it took the entire dozen to tow Ysbet home. She could see them beyond the edge of her Wing, straining against their tethers, laboring in a flight that would have been difficult and tedious even without her weight dragging behind them.

The valley which surrounded Ula t'Cwa crept slowly into sight around the edge of a monstrous, snow-capped mountain. The Ula reappeared, an eccentric jumble of rooftops and balconies clustered at the peak of a mountain. Suddenly, claws skittered on the fabric of Bet's wing: the onfrit pair Ata and Iil were releasing the astil cords from the Wing, as they had been trained, so that Bet and her Aeyrie escort could land unencumbered.

Starting with shallow glides down a cleared slope, and graduating to higher and steeper starting points, Bet had been practicing her landings every day since early spring. She had cut herself repeatedly on the unforgiving glass, twisted her ankles, bruised every part of her body, and once, in a particularly spectacular crash, had wrecked the Wing so badly that the inventors had to start over again from scratch.

"Use your s'oleil," Arman had begged her, as if she could create out of thin air an ability which had never been visited on her kind. In the end, the Aeyries could not teach Bet how to land. She had taught herself.

Arman swooped past, to kiss ids hands and offer them to her in a formal gesture of good luck. If she crash-landed, then ids invention would still be a success; but where would id find another Walker crazy enough to agree to fly it?

The Wing felt different now: looser, and lighter.

Sometimes it bucked slightly, like a draf in spring. The Aeyries would be circling overhead now, coiling up their lines and watching Ysbet as she dropped slowly toward her rendezvous with the harsh glass.

Astonishing, how swiftly the earth leapt up at her now. Reluctant to end her flight so soon, Bet hoped for a chance updraft to slow her descent, but the weather sh'man had not been wrong in ids guarantee of a calm day. The Wing tipped and turned obediently at Bet's command. Far from the unpredictable edges of mountain and canyon, Bet brought herself to a smooth plain and began to spiral downward. In moments she could distinguish the fissures and rubble amid the thick cushion of the astil. She straightened out of her turn and the earth came at her. She swung her feet forward, pulling the leading edge of the wing up into a stall, and landed running.

The Aeyries landed all around her: first Arman and the escort in a rush of iridescent wings, whooping and shouting and dancing in ecstatic circles around each other. A few moments later, the healer landed, laden with bags of unneeded supplies. Arman came over to Bet at last, to help her loosen the buckles of the harness and to pat ids kissed palms on her cheeks. "I never thought you would go through with it."

Shortly, other Aeyries began to land: people from the Ula who had witnessed the flight and now arrived to congratulate Arman and the others. They brought c'duni and sh'duni to nourish the tapped-out flyers. They patted Bet's shoulders with their long-fingered hands. "The world is yours," they said.

And then, at last, Laril landed softly as a leaf in the midst of the crowd, the sun outlining a lacework of red blood veins in ids wings. "The world is yours." Id kissed Ysbet softly on her mouth.

In the chaos and confusion, she found she could not collect her thoughts to reply. The Wing was being dismantled for the journey back to the Ula. Bet felt very odd: heavy, disoriented, earthbound.

"Look, Bet," said Laril, pointing skyward. Overhead, an Aeyrie black hovered, huge wings beating like an onfrit's, legs ruddering smoothly back and then forward to hold ids nearly impossible balace in the air.

"Not many Aeyries can hover like that," Bet said.

"It's Eia. Id arrived at the Ula in time to witness your landing."

"Eia Stormtamer? What is id doing here?"

The graceful flyer found a space in the crowd below at last, and landed neatly, tucking in ids wings at the last moment to avoid buffeting anyone standing nearby.

Bet wrapped her arms around herself. There were too many furred bodies, too many sun-warm, leather-soft wings. "Has the entire Ula come out?"

"It looks like it."

"Why is Eia here?"

"Id wanted to see the caricha farm. And your garden."

"The Stormtamer didn't fly all the way here from Triad just to examine our agriculture."

"Ysbet," Laril said, gently enough, though it still sounded like a reproof. "You still do not realize what a revolution it is, for Aeyries to do their own farming."

"It almost caused a revolution," Bet muttered. But that was history now.

Eia wedged ids way through the crowd. Some, recognizing idre, gave way respectfully, but most did not notice ids presence. Gray salted the shiny black of ids braided mane, but the rest of ids fur remained the velvet black of a night sky. Sweat still plastered down the fur of ids torso, where id had recently removed a flight vest. No ornament set id apart, no symbol or vestment. As id held out ids hand to greet Bet as a Walker would, the Quai-du master's triangle branded in ids wrist turned skyward.

"The world is yours," Eia said, grasping and then releasing her hand.

"The world will never be mine! Why is everyone telling me it is?"

Eia grinned, delighted at Bet's bad manners. "It is what we always say to a l'shil who has just completed ids first flight."

Appalled, Bet turned to Laril. "It's bad enough that you tell your hatchlings that the world is a good place. But to tell the l'shils that the world is theirs! Why do you lie to your children?"

"Ysbet!" Shocked speechless, Laril could not continue.

But Eia's mouth, gone slack for a moment, twisted ironically. "It is just a wish, my dear, not a prediction."

The furry bodies which had packed around them had begun to ease away, following on foot the inventors who carried the Walker Wing in triumph back to the Ula. Eia took Bet's hand once again. "I want to talk with you. Will you walk with me?"

Beside the slight, muscular, sleek figure of Eia, Bet felt heavy and ungainly, weighed down by her heavy muscles and heavier bones, her padded clothing, and the helmet tucked under her arm. The ground underfoot felt hard and ungiving, offering only the harsh support of gravity. "It would be easy to become scornful of the people who have no choice but to walk on the ground," she said.

"Did you love your flight, then?"

Eia had spoken in the Walker language, so Bet replied in it. She spoke in her native tongue so rarely that it had begun to seem unfamiliar to her. "I loved flying," she said, "and I also hated it. I hated it because I can never fly like an Aeyrie. I hated it because the Aeyries will always be amused by the Walker Wing, and the Walkers will always be shocked and horrified by it. I hated it because there is no one in the world who can understand why I loved it."

They walked more slowly than the other Aeyries, who passed them in groups of twos or threes. Hearing the unfamiliar syllables of Walker speech, many of them turned their heads in curiosity. Recognizing Eia, they usually gestured a respectful greeting, and walked on.

"Living with one foot in each of two worlds is wearing away at your spirit? It's a lonely road you've chosen."

Perhaps Eia was the pivot upon which turned the

fragile peace between the Aeyrie and Walker people, but Bet had learned to think of idre as a friend. Eia lived with the Walkers as she lived with the Aeyries, inhabiting both worlds and belonging to neither. Except for Delan, who had been raised as a Walker, Bet understood no other Aeyrie better, not even Laril. So she could say, wearily and honestly, "I don't remember ever choosing it."

"And all is not well between you and the taiseoch," Eia continued.

"Laril is no longer a l'shil, free to do as id chooses. Id is a public person, who can never lock ids doors against interruption. Every day, I seem to embarrass idre. I think Laril wishes I were an Aeyrie."

"Laril would benefit from greater maturity, I think. Id's wing year is only four years in the past. In all the history of the Aeyrie people, a taiseoch has never been named so young."

"And I am old enough to be a grandmother."

"So young? No wonder the Walkers have overrun the lowlands in only five hundred years."

The Ula's hollow mountain loomed before them, its lower door gaping open to allow entry. Airborne Aeyries also swarmed around the town perched on the mountain's peak. Once there had been hundreds of such towns, perched on mountains hollowed out by forgotten science or magic. The mountains still stood, but of the Ulas only three remained. Even the names of the others had been forgotten.

And still, despite all the treaties and trade agreements which Eia had forged to help guarantee the people's future, the Aeyries remained a dying race. Slowly, almost too slowly to notice, their population continued to decline. When Bet asked why they simply don't hatch more eggs and raise more children, they could not seem to answer her sensibly. "There is not enough food," they would say, or, "Raising a child is difficult work." They would point out the rate at which the Walkers were overrunning the lowlands. "We cannot live wingtip to wingtip like that. We need the room to fly."

The truth was that the Aeyrie people had lost their will to survive. They blamed their decline on the Walkers, whose domination of all the fertile land made it impossible for the Aeyries to acquire food except through trade. But trade was dependably lively, and the Ulas actually had large surpluses of food and credit. The tentative peace between the two races became, with every day that passed, more stable. Yet the decline continued.

They entered the door and started up the long staircase, their footsteps echoing in a dry whisper against the crystal walls. "I thought you came to t'Cwa to explore your mage gift," began Eia.

"What gift? I can make myself invisible and I can unlock doors. I can write with my fingertip words that glow in the dark. I hear strange sounds that no one else can hear. I have waited, like the mages instructed me, and listened, and held myself silent. But the secrets I once knew and lost are not revealed to me anew. What Raulyn stole from me, id stole forever."

A dark shadow against the gloom of the Well, Eia murmured, "Well, you are right to be angry."

"I have to get into a better mood soon, or I'll spoil Laril's party."

"I want you to come to Is'antul with me."

"What?" After twelve years of experience, Bet had become reasonably proficient at reading Aeyrie expressions, but Eia's sculptured face and dark, shiny eyes gave Bet no clues. It would drive a Walker mad, she thought, to try to negotiate with a face like this, which gave nothing, took nothing, merely waited for a response. "Why?" she said, because there was nothing else to say.

"The Ulas have always negotiated our Walker trade agreements one year at a time. But this year, I demanded a ten-year agreement. The Walkers do not want to admit that they have become nearly as dependent on Aeyrie technology as we are on their food. They want us to design a fleet of trade ships for them. And they want us to build them a field of windmills with which to irrigate the Altingale waste. I have agreed to contract for these projects, but only in exchange for the trade agreement. They will not even consider ten years. They will not consider five. We are at a standoff.

"My people are dying out before my eyes. I have to get them something they can depend on. I need a catalyst, something to break the stalemate. And I think that you can be that catalyst."

"Eia, I am no catalyst."

"I must disagree." The consummate negotiator, Eia knew when to speak and when to be silent. They climbed the staircase through the gloom, toward the welcoming glow of the open door above. The spicy, rich scents of festival food drifted down the stairs as the cooks made their final preparations. At Laril's insistence, they were giving her a wingday party.

They reached the top of the stairs at last, Bet with her breath rasping in her throat, Eia scarcely breathing heavily. In the common room, earlycomers had already gathered to sample the summer wine and other delicacies. Musicians with tambors and lap harps, flutes, bells, and fiddles, tested their instruments. After the meal, there would be circle dancing, the intricacies of which Bet had given up hope of ever mastering. Perhaps, in her honor, they would attempt some of the box and line dances which she had taught them. But they would refuse to stamp or clap, and would find it impossible to follow their dance partner's lead.

Arman, surrounded by Laril and a few of ids advisors, talked excitedly, waving ids long fingers in the air, so drunk on success that id would surely need no wine tonight. Laril slipped away from the group when id spotted Bet and Eia. "Do you think there are many other Walkers who would be willing to try flying, much less want to purchase a Wing of their own? Arman thinks the Wing will be worth a fortune in trade. But I think Bet is exceptional, and we will never find another Walker willing to try this."

"Who knows?" said Eia. "The Walkers are not nearly so cautious as we would like to believe."

"You mean you really couldn't tell that I was terrified?" said Bet.

Laril slipped an arm around Bet's waist, ids soft wing brushing across Bet's shoulders. Id smelled of summer sweat and sweet herbal wing oil. Silver fur, tipped with white by the sun, tickled her cheek. "Is that why you've been so cranky?" Id leaned against her gently, forgetting appearances for once. What a friend id had been to her: a partner in laughter and in pain. For four years they had studied together, plowing through the vast libraries of t'Cwa like ravenous children in an unguarded pantry, dreaming together of how they would change the world. But the day Ishta died, all their exploring had come to an end. Now Laril had no time to spare, and Bet had all the time in the world to discover the folly of living in a community where her lover was her only friend.

"Laril," she said, "I'm going to Is'antul with Eia."

Laril drew away from her, startled. "When will you be back?"

"I may never come back," she said.

After that, there was nothing to say.

Chapter 2

Summer, Day 48

This is my first memory: It is a thought that has no words, a piece of music that has no sound. It slices deeply through the substance of my being, deeper than awareness, deeper than thought, into the darkest, remotest, simplest part of my mind. It slices into me without blood, or pain. I feel only a kind of shock, as if I reached out casually with both my hands, and grabbed hold of a lightning bolt.

This is my next memory: I see light, and only then realize that I have been blind.

Later, I cannot say how much later, I hear something: a commonplace sound like the rustling of cloth. I realize that I have been unable to hear.

The wordless, soundless, musical slicing, and the accompanying shock continue. I begin to wonder confusedly who and where I am, and what is happening. I begin to feel pain, just a small amount at first, but it grows into unendurable agony. I thrash about, and only then realize that I am lying on a bed, and, until just now, had been paralyzed.

"We'll stop for now," a voice says.

Shadow moves across light.

"There is a great deal of pain," says another.

Shadow moves across light once again. I feel a nearness, a heaviness in the air. The voice says, "Do you remember your name? It is Arman Orshil Tsal. You will find that you cannot speak yet. You are at the Triad Hospital. Some t'Han Aeyries carried you here, *having found you severely injured along one of the flightpaths. There was a storm; perhaps you were caught in a hellwind."*

I try to speak, but can only make a formless, moaning sound. What is happening to me?

"Your wings have been shattered. And you have suffered brain damage," the voice says dispassionately. "Your will to survive kept you alive for at least seven days before you reached the hospital. We decided to respect that will and save your life, even though your life may be far different from what it was. You are an explorer, your friends and relatives have told us. You will welcome the opportunity to track new ground."

I try to speak again: What is happening to me?

"Right now, the Mers and healers are working together to repair the injuries to your brain. You must understand, Tsal, that you will not be the person you were. We are saving everything that can be saved, but there is much that is lost beyond reclamation, some of your memories, even some of your personality. We regret that we could not give you a choice before we began this work, but we offer you that choice now. If you would rather die . . . it is up to you."

I had yet to learn exactly how much that fall at the whim of my fey lover the wind had cost me. But my curiosity, at least, had survived. So I chose what proved to be an anguished, frustrating, confusing, and terrifying thing. I chose life.

In preparation for this journey, I read all of my old journals, which were shipped to me at my request from the archives of t'Cwa. I do remember, after a fashion, most of the journeys and events which I describe there. It is the author I do not recognize: an errant, restless wanderer, an outgoing storyteller, a flyer of fast-moving winds. I cannot move as quickly now; and I am, I think, far more thoughtful. But I still passionately love that harmonious, poetic interaction of land and sky. The wind still calls me, and I still cannot resist its sweet seduction: to see new lands, to throw myself once again at the weather's mercy, to measure the aching loneliness of the wilderness. I have packed my mapmaker's tools, and I have begun a new journey to the south of Sa, where the lowlands come to an end and the mountains meet the sea. Over a hundred years ago, an explorer named Beno mapped that area, but ids maps are notoriously incomplete and inaccurate. Beno may have been a brave flyer, but id was not much of a mathematician.

Of course the Triad healers did not want me to leave so soon. A winter, a spring, and most of a summer have passed while I learned, under their care, how to function as a person once again: how to think, talk, walk, and finally—oh, joyous day—to fly. But if I remained at Triad much longer, I would have been forced to remain for yet another winter. After being grounded so long, I wondered if I would ever leave at all. It is so comfortable there; the community runs with the precision and discipline of the Walkers and the inspiration of the Aeyries; and that sweet sea wind . . . I could stay forever.

I had to take this journey, not because of the need for accurate maps of the wilderness, but because I need to map out my new self before winter sets in. For three seasons I have belonged to the healers and the Mers who re-created me. Now I must claim myself.

Summer, Day 52

This evening, as sunset neared, I found myself far from a decent campsite. Here at the edge of that strange wasteland known as Ara's Field, there are no mountains, no hills, no trees: only flat, barren stone. I passed a final Walker community, which is centered around one last patch of good soil. When I saw only barren wilderness before me, I turned back, and landed at the edge of the farmstead, and walked boldly into the community.

Most farming Walkers sleep during the hot afternoon and, being able to see much more clearly in the dark than Aeyries, will work far into the night. I found the business of the farm in full swing: the gardens being weeded, the irrigation channels being tended, the harvest being brought in, the drafs being fed and groomed.

As I walked among their barns and outbuildings, I know I must have been a shocking sight, for these people surely have never set eyes on an Aeyrie before. But they continued determinedly with their chores, a crowd of busy people brightly dressed in clothing touched by the sunset's fire, constantly turning their gazes from their hands to me and back to their hands once again.

Finally one approached me, an older female with her hair tied up in an intricate knotted style which I vaguely recall is symbolic of high status. "Welcome, stranger," she said cautiously (in the Walker tongue).

I gave her a Walker greeting, a shallow bow with the hands held out respectfully (I must say, I felt like a fool doing it). "Madam, please pardon me for interrupting the important labor of this community. I am flying on a journey of exploration, and I will be sleeping outside of your community this night. As I am sure you must know, an Aeyrie cannot fly from flat ground. May I use your barn roof as a flight platform tomorrow morning?"

She asked me many careful questions for clarification. The welfare of the barn was her responsibility and I suppose she needed to make certain that I did not plan to set it on fire or somehow damage the roof.

In the end, she gave me permission, and even offered me a drink of water from their well, which I gladly accepted. (It was an old, hand-turned well. This community could use a good windmill.) As I sat on a stone, sipping from the dipper she gave me, the children finally began to appear, creeping from the gardens and fields, holding tightly to each other's hands, and staring at me from a distance. I waved one of the bolder ones to come over, and spread my wings for him to view, and offered to let him feel the membrane. Soon they had all surrounded me, fondling my fur and my wings with a curiosity no less uninhibited than that of an Aeyrie child. When they began to ask questions, I told them I would answer only if they also would answer my questions.

By this time, of course, some of the adults had drawn near out of concern for the young, so I took great care in the wording of my questions. The children asked me where I had come from, where I had been, and what it was like. I asked them about the land: did they have earthquakes, when did they have rain, when did they have wind, and so on. We actually know very little about this part of the world, I explained. Soon the adults were answering questions as well, and even asking a few of their own.

The children wanted to know why my membranes are reinforced with wingtape, and why I have metal braces screwed into my wingbones. I have not had to explain my injuries to anyone before. The children, having so little experience of pain and fear, were more fascinated than anything else. After a while, I became a little fascinated, too. As little as two years ago, I told them, far less serious wing injuries would have meant I could never fly again. But now, the metal braces actually make my bones stronger than they were before. "Does it hurt?" the children asked me, and I answered honestly, "Not as much as it would hurt to be unable to fly."

Though they are forever earthbound, they seemed to understand me.

When I asked them to tell me about Ara's Field, this is what they told me:

Long long ago, long before Grandmother Tinta was alive (I think that Grandmother Tinta is the high-ranking female who first greeted me), there lived a farmer whose name was Ara. One night, he dreamed of the perfect field, where there are no weeds, and the lush crops yield great harvests; where the streams turn themselves this way and that, to irrigate first one part of the field and then another. When Ara awoke from his dream, he decided to search the world over until he found this perfect field.

So, over many years he traveled, from one end of the earth to the other. At last he found the field of which he had dreamed. It was even more beautiful than he had imagined, and it stretched from the ocean's shores to the edge of the mountains. When he planted it, the field yielded enough food to feed a city, and some of the seeds bore fruit the like of which Ara had never seen before: bigger than he could carry, sweet as honeydew.

So, rejoicing, Ara sent for all his old friends and family, so they could come and share his field with him. They came, and when they saw Ara's field they were astonished beyond speech. But soon they began to be jealous, even though Ara had invited them to share in his wealth. "What if he decided to make us leave?" they asked. So they killed Ara, and they took a plow and plowed his body into the soil of his field.

In the morning when they awoke, Ara's field had turned completely to stone, from the shores of the ocean to the edge of the mountains. So it remains to this very day.

This simple story astonished me, not because of its contents, but because it was Walkers who told it to me. The Walkers, after all, have single-handedly endangered the survival of the Aeyrie people because they claim all fertile land for their farms, leaving my people with nowhere to gather food. Yet they are still able to tell stories like this one, and see in it no irony.

As I write these words I am sitting out in the rocks of Ara's Field, working by lanternlight, as my baggage kite creaks on its tether, passing its shadow gracefully across the moon and the stars as it rides the high wind. I think I will have quite an audience when I mount the barn roof at daybreak tomorrow.

Summer, Day 53

This has been an astonishing day.

It dawned soft and clear, the sky filled with color, from the deep red at the horizon to rose, and pink, and pale yellow, and gold, and finally green and multitudinous shades of blue. Of course the whole community was waiting when I arrived to climb to the barn roof, towing my baggage kite behind me. When I leapt off the edge of the roof, they uttered such a cry of fear and astonishment that I missed a wingstroke and nearly *crashed, accidentally giving them more of a show than I had intended.*

I followed the shoreline southward, with the colorless, burning desert of stone to my right, and the deep, rich hues of the ocean to my left. When I flew over the restless surface of the sea, its lush scents enveloped me, and I could see far into its depths, where fields of caricha, and red and lavender fronds of sea plants swayed gracefully back and forth as the swells passed them. When I flew over the desert, the air smelled only of dust.

As the afternoon turned toward evening, I began to search for a high stone which could serve as my flight platform in the morning, and, having found such a stone, I ended my day's journey early. My mended bones were aching, and I had been sternly warned about getting adequate rest.

Having drawn in my kite and set up camp, I sat on a rock where I could look up from my mapwork and watch the sea. I had been sitting there for a while, making notations of changes in the shoreline and wind currents, when I became aware that I was no longer alone.

I climbed to the high rock which would be tomorrow's flight platform, and surveyed the rocky landscape. I could see nothing unusual: no movement, no color. Yet my awareness of another's presence persisted. I asked myself if some undiscovered quirk in my new brain had suddenly surfaced. I shut my eyes, breathed deeply, and concentrated, as the Triad healers taught me to do, on the actual process of my thinking. So I realized that I felt I was no longer alone because I sensed someone's attention focused upon me. The sensation was strikingly similar to the telepathic attention paid me by the Triad Mers when they viewed me from within, checking to see that the new thought pathways which they had forged for me were functioning as intended.

I opened my eyes and looked out to sea, and saw there the bobbing head of a Mer, just beyond the breakers.

I greeted the Mer in my thoughts. I am no se'an, but since she was paying attention to me, she must have received my greeting. I think my simple communication startled her, for she instantly withdrew her attention. But, as the sun set into the grip of the mountains, I still saw her, not too far out in the water. And sometimes I sensed her attention once again, focusing on me briefly as if to taste once again an alien food, and then drawing quickly away.

She obviously is alone, having somehow been separated from her herd. If we can learn to communicate with each other, I will inform her of the Triad herd and how to find them. I feel an obligation to help her, after all the Mers have done for me. I know that without the company of other Mers, she will inevitably die.

Summer, Day 54
All day she followed me southward. This evening, once again, we faced each other across the boundaries that separate us: the water, in which I would drown, and the air, in which she would suffocate under the weight of her own body. The rocks were not so cruel here, and she negotiated herself closer to shore, so that I could see her flat, large-eyed face, and sometimes her hands as she lifted a leaf of red seaweed to her mouth. Her brown fur was dappled with white and black.

I feel her attention on me now as I write. I want to tell her that the Triad Mers teach each other how non-Mers communicate with each other, for the concept of language is difficult for Mers to understand. I want to tell her that she and I need to communicate through the senses which her kind and mine have in common: sight, sound, memory, and music. But I cannot think without avoiding the words which will mean nothing to her. Perhaps I should try singing.

Summer, Day 55
Singing while flying is extremely difficult. I hummed to myself instead, throughout my day's journey. Sometimes, I flew out to sea, where Ara (as I have taken to calling her) swam in the strong offshore current. With

the help of the current, she kept good pace with me, even though I have been helped along by a friendly wind today.

I noticed some changes in the deepwater vegetation that I do not think have ever been recorded before. Many plants, rather than being a deep red color, have brightened to a harsh, ugly orange. I also noticed that the stark shoreline began to be littered with debris: not just seaweed, though there was plenty of that, but other things. The rich scent of the ocean became too rich: cloying and sweet, the scent of death.

There was a worried, anxious itch in my mind. When I flew out to sea once again, I could not find Ara, and I wondered belatedly if that itch had been her attempt to communicate distress to me. I had retraced perhaps half the afternoon's travels when at last I saw her leap out of the water—out of excitement, or in an attempt to help me spot her? In either case, she has apparently learned a great deal about my thinking processes and perceptions. I wish I could learn as much about hers.

Summer, Day 56

I only just awakened, thinking, "How extraordinary; I dreamed that I was Mer!" But how could an Aeyrie, who has never since the day of my hatching been under water, imagine in such detail what it is like to swim? The dream must have been a communication from Ara.

I dreamed I swam among other Mers, a member of the Mer gestalt, with shared experiences, and shared memories. The water surrounded me/us in the steady pressure of its cool embrace. Something important and distressing had recently occurred, and I/we considered as we drifted, remembering an ancient memory which had been saved like a treasure from the past and handed down, from generation to generation. I/we remembered a time when the ocean's water—

Later

I understand now. I dropped my journal earlier, and rushed down to the seashore, where dead caricha, mollusks, plants, and many other unidentifiable dead things

lay stinking and moldering among the stones. I shouted
Ara's name, but though I knew she heard and understood me, she would not come in to shore. Of course
she would not; she is staying clear of the tainted water
because exposure to it will kill her, just as it has killed
all these other inhabitants of the sea. She knows her
danger, because she remembers the last time the ocean
was poisoned, many generations before her lifetime
actually began.

Do the Mers actually remember the Forgotten Times?
It was then that the Aeyrie people nearly disappeared
from the surface of the earth, and all of our technology
and culture was destroyed. Over five hundred years
later, my people still have not begun to recover: not in
population, and not in knowledge. And we do not
know what happened, or why. Now the water is poisoned once again.

I do not want to believe Ara. I suppose that the
possibility of this awful thing happening again to my
people is too painful to contemplate. But I am a person
of intellect (at least I am now; I do not think I used to
be nearly so logical) and I cannot argue with what she
showed me in the dream. Either it is true, or she made
it up; but I know that Mers do not understand fiction,
and cannot lie.

The source of the poisoned water is an underground
river not far south of here. As I write these words, Ara
tells me that, long ago, the river flowed on the surface
of the earth. But a tide of molten glass covered the
entire land, including the river, and even spilled into
the sea before hardening once again into the colorless
rock of Ara's Field.

. . . It is a very strange sensation for another being
to follow my thoughts like this! Ara, if you understand,
this is what I am going to do. I will continue my journey southward, and try to find the outlet of this underground river. Then I will explore inland, to try to
determine where it flows. Despite its shell of rock, there
will be signs that I can follow, for the surface of the
earth has been the study of my lifetime and it cannot
fool me. You must wait where you are, lest the poison

harm you. If you like, you may accompany me none-theless, floating in my brain like my baggage kite floats behind me in the wind. I do not mind your company, Ara.

Summer, Day 57

Found the river outlet; marked it on map. Will follow inland tomorrow. Exhausted. The day unbearably hot. Ara still travels within me, watching and waiting.

Summer, Day 58

Never in my life have I seen a land so flat. Now that Ara has told me that this area was completely covered by molten glass, I see that the history of the rock is written in its own bubbled, rippled surface. Are mountains missing, which have been melted by some unimaginable force, and poured into the sea? This is a puzzle for better geologists than I.

The course of the underground river is easy enough to trace from the surface of the land. I am not trying to map it accurately, for the calculations and measurements would take too long, and my silent partner, Ara, is increasingly anxious to return to her herd. But I must wonder what, if anything, I will be able to discover from the land's surface (or from overhead, if I ever find a decent flight platform in this flat land) which will resolve an underground mystery. At least I have plenty of supplies, including water, in my baggage kite; and the winds so far have been sufficient to launch it without my wings to assist it.

Summer, Day 59

I never thought about how hot it would be down here on the bare rock. I feel as if I have been walking in a frying pan. The rock is not as smooth, either, as it seemed from above. After a morning of walking, my feet feel as if they have been sandpapered. However, I have arrived at a place where the river's stone ceiling has collapsed into a surprisingly deep canyon. At the bottom, the river winds among monuments of broken stone. Tomorrow I will use this canyon to launch

myself into the air and fly back to the sea. This after-
noon I plan to explore the canyon on foot, to see what
secrets it may yield. Then I will fly up the Panicblood
to Ula t'Fon, and try to pull together a crew to help
unpuzzle Ara's mystery. My mapping project will have
to wait until another year after all.

Later

I have found a place through which I may be able to
enter the underground cavern in which the river runs. I
will try to enter, just to see what I may see.

Chapter 3

After the food had been eaten, the wine bottles emptied, the dances danced, and the jokes and stories recounted, Bet and Laril faced each other once again, across the plain bed they had shared these last five years. "I need my own kind," Bet said at last.

"You are the one who insisted that we love only each other."

"Why can't you listen to me?" But Laril had closed idreself up like a box slamming shut. Bet left the room quietly, and lay that last night in a strange bed, with the window open to the summer wind. She watched the stars spin and the moons dance, and she turned her thoughts over and over in her mind. Laril could never understand the loneliness of her life, no more than she could understand the obligation and traditions that snatched away all of ids choices, leaving only the illusion of freedom.

They had reached the end of their wind. Bet had expected and dreaded the day that Laril would abandon their exclusive relationship in favor of the sexual license which seems more natural to the Aeyries. But, in the end, it had been she who chose freedom, and it was Laril who was left dumbfounded.

"But how could anyone live their entire lives, suspended between two worlds, belonging in neither? I need to find a place among my own kind, if it is not already too late!" These words she said to herself, as she watched the stars turn. But her belly, and her chest, and all of her bones ached with grief.

*   *   *

She arrived in the *h'shal talan* shortly after day-break, having awakened exhausted. In the eastward-facing windows, the edge of the sun decorated the peak of a mountain like a brilliant jewel. At these ancient, often mended tables and chairs, generation after generation of t'Cwa-dre had come together every evening to eat their communal meal. Here they conducted the business of the Ula; here they elected and dedicated their taiseoch, here they celebrated or mourned the passages of the people. This room, the only one large enough to contain every member of the Ula, was the heart of the community. Now it was empty, except for Eia and Laril, who sat together at the end of one long table, sharing a pot of tea.

"Excuse me," Bet mumbled, as Eia and then Laril turned their heads at her entrance.

Eia stood up stiffly. "The wind does not carry me as lightly as it used to. I want to visit the baths before we leave. Did Arman ever find you last night?"

"Great Winds, what does Arman want now?"

"Id's heart is breaking," said Laril dryly. "Who will complete the tests on the Walker Wing if you are gone?"

"Let id find some other damn fool."

Bet turned toward the kitchen, but Eia picked up the teapot and pursued her, clasping her by the elbow at the doorway. "I'll get you some tea," id said firmly. "Do you want some bread, too? Never mind—you have to eat. Go sit with Laril. Do it, or I'll slap you."

"I would slap *you*," Bet murmured. "if I weren't bigger than you are."

"You've made worse mistakes," said Eia, and shoved her firmly in Laril's direction.

Laril began talking before Bet even sat down. "Arman wants you to use the Wing to travel to Triad, and maybe even to Isan'tul. With an escort, of course."

Bet did not reply. The Aeyries made the journey to Triad in ten days, and to Is'antul in another ten. The Walkers, forced to travel by the circuitous land routes, took twice as long to cover the same distance. To travel as the Aeyries do, unencumbered, limited only by the winds, seemed a delightful prospect. But to spend one long day after another strapped to the Wing, with those bruising buckles digging into her flesh—it was an appalling possibility.

Laril drummed ids nervous fingers silently on the tabletop. "I apologize about last night. I behaved badly."

"Well," Bet began.

"You could have been more gentle."

"I could have. I'm not famous for my tact, as you may have noticed. I apologize if I wrecked your party."

"It was supposed to be your party."

Bet held her tongue with difficulty, but Laril looked up as sharply as if she had spoken, ids eyes dark and liquid behind the shaggy shield of ids unkempt mane. "I want you to come back. In two seasons—even a year. I know I can't make you stay at t'Cwa, but I don't want our friendship to end like this, without saying the things that need to be said. You have been important to me—more, maybe, than I have let you know. For a time, we could not have survived without each other. I have not forgotten that."

"Neither have I."

"You have been more than a lover to me. You have been a true friend. It hurts my heart to see you go, knowing that, wherever you go, I will never be able to seek you out there. Say you will come back, Bet, if only to say good-bye properly and leave once again."

She had to hold herself back then, to keep from saying everything Laril wanted her to say: that she would stay, that she loved idre, that they would be together forever. "I will try to come back, to say good-bye properly," she said.

So she left t'Cwa soon after sunrise, riding on the Walker Wing, accompanied by Eia, Arman, five onfrits, two baggage kites, and seven out of the dozen original Aeyries who had escorted the Wing the day before. Only Laril, the weathermaster, and a few casual bystanders witnessed the second launching of the Walker Wing. Bet found it to be only slightly less terrifying than the first time. But, once airbound, with the element-carved landscape slipping slowly past below her, the silence and solitude seduced her. No wonder the madhouse of the Aeyrie Ula did not trouble its inhabitants, when they could always ride the wind alone. With the entire sky for the having, who needed peace, or quiet, or privacy, at home?

At the half-day mark, Bet landed in a sloping field of ast. Because her legs had gone numb, she stumbled, but the springy ast absorbed the worst of her landing. She sat in the ast, as her companions sat nearby on stones, sharing loaves of cheese-studded bread with the onfrits, and passing the water flasks from hand to hand.

This gentle mountain slope dropped into a crooked valley, crossed by many brooks and lushly overgrown with sucker plants. It would have been a good site for a farm, had there been any soil. Bet and Laril had once dreamed up a grand scheme to turn mountain land into farmland, with the help of a herd of drafs to transform ast into manure. But to truly be successful, soil would have to be imported from the lowlands as well. Ishta, and now Laril idreself, had refused to finance such an expensive experiment.

Eia, with the onfrits flocking behind idre, walked up the hillside to squat beside Bet. "Is all well with you?"

"I must admit, it feels good to sit on the ground."

"This is a strange way to travel." Eia gestured vaguely at the crowd of Aeyries, the sulfur yellow of the baggage kites and the brilliant red and blue of Bet's Wing.

"Is it more trouble than it's worth?"

"I can't see traveling by air becoming commonplace for Walkers, if it takes so many Aeyries to keep you afloat. But for emergencies and urgent business—well, maybe. For those who can afford to pay."

One of the onfrits timidly accepted Bet's proferred

bread offering, and perched on her knee as she ate, digging claws into Bet's padding for balance.

"According to the onfrits, a friendly wind ahead of us flows east-west. If we follow it, we could save ourselves a day or so in the journey time between here and Ula t'Han. But the wind also will take us away from the main flight route. It'll be a harder journey without the shelters and the dependable water supply. Do you want to do it?"

"What do the others say?"

"It's up to you."

"Yes, but what do they say?"

The corners of Eia's mouth twitched. "We make a sport of traveling from one place to another in as little time as possible. That way, we have something to boast about when we reach our destination. And a broadsheet all about your flight yesterday was published last night—it would be amusing to arrive at t'Han before the news does."

"So everyone wants to follow this friendly wind, but they don't expect me to agree, because I won't understand this sport of yours. Well, they are right: I don't understand it." Bet sighed heavily, thinking of how the harness had already bruised her, and in places had begun to rub her skin raw. "But I suppose I have to agree, rather than spoil everyone's fun."

Eia took a map from the long, cylindrical case hanging at ids waist. If they departed from the main flight route, which was clearly marked with flags driven into the glass, they would have to depend on other, more easily mistaken reference points: certain distinctive mountains and watercourses, and triangulation markers, survivors of a seminal survey which predated the Forgotten Times. "And there are always the onfrits," added Eia.

Bet responded with a sigh, stretching her aching muscles and unfastening her flightsuit, for she was beginning to swelter in the warm sun. Too soon, they had to climb up the mountainside to find a good launching point, and leap into the air once again.

That night, and the next three nights which fol-

lowed, Bet slept on the craggy ledge of one or another
towering mountain, with no padding except that of
her flightsuit to insulate her aching and bruised body
from the glass. Since she could not possibly land her
Wing on these narrow ledges which the Aeyries
favored for their very inaccessibility, she had to land
where she could, and allow herself and her Wing to
be hauled up the mountainside with ropes. But by the
end of her second day of flight from sunrise to sunset,
Bet could have slept anywhere, and of the vestiges of
her fear of heights, nothing remained. She slept at the
edge of the cliff over which she flung herself in the
morning. She made dangerous landings that she would
have sworn she would never attempt. And she dreamed
that she had sprouted wings and could fly as freely as
the Aeyries.

Unlike the Walkers, who tended to travel in cara-
vans, rarely did Aeyries travel in groups of more than
two or three, so they attracted an inordinate amount
of notice when they approached Ula t'Han five days
after leaving t'Cwa. Half the community turned out
to watch Ysbet land at the foot of thcir mountain.
Fortunately, despite her exhaustion, she managed a
decent landing, and received for her efforts an appre-
ciative yodeling from the onlookers. After that, there
was the grueling climb up the center of the mountain,
with only an onfrit to keep her company. She arrived
at the top wobblc-kneed, her head aching, only to be
confronted by a crowd of Aeyries and a cacophony of
questions.

Eia rescued her from the enthusiastic crowd, presented her to the taiseoch C'la, whom she had met
before at Laril's dedication, dispatched her onfrit companion to the onfrit house, and then towed her firmly
out of the room. "Don't let Aeyrie curiosity get a grip
on you. They'll eat you alive, just to see what you
taste like."

They had to stop then, because she had begun
laughing so hard she could not catch her breath.
"Great Winds, I'm tired," she gasped at last.

"How about a bath?"

"I think I want food more—real food, not flight food."

"I've already arranged for food to be brought to us. You do know that t'Han is famous for its cooking. The preparation of food, after all, is one of the arts."

They walked together down the hallway. The common room had been so crowded and noisy that Bet could not appreciate its decor, but now the rich colors and fine wood, the shape and breadth of the hallway, even the lay of the light and shadows, caught her attention. "This is a beautiful place!"

"Yes," said Eia, a trifle sadly.

They walked together in silence, through plant-filled solariums, past cluttered and crowded studios, past a closed door behind which rumbled the distinctive sigh and clatter of a printing press. "T'Han is the home of Aeyrie culture and art. But it has too much the feeling of a museum," Eia said finally. "It's missing something—that ragged edge, perhaps, where the present is already cutting eagerly into the future. Twenty to thirty years ago, it had a vitality . . . sometimes it could be almost frightening. But not anymore. T'Fon is the same way: a town famous for its inventiveness and eccentricity, but in the last ten years, the best inventions have come out of t'Cwa rather than t'Fon. Here; these are the baths."

Behind the wooden door was an extraordinary place, a fantasy world of warm streams and waterfalls flowing across mossy glass, filled with misty light which filtered from skylights overhead, and crowded with lush, blooming plants the like of which, Eia said, had never been seen in the wild. "They are grown in the greenhouses here; propagated from generation to generation. No one knows where the original plants came from: a faraway land, perhaps, visited by an Aeyrie long ago, before our Universe began to shrink."

Bet took a cake of soap and found herself a small private pool, only a few inches deep in deference to Aeyrie fear of water, with a warm waterfall in which to rinse her hair. Afterward, she walked naked into the warm room where a few Aeyries lay on benches, oiling their wings and drying their fur. They gave her a collective, startled glance, then hastily turned their gazes politely away.

Bet sat down next to Eia on a platform. "I guess t'Han doesn't get many Walker visitors."

"Oh, there are plenty of traders and such, but you know how Walkers are about privacy. I don't think there are many in t'Han who have seen a Walker without clothes on."

"You'd be more self-conscious, too, if you didn't have any fur."

"No doubt. This must be our food."

An older child, a l'shan, had appeared, bearing a tray, which id set down on their platform rather hastily. "The cooks beg you to eat the fruit first," id stammered, "since it will warm up quickly and the flavor will be spoiled."

"Thank you very much."

The child gladly retreated.

"Well, that will give one l'shan a story to tell ids friends." Eia picked up a spear of fruit, which had been wrapped in a slender leaf and pierced through with a flower. "One is supposed to feast one's eyes first, but I'm too hungry."

After her fourth piece of fruit Bet was able to begin to savor the flavors: the tang of the herb and the musky sweetness of the melon, the fragrant, honey-flavored flowers, the crunch of the fried noodles and the delicate spicing of the steamed buns. Between the two of them they devastated the tray, then Bet asked with a sigh, "How long until supper?"

She offered to oil Eia's wings. Id lay in preoccupied silence as she rubbed the fragrant oil into ids leathery wing membranes. "You can't lose your hope," she finally said, though it felt very strange to her to be inviting confidence like this.

Eia sighed. "What hope? Five years ago, when you and I first met, I thought the world was on the verge of a breakthrough. The Aeyries and the Walkers were learning to trust each other; never had there been such interaction between the species. And now the Aeyrie population is plummeting; even the separatists have ceased their passionate protests . . . Great Winds, I actually miss them. Our l'shils, even the best and brightest of them, seem weary and dispirited. I fly from Ula to Ula, begging the taiseochs and their counselors to imagine the future. 'If you can imagine it, then it can be created,' I say to them. I am not lying to them; every word I say is the truth. But they have forgotten how to imagine. They dream small dreams, and even then they ask themselves, at every turn, 'But how much will it cost?' The Walkers—the predictable, pragmatic species—they do not interfere with their own progress half so often."

Bet stood with her fingers in the oil pot until finally Eia turned ids head and said worriedly, "There are not many people I can say such things to. . . ."

"What you're saying, it's like a missing piece of a puzzle. I could never say this to anyone either, not even to Laril—that I find the Aeyries to be fascinating, delightful people, but they are wasting away their lives in trivialities. I always thought I was just intolerant. It never occurred to me that I might be right."

"Well, I think you are right. This is what I have wondered: I have wondered if this new decline is my fault. I am the one who has encouraged the Aeyries to intertwine our future with the Walkers. Now, nothing happens in the lowlands which does not reverberate in the Ulas. Have I taken away from my people the last thing which kept us alive; our fierce independence?"

"What choice did you have? The Aeyries were starving to death."

"But at least they were alive until the moment they died!" Eia rested ids sharp cheekbone against the smooth wood platform. "I am at a dangerous age, Ysbet. My youth is behind me. With each passing day, I feel my own death draw a little closer. The struggle to make peace between the Walkers and the Aeyries and save the Aeyrie people from extinction has been the project of my lifetime. If it fails, then my life is a failure. I am too old for a second chance, but young enough that I will have to live a long time with my failure."

Bet was too honest for platitudes, and too convinced of the truth of Eia's words to argue. She sat on the bench in the bath beside Eia Stormtamer, Ambassador of the Aeyrie people to the Walkers, and could not think of anything to say.

Six days later, they flew into Triad.

Chapter 4

Five years ago, when Bet and Laril left Triad for t'Cwa, the community had still been reeling under the devastation wrought by the mage Raulyn's final, magnificent storm. Of the barn and the outbuildings, only the foundations had survived the wind. Trees had been uprooted, the boathouses had been destroyed, and even the shape of the coastline had been altered. But the great stone building which housed the Aeyries and the Walkers had remained standing. Now, Bet saw from the air as they circled in wide spirals overhead, the outbuildings had all been rebuilt, the trees replanted, and the entire diurnal community seemed to be out working in the fields on this balmy afternoon.

The soil here had always been judged too sandy and salty for farming, until the people of Triad proved differently. Now, several other farming communities had settled in the once empty land. Their young woodlands and cultivated fields and fenced pastures swept past Bet; and then once again she saw the sea's polished surface, and the red-painted ship riding off shore.

Four days earlier, flying with her companions through a narrow passageway between mountains, the steep, harsh slopes had seemed to step aside. There lay the patchwork vista of the lowlands, where woods gave way to fields, and Walker houses and barns clustered in orderly little communities, or piled on top of each other in the occasional crowded city. When Bet landed in a grassy meadow that evening, she lay down on her belly in the soft grass, and breathed in the scent of the earth. Her heart sighed. The mountain air was clear and clean, but this was the true smell of home. How weary she had grown of the harsh, spectacular, brightly colored landscape of the mountains! These soft greens and gentle textures, this was where she belonged.

Now, as she circled slowly above the tree-lined fields of Triad, Bet's onfrit swooped in under the shell of her wing to chirrup, "Time to land."

"I don't want to land accidentally in the vegetables, Kathé. Show me a good place."

The trained onfrits untethered Bet from her weary escort. Once again, as the Wing was freed, it trembled on the wind, like a spirited creature forced to spend its days in confinement. Though the long journey often digressed into tedium, these brief moments of freedom as Bet spiraled from sky to earth had never grown old. To turn and to glide, to control for a little while her own destiny, this impassioned her. At night, in her dreams, she could fly as freely as the Aeyries, but by day she knew it was only a dream.

Wings flickering in the sunshine, Kathé guided Bet to an uncultivated field. There, yet another astonished audience, this time Walker as well as Aeyrie, watched her land. Then, with screams and shouts of delight, the children came running. "A Walker! A Walker with wings!" Aeyrie and Walker child alike hovered over Bet as she unharnessed herself. She sat wearily on the ground and let them have at it: if the Wing couldn't survive the attention of a group of children, each of whom wanted to try it first, then it had no business being up in the air either. Soon the children wanted her helmet, too.

A Walker female came in from the field to offer Bet a drink of water from a jug. "They already play at flying all the time," said the Walker worriedly, as if she thought the children would all start jumping willy-nilly off the flight tower, now that they had actually seen a Walker fly.

The rest of Bet's companions scattered across the

field as they landed, bringing down the baggage kites with them. Kathé came to perch on her knee, gazing shyly sideways at the Triad onfrits who flitted excitedly nearby.

"How is your arm?" the Triad Walker asked. "Did it heal straight after all?"

Bet remembered her then. When Bet broke her arm and cracked her head in wild tumble into a dry gully, this woman had been one of several who nursed her. "I've almost forgotten that I ever broke it," she told the woman, holding out her arm for inspection.

Much to the disappointment of the children, Arman began dismantling the Wing. Eia, toting a bundle from the baggage kite, gave Bet a hand up, and they walked together toward the central building.

"They tell me Delan's been up in the attic painting for two days," said Eia. "We'll go up and let idre know we are here. Then I want to spend some time with my children—they are growing up in my absence."

"I want to visit Orgulanthgrnm."

"The Orchths have their own community now." Eia pointed out a cluster of low, thatch-roofed buildings that nestled among trees at the other side of the compound.

"You have more land under cultivation."

"More of everything," said Eia. "More people, more internal conflict, more financial complications, more business at the hospital. Eventually we'll have to build a new hospital outside of the community, probably in the nearest town. But we're hoping to put it off for a few more years."

"It's not a problem to move the hospital so far from the ocean?"

"Apparently it doesn't make any difference to the Mers. They claim they could communicate with their chosen friend from anywhere in the world."

"How does Delan find time to paint, with so much business to take care of?"

"Actually, Triad still runs itself, pretty much. Delan does not even try to manage the community's everyday business—there are others who do that."

They mounted the steep main staircase. On the second floor of the building, where more Aeyries than Walkers lived, the hallway felt more like that of an Ula, with bookcases lining the walls and most of the doors hanging ajar. An Aeyrie with a fussy hatchling walked up and down the length of the hallway, swaying the infant rhythmically in its arms, and singing softly in h'ldat.

Eia and Bet continued up the second, narrower flight of stairs, to the low-ceilinged attic where a row of skylights let in the sun, and a couple of open windows could not entirely disperse the stuffy air. Here, in a litter of stools, canvases, dusty storage cabinets, and crumpled sketchbooks, pale-furred Delan the seer stood at an easel, color-smeared palette in hand, staring distractedly into space. Eia, tapping a finger on ids lips for silence, stepped softly amid the clutter, working around behind Delan until id could see the easel. Id paused then, eyes narrowing, and stepped back with a frown. After a moment id turned, looking for Bet, and gestured her over.

As she came up to ids side, Eia's hands spoke in the language of flight: *What do you make of this?*

An explosion of fierce, agitated color covered Delan's canvas: reds, yellows, and oranges, streaked through with an occasional unsettling bit of lavender or blue. The color radiated out from the center, where there was nothing: only a disturbing darkness, like a night sky from which the stars have all been methodically removed.

The painting dizzied Bet strangely. She could not bear to focus her gaze on it for more than a moment, and she found herself wanting instinctively to put more distance between herself and the chaotic energy of the canvas. She took a nervous step backward, bumping into a stool and knocking over the empty can which had been perched on top of it.

At the sound, Delan turned ids head slowly, as if id were drugged or not entirely conscious, and looked at them.

"I'm home," said Eia.

Delan's mouth moved, but no sound came out. Eia stepped forward to pluck the paintbrush out of Delan's hand. Then id carefully turned the easel around, so the painting faced the wall. "How long since you last ate?"

Delan swallowed, and this time ids voice could be heard, hoarse with disuse. "What day is it?"

"Great Winds, Del! Come on downstairs, and I'll get you something to eat."

"The painting isn't finished."

"It looks finished to me."

"Something is missing. Something—" Delan turned, looking for the painting. "It's important."

Eia tapped ids drawn cheek with the tip of the brush taken from ids hand. "Look: it's dry. You've been standing here without doing any painting for most of the day. The painting is done."

"But something is missing."

"Then something is supposed to be missing."

Bet helped Eia remove Delan's apron, and between the two of them they pushed and pulled the reluctant artist out of the room. At the top of the stairs, Delan rubbed ids face with ids hands and said less thickly, "Eia? What are you doing back so soon?"

"I'm glad to see you, too, love. Food first."

Delan followed Bet down the stairs to the common room, but by the time Eia had fetched soup and bread from the kitchen for all of them, id had fallen asleep with ids head on the table and had to be awakened to eat. But the food seemed to bring id into focus, and id belatedly welcomed Bet and asked about Laril's welfare, though id seemed too distracted to care very much about the answers. "Tell me about the painting," said Eia.

"There is emptiness. And fire. Not the kind that warms a room on a cold night, but the fire that consumes." Delan's spoon dangled from ids hand over the half empty soupbowl. "Hunger," id said. "Ravenous, unimaginable hunger. That is the painting."

While Delan slept, and Eia, frowning with worry, went to claim ids youngest child from the caretakers,

Bet left the building and followed a stone path to the Orchth community. The painting came with her, hovering in her vision like the shadow which comes after staring too long at the sun.

Delan was better known as an artist than a seer. Ids predictions, if predictions they were, were metaphorical at best. Of course, ids paintings hung in every Ula, and in every Lanhall of Is'antul, even, it was rumored, in the palace of the A'lan herself. And there were some hysterics, Walker and Aeyrie both, who swore that the paintings were to blame for all the terrible changes which had happened in the last thirty years: the trade pacts, the peace, the exchanges. Somehow, they said, Delan's visions of this intolerable future had caused it to be brought to pass.

Delan only laughed at this kind of talk; but Eia, at least in private, would frankly say that Delan's visions of peace; both the commonplace and the extraordinary, had done more to improve the relations between Walker and Aeyrie than all of ids own painstaking negotiations and careful diplomacy.

As far as Bet knew, a painting like this had never before come from Delan's hand. She could not imagine what it might portend.

In the Orchth community, plain, windowless mud huts clustered like overturned earthen bowls amid the high grasses of midsummer. Woven grass mats hung across the doorways to block out the midday sun and protect the Orchths' sensitive eyes. Delicate, surprisingly ornate designs, pressed into the mud with fingers or sticks when it was still wet, decorated the doorways. Stepping softly so as to avoid disturbing the sleepers within, Bet examined each doorway in turn, until she found one which had been embedded with an extensive collection of blue and lavender glass pebbles gathered from the seashore, frosted and rounded by the waves and tides. "Orgulanthgrnm," she said softly.

"I smell a friend," rumbled a voice within.

"Cover your eyes; I'm coming in."

She held aside the grass mat and slipped in, letting

it fall shut behind her. Within, on a thick bed of fresh-scented grass, lay the Orchth, taking up nearly half the available space with his furry bulk. At the base of the other wall, a few clay pots were ranged. Orgulanthgrnm's stone flute occupied a place of honor on the only shelf. Bet knelt down and took one of the Orchth's hands in hers. "Pardon me for awakening you."

"Sleep," said the Orchth with a snort. "In summer, the days are long. Much time has passed since you last walked here, Bet."

"Five years."

"Good years, or bad?"

"Good and bad. I don't know—I thought I was making so much progress and learning so much at t'Cwa. But the last few seasons, I have doubted everything. Now I wonder if I have just wasted another five years. My whole life could go by like this, and I could die wondering if I did anything worthwhile or not."

"You are like an Aeyrie with your questions." The Orchth's shaggy head bobbed with amusement. "If it is good, you do not accept it. You must ask what it means."

"It must be a curse."

"Perhaps, perhaps." Orgulanthgrnm lifted his massive body from the ground and stretched all four of his running legs, one at a time, finishing by reaching his arms above his head just as Bet did when she awakened in the morning. "Among my people, there are only a few who ask such questions, the shamans. But their lives are too short, because they cannot eat or sleep until their dream is accomplished. It was one such who brought us here, the shaman Grnlmagdlm . . . I have often asked myself what she would think of us now, had she lived."

"I never heard the story of how you came here," said Bet. She moved the water jar closer to Orgulanthgrnm, then settled herself comfortably on the floor.

"Oho, it is a story you want. Then where is my story gift?"

"If you tell me the story of Grnlmagdlm, I'll tell you the story of how I learned to fly."

"A trade? Well, then." Orgulanthgrnm settled himself once more onto the grass bed. "I remember Grnlmagdlm, for I was her friend. So you will hear my name in this story, but you must remember that it is not my story, it is hers." The Orchth poured some water into the clay cup which lidded the water jar. He took in his breath, and began: "In early springtime, Grnlmagdlm came into her season of power. River Across Singing Stone the elders had named her, for her speed and suppleness, and for the passion with which she sang the old songs of the hill people. 'It is a mighty name,' her mother had said doubtfully. But on the night River came into her season, she rose up before sunset and took herself into the hills to be alone. She knew that when a young female awakened early, with her blood thrumming in her throat like a power chant, it can mean only one thing. And this night, of all nights, she wanted to be alone.

"She wandered the blooming hillsides, working her way gradually westward. At her back, the giant crystalline fingers of the mountain wilderness scratched against the sky. Ahead of her, the hills knelt into the sea, where one small moon floated like a pearl on the swelling belly of the ocean. River paused on the last hilltop, astonished that she had come so far.

"On these shimmering beaches, where a pinch of sand contained grains of glass ground from mountains across the world, the Orchth gathered each autumn to collect and dry the seaweed strewn across the sand. Here River had met that sweet singer of the Grass People, Orgulanthgrnm, He who Cries into the Wind. Remembering how he had openly admired her sleek fur and muscular flanks, and how after the throat singing that night had taken her aside to compliment her on her voice, River felt a flush of heat course through her body.

"She lay down on the last hilltop to watch the moon sink into the ocean. She did not need to turn her head to see that the western horizon had begun to pale, for she could smell the rising sun. River lay in the warm dawn, power thrumming in her blood, and wondered if it had only been her memory of Orgulanthgrnm which had brought her to this place. For the first time she understood why the elders had replied so indulgently when she first announced to them that she wished to become a shaman. 'What you wish,' they had said to her, 'has little to do with what will be.'

"She took refuge from the sun in a sea cave. All day long she could hear the voices of a herd of Merfolk, harvesting caricha in the seaweed forest just beyond the breakers, but by sunset they had gone out on the tide. She had drunk her fill from a spring known to her, and once more waited on her hilltop, when a winged being no larger than her two forehands clasped together came flying down the beach. She was half hidden by the lush grass and blooming flowers of spring, but she stood up and the being veered toward her.

"It hovered before her face, just out of reach of her powerful forehands.

" 'This is my season of power,' River said to it. 'I will not hurt you, and you cannot harm me.'

"The being cocked its head, as if puzzled or intrigued, and examined her intently out of eyes like wet stones. A four-legged creature, it flew on wings like cleata-skin stretched over a basketframe, its forepaws tucked to its furry chest. A harness, discolored by dirt and sweat, strapped a small package to its back. 'I seek the Lost,' it said.

"River breathed in the being's scent, and felt her power shudder in her body. She smelled his maleness, his weariness, and his hunger, truths any youngling could have detected. But she also smelled his journey, long beyond imagining. She smelled the salty sea in his fur, the aged, oiled wood of a sea vessel, and the faded scent of fear. She smelled the older scents of his homeland: the smell of rich earth freshly turned, and the body scents of alien persons far more complex and contradictory than this simpler being before her. She smelled urgency and anxiety, and she smelled need and an old, unforgotten love. On last thing she smelled, which set her skin to tingling.

" 'I will help you,' she said. Out of her sidepouch she offered him nuts and dried fruit, the last of the winter stores, hard and stale now. The being landed on her slender back, and soon slept there, his small clawed feet clutching her fur. When he awoke, River was already climbing the steeper slopes where the hill people lived at midsummer and gathered wild apples and berries, though she was still a goodly distance from their winter home.

" 'I am River Across Singing Stones,' she said, 'And I am a shaman.' For she already had learned this one small thing, that by saying that a thing was true it often became true.

" 'I am Ch'ta. I am Speaker for the mage Delan.'

"So, it had indeed been power which River smelled in the being's fur. She paused at the top of the slope, not to catch her breath, but to turn her forebody and fill her nostrils once again with the scent of the Speaker's truth. Now she could smell the mage clearly, though the complexity of the scent challenged even her heightened awareness to completely sort it out. 'Who is the Lost?' she asked.

" 'Brother Och,' the being said again. 'Brother Lost.'

"Once again, River smelled Ch'ta's love. 'I am bringing you to the elders of my people," she said. The shortening spring night had already run half its course; she dropped her forelegs to earth and ran as only the six-legged can, swift and smooth as water. Even so, the sun had begun to brighten the sky when River stumbled down the steep slope into the sheltered valley of Winterhome.

"In the largest cave the elders gathered, six who had survived a hundred journeys from winter to summer and back to winter again. The memories of a thousand snowfalls, of the many generations of cubs bumbling after their mothers, surviving or not surviving, of the voices of the people, singing the stars into the sky, all these memories lay in their lined faces and their deep eyes. Like all cubs, River had feared them. But in her season of power she could smell the anguish and peace of their long lives, and she feared them no longer.

"She lay respectfully on the ground before them, bowing even her head into the shelter of her folded forearms. She did not need to tell them that she had entered her season of power, or even where she had been these last two nights. They would smell the sea-salt and the power, and they would know.

"River had rested this day in her motherclan's cave, but once again she had neither eaten nor slept. The cubs had looked fearfully at the Speaker riding River's shoulder, but the other females greeted her with gentle hands, those who remembered their first season, and those still too young to have anything to remember. By nightfall, several males of other clans had gathered outside the cave, carrying gifts of succulent greens and roasted nutmeats. River acknowledged their presence as she walked to the cave of the elders, but she did not accept their gifts.

"Yet her body was still burning as she spoke to the elders. 'This is Ch'ta, Speaker for Delan the mage. He has crossed the ocean seeking an Orchth called Lost. I have said I would help him.'

"One by one the elders smelled the Speaker's fur. They conferred among themselves, and at last Mrklglmn spoke. 'It is your right to do as you will, River Across Singing Stones. We have only this to say: For a thousand thousand years the Orchth have walked this land. Do not do lightly that which will change our people forever.'

"At these words River felt ashamed, yet she replied boldly, 'I do as I must.'

" 'Then hear these words, and do not forget them. When your mother's mother's mother first suckled at her mother's teats, the people who rode on water and walk on two legs first came into our land. We Orchth fear no creature, but we learned to fear these, who killed though they were not carnivores, and stole our young from their mother's caves.'

" 'Yes,' said River, for even though it had happened long before her time, there are some things that the people cannot forget.

" 'When you were a cub, one of those who had been stolen returned home to his people. We who stand before you have spoken with him, but we are not the bearers of his story. It is among the Grass People that you must seek his memory.'

"With astonishment River's fur ruffled along the ridge of her backbone. 'If his story is known, then why is it not told at the seashore gathering? For I have never heard it.'

"Once again the elders conferred with each other, their voices a low rumble in the heavy silence of the cave. River could smell the scent of their concern, and for once did not envy them this power of theirs. She had begun to understand that with power comes the weight of responsibility, a burden that grew only heavier with each passing year.

" 'These are questions which we do not lightly answer. Understand, River Across Singing Stones, that to be a shaman is to know when to be silent.'

" 'I understand this,' said River.

"Then we tell you this, that there are some things which it is better to forget than to remember. The elders have decided that the story of the lost Orchth is to be forgotten. It is for the sake of our cubs yet to be born that this is so.'

"Once again River lay silent in astonishment, for this was a thing she had never known, that the elders decided what the people would remember, and what the people would forget. She wanted to ask them how they decided such a thing, but the elders were already leaving the cave. Her audience with them was over.

"After they were gone, the Speaker on her shoulder, who had listened in silence, spoke suddenly, his voice cracked like an old seed jar. 'Brother Och is dead?' he said.

" 'No, he is not dead, for he is still remembered,'

said River. She smelled his grief, and turned her head to lick his fur, marking him with her friend-scent. 'He must have been very old, Speaker-for-Delan, for very few elders are alive who lived in the Days when the Orchth Learned Fear.'

" 'He was my friend,' said the Speaker.

"River knew that she could do nothing for his sadness. She rose up from the cold cave floor, shaking a lingering stiffness out of her muscles. 'I must bid my mother and clan farewell, and then I will take you to the Grass People.'

"River's mother and her sisters promised to remember her. The males who still gathered hopefully at her motherclan's entrance watched her leave in disappointed silence. The older females rarely take more than two or three lovers, but a youngling like River could have satisfied a dozen or more before her season burned itself out. She walked too swiftly away from them, her loins sticky with her hunger.

"She crossed the steep cliffs and sharp ridges of the rugged land to the north of Winterhome. By the third night she had reached the Downs, where the stars hung low over the bowed over remains of last year's grass, which covered the rolling hills like matted fur. A deep breath of the wind brought her the scent of the ancient stone village of the Grass People, but she had to spend that day in a damp rock cleft, shielding her eyes with her hands. She did not arrive until the middle of the next night.

"The people were scattered across the hills, but as she drew near, an entourage of males attracted by her scent accompanied her to the cluster of round stone buildings which was their Winterhome. They were puzzled but not put off by the alien rider on her back, for a female in her season of power does as she chooses. They offered her beautiful, cleverly woven grass baskets filled with sweet oxrka seeds, but she accepted only some dried fruit and nuts from one of the motherclans, which she put into her sidepouch for

Ch'ta. Then she went into the abiding place of the elders.

"The thick stone walls and sod roof plucked out the teeth of the biting wind, and a smoldering dung fire gave forth a welcome warmth. River lay down on the earthen floor, her eyes watering from the smoke. 'The elders of the Hill People greet you,' she said politely. 'I am the shaman River Across Singing Stones.'

"The elders of the Grass People listened in silence as she introduced the Speaker for the mage Delan and told them the purpose of her visit. They held their silence long after she had ceased to speak, and then, with a sigh like wind in the ocean pines, the eldest among them, whose hair glowed white in the dim dwelling, spoke only two words, reluctantly, like heavy stones rolling onto the seashore. 'Orgulanthgrnm remembers.'

"She smelled their concern, and even something like fear. 'My power has brought me here,' she said. 'How can I do any harm?'

"The elders sighed as one. 'Many shamans have walked through this door, Grnlmagdlm, and every one of them has been very young. Each one asks us that question, 'How can I do any harm?' The answers to that question are like the stars in the sky. We are weary of trying to answer that question.'

"She pressed her face against the cold dirt floor. 'Why are the elders afraid of the shamans?' she asked.

'It is because you do not know, and will not believe, how much harm you can do. But we know, and we believe.'

"Outside of the elders' hut, Orgulanthgrnm stood apart from the crowd of suitors. He bore no gift with which to tempt her favors, only a carrying basket full of fresh greens. Even from the distance that separated them, River could smell in his fur the sweat of long, swift journeying, and the dampness of a remote, muddy river. Sometimes, cubs fell ill in the springtime after the long winter without any greenery, and it became a matter of life or death to find a supply, and quickly. Orgulanthgrnm had undertaken this urgent project.

"River went to his side, hearing the males sigh with regret in her wake. 'He who Cries into the Wind,' she greeted him. 'I am a shaman.'

"He looked at her without replying, as the vagrant wind brought a puff of smoke and the sharp scent of roasting nuts to River's nostrils. A young cub yowled at a corner of the village.

"At last he said regretfully, 'It is a rare thing, to be a shaman.'

" 'The elders have told me that you remember Och. This my companion has traveled from a far land in search of him.'

" 'Yes,' said Orgulanthgrnm. 'I remember Och.' Then he sighed deeply, and she smelled in him, not the disappointment of frustrated desire, but a much rarer thing. She smelled that he loved her.

"River walked beside Orgulanthgrnm as he doled out the contents of his heavy basket, and he told her and Ch'ta what he remembered. The kidnapped Orchth known as Och, or "Lost" had traveled with many others across the sea. There, with the exchange of something called money, he had passed into the control of another of the two-legged land walkers, who once again took him on a journey by ship. After nearly a year of traveling from port to port, he was sold again, in a land which became his home.

"In this land, said Orgulanthgrnm, there were flatlands along the edge of the sea, and there were mountains, jagged crystalline ranges, which reached from the edge of the flatlands to the end of the earth. In the fertile flatlands, wherever there was room to build a house, lived the two legged people, the Walkers, who fancied themselves the rightful rulers of the land. It was a Walker once again who purchased Och, and put him in a cage pulled by drafs. Along with many other creatures of the earth, also in cages, Och traveled from town to town, where Walkers paid for the privilege of staring at him. For the rest of his childhood and well into his adulthood, he lived like this. By then, he had learned a few words of the Walker language, and gone more than a little mad.

"At last, an Aeyrie named A'bel, injured and captured by the Walkers, was caged and made part of the traveling show. Over the long days and long nights they became friends and came to call each other brother. One night A'bel escaped from his cage and set Och free as well, and they parted in haste, with scarcely the opportunity to say good-bye.

"Och nearly died that first year. The Walkers, who could see both in daylight and in the dark (at this River sighed with wonder) were difficult to avoid except when they were hibernating in winter, and they fiercely protected the fruits of the land which they considered to be theirs. At last Och found a cave in a remote area, and there he settled down to live his solitary life.

"It was many, many years later that a young Aeyrie, unable to fly because of an injured wing and pursued by a Walker sorcerer, stumbled into Och's territory. Remembering A'bel, Och had helped the young mage Delan to escape. Later, Delan had come to him in the form of a ghost, asking him for help, and so in a great battle between the Walkers and the Aeyries once again saved Delan's life.

"It had been Och's old friend A'bel who, along with Delan, put Och onto a ship which at last took him home. Och had been a great singer, and so he and Orgulanthgrnm became close friends. He had died two years previously.

"Orgulanthgrnm did not finish telling all that he remembered until the night was nearly over, and they rested together in one of the sod huts as he roasted grass seed and stewed dried fruit for himself and the onfrit. River turned her head to see that Ch'ta had undone the harness and taken the package off of his back. The onfrit unwrapped layers of a soft, shiny cloth, as light as air, to reveal at last a shard of pale blue crystal. River drew near to the crystal, smelling magic.

" 'Och is dead,' said the onfrit. 'River and He Who Cries, they remember him.'

"The crystal clouded, as if a blizzard of snow had crossed its face. And then it cleared, to reveal a face captured within its depths, a face like none River had ever before seen: narrow and pointed, softened by silver-gray fur. Orgulanthgrnm drew near as well, then drew back, frightened, muttering, 'This is shaman's business.'

"The face in the crystal began to speak, a strange, soft, liquid language, so airy and lilting in comparison to the deep, growly speech of the Orchths that River did not quite realize that it was speech at all. But then the onfrit began to translate. 'This image which speaks to you is only a memory,' said the onfrit. 'I have tried, but I cannot scry across the sea. I think of you every day, brother Lost. Ch'ta has news of all your old friends, all of whom still remember you.'

"At this, Ch'ta chittered sadly to himself, and then had to speak more quickly to catch up once again with the image speaking in the crystal. 'I have just been named taiseoch of the Triad, my brother, for Pehtal is ill and not expected to recover. Here, the uneasy peace we have made with each other, Walker and Aeyrie and Mer, continues to deepen and to spread. When we named our community Triad, we did not know that in fact there are four races of sentient people living on this earth. This my heart is telling me, that your people belong here, too, in the home of peace. We need your strength and your wisdom, for these are dark and troubled times. I am asking you to come back, and to bring some of your fellows with you.

" 'Ch'ta has come to you in a sailing ship owned by Triad. The ship will return to pick up Ch'ta sixty days after it drops him off. I know it is a long, uncertain journey to a strange land, and I can scarcely believe that I dare ask you to undertake it. But I am speaking to you as a mage and a seer. We need your people, not just for our sake but for yours. Please, for the sake of our friendship, go with Ch'ta to meet that ship, and come back to us.'

"The light in the crystal faded. Orgulanthgrnm lay on his belly, his face buried in his forearms. River reached out and picked up the crystal, and cupped it in her hand. Her power thrummed in her blood, quivering through her muscles, shuddering in her great, thundering heart. She thought about all the elders had told her. Rightly had they feared to remember Och, who had returned from his long exile to speak, not only of hatred and slavery, but of other gentle and wise people who had called him brother and friend. For how many generations had they restrained the wanderlust and curiosity of their youth by the use of fear? And without that fear, how could they retain their ancient culture intact and unchanged?

" 'They cannot,' River said out loud. 'From the day Och came home to us, we were a changed people. The elders themselves knew that so important a thing could never be forgotten.' Her hunger lay in her belly, not a hunger for food or for sex, but for the sight of a strange sun setting on a strange shore, for the sound of songs that the Orchth had never dreamed of, for the wonder and mystery of all she had thought she could never know.

"It was this hunger speaking when River had first announced her intention to become a shaman. More than her hunger for love, or food, or to bear cubs, or to walk the safe grounds of known lands, or even to live, she had hungered for that strangeness, for the knowledge which would fill her and change her and make her an alien to her own people. So she had chosen, and now she knew her destiny.

"It was the elders who remembered the past, who told the people when to wander and when to settle, when to plan for a hard winter and when to anticipate the warming of spring. It was the elders who told the tales and sang the songs of the people, who named the cubs and remembered the dead. But for a journey such as this, a break from the traditions of the people and a defiant leap into the unknown sky, for this the people would only follow a shaman.

". . . It was Orgulanthgrnm who carried her, half in his forearms and half on his back, down the swaying gangplank onto the sighing dock. River Across Singing Stones had never seen so clearly as she saw this bright evening, with the sunset still gleaming the sky with its eye-aching light. Behind Orgulanthgrnm, following not him, but her, the people came; mostly young, a few older who had never forgotten the restlessness of their youth. They looked with wondering eyes at the people grouped on shore, at the singing Mers exploding joyfully from the glassy surface of the swelling sea.

"River looked for one last time at the ship which had carried them so gently across the uncertain sea. Sixty days, maybe longer; as her visions took her, she had lost track of the days. Then she looked forward, at the people waiting so quietly on shore. The mage Delan stood out among them like a white flame, holding a suckling cub in the crook of one arm. Other Aeyries, black and brown, red and golden, quietly shared the shore with Walkers of all sizes. A few Mers had allowed the sea to wash them onto the beach, and lay on the wet sand. Beside one, a half-grown wingless Aeyrie crouched, gently stroking the wet fur.

"River took a deep breath of their scent, and smelled their minds, open like goblets, and their power. The elders had cried out against her as she led the people away, calling her mad. 'All shamans are mad,' she had said to them. At last she knew, beyond all doubt, that she had brought her people to the right place, to a land which they would one day call their home.

"Orgulanthgrnm laid her gently onto the dry sand. 'We are here,' he said gruffly. 'Now will you eat?'

"She looked at him gently. Of course, he knew that it was much too late. Some shamans outlive their season, and some do not. In full knowledge of this truth, River had made her decision. Orgulanthgrnm bent over to stroke her wasted cheek with his tongue, as

Delan and another Aeyrie drew near. A rare thing, this love. A guarantee that she would always be Remembered.

" 'I am the healer, Gein,' said the red Aeyrie. 'How can I help?'

"Orgulanthgrnm raised his heavy head. 'River Across Singing Stones is our shaman. If the shamans of our people sleep, or eat, or make love, it will end their Season of Power. And River has led us on a very long journey. She should not have lived this long.'

"The red Aeyrie seemed to understand more than had been spoken. After a brief, low-voiced discussion with the healer, Delan the mage came forward and dropped gracefully to one knee, laying a warm hand onto River's forearm. 'Had I known what I was asking, I still would have asked it.'

" 'And I still would have come,' said River, in the whisper that was all that remained of the voice with which once she had set the echoing canyons to shivering.

" 'Welcome, to your new land and to your new people. We will always remember you.'

"So the shaman River Across Singing Stones shut her eyes and slept, the sleep from which there is no awakening. Her Season of Power was over. But she is Remembered to this day."

Chapter 5

A day later, at dawn, Bet strapped herself into the Walker Wing once again and waited, at the top of the Triad flight tower, for Arman to finish organizing the other Aeyries and give the signal which would start the day's journey. Even the Aeyries had clamored their objections when Eia announced that they would rest at Triad for just one day. But there could be no delays, Eia insisted, so forcefully that for the first time Bet began to wonder just exactly what it was that Eia had up ids sleeve.

The sun rose through a pastel nosegay of soft summer clouds. The Aeyries launched the baggage kites, as bright as flags, onto the gentle morning wind. "Are we ready?" Arman cried.

Someone answered that Eia had not yet made an appearance, and there were mutters of irritated discontent. With a sigh, Bet leaned against a railing. The Wing's harness straps already were awakening the bruises and abrasions accumulated on this interminable journey. She considered unstrapping herself again, but, no, Eia appeared at last on the tower stairway, with Delan at ids side, and waved apologetically. Both Eia and Delan wore flightsuits, Bet noticed, and Delan had a case similar to Eia's map case strapped between ids wings—for a sketchbook and pens, Bet guessed.

"Is Delan joining us?" cried Arman in astonishment.

Eia gestured: Yes.

Shaking ids head in disbelief, Arman signaled Bet
and her escorts to prepare to launch. The onfrits flew
up in a chattering cloud of flickering wings, and the
baggage kites floated sunward, their astil wings bil-
lowing in the soft wind.

Their journey now took them along the jagged
northern coastline, where, except for an occasional
fishing boat dragging its nets through pale caricha
beds, and an occasional fishing community bravely
perched on the cliff's edge, the land was abandoned
to the domination of rock and water and sand. Here
cleata lizards sunned themselves on the rocks along
shore, or swam sinuously through the smooth water
beyond the breakers. Sometimes, when the wind died
down, the restless surface of the ocean lay still and
shiny as an iced-over pond. Bet could see the ocean's
floor, with sunlight glittering on ground glass, and
bright-shelled snails climbing the feathered towers of
the pink and golden coral.

That first night, they camped on bare ground and
ate only cold camp food for their supper. The t'Cwa
Aeyries quarreled among each other. Even Arman
could not summon up the energy to chat with Bet
about the day's flight. Just to get away from them,
Bet climbed the cliff to the water's edge. The tide was
rising, and soon she waded, knee-deep, through the
cool water. Two moons rose, and then two more.
Bet's ears were filled with the hush and sigh of the
sea.

Then she heard someone calling her name, and she
made her way back to the cliff, where Delan, silver
in starlight and winged in ghostly white, stood on a
last sandy beachhead. In this uncertain light, an
Aeyrie would be all but blind. Bet took Delan's arm
to show idre the way up the cliffside. "You didn't
have to come. You know I can take care of myself."

"I wanted to get away from them, too. What nasty
moods all of us are in."

It was strange to hear an Aeyrie speak h'ldat with
a Walker accent. Delan's arm was so thin Bet could

close her fingers around it: bone, clad in muscle, with not even a hint of fat.

"I thought you would convince Eia to postpone this trip, because of the painting."

"I know better," said Delan.

They climbed the steep cliff; Delan, with ids s'oleil and heightened sense of touch climbing it almost as easily as Bet, even though id could not see. At the top of the cliff, they turned to look at the ocean, which the moons and the stars had clad in silver thread. "This has been a long journey for you already, Bet. And I think we are all of us going to journey much farther than we expect, before we are done."

"Why did you come along?"

"Because I know something is going to happen in Is'antul."

Bet shivered in the cool wind that blew across the surface of the sea. Without another word, they turned and walked back to where the warm light of an air lamp flickered among the stones.

The next evening, before sunset, they landed near the shores of the Is'isre Inlet, a shallow, warm sea, choked with lush seaplants and richly fragrant in the summer heat. Here many Walkers dove for shellfish, piling their flat-bottomed boats with their harvest and then poling in to shore where small cottage factories processed and pickled them for the Is'antul market.

Eia led them to a nearby travel house which presided over a wagon track aspiring to be a road. Here the innkeeper greeted them effusively in broken h'ldat. The public room was empty except for a boy halfheartedly cleaning ashes out of the stove, but soon the local Walkers began to trickle in, calling loudly for beer and pies and tossing their coins onto the tabletops. Divers and boaters, most of them were, with a few hardy homesteaders, their backs broad and bowed from struggling with the rocky soil. They stared somewhat askance at the large crowd of Aeyries, but most of them greeted Eia by name, and it soon became clear to Bet that the modest travel house would not normally have a tenth of the customers, if not for the attraction of the Aeyrie ambassador's presence. Uninvited, the Walkers pulled up chairs to Eia's table to express their opinions on this or that subject. Eia welcomed them warmly, and plunged cheerfully into the heat of debate.

Soon, Walker and Aeyrie alike were engaged in cheerful, awkward, halting conversations, punctuated by much gesturing and nodding of heads with which they filled the gulf of language. When the Aeyries called on Bet to translate, she firmly refused. "You should have studied harder when you were a l'shan. Now let me eat my dinner in peace."

But she herself could not escape the attention of the Walkers for long. They bought her drinks she did not want, and eagerly asked her, not what it was like to live with the Aeyries, but what it was like to fly. She tried to explain that she was not in fact flying at all, but merely gliding behind the Aeyries like their baggage. She told them that all she could do under her own power was leap off a high place and ride the wind to the ground. Their eyes grew wide and blank with wonder and desire, and they swore they would come to the landing place in the morning to watch.

And, indeed, they were there in the morning, they and all their friends. Bet, feeling Eia's gaze focused a little too sharply on her, turned to ask idre a question, only to find id looking innocently away.

From Is'isre they flew inland, bisecting the great peninsula which curls around the Is'antul harbor. For three days they flew over lush farmlands divided into tiny plots, each one farmed by a single family. Each generation, the farm plots had been divided into smaller and smaller portions until now they were scarcely big enough to feed a family. The farmers here were the poorest in the Walker lands, but they refused to pool their land and labor into communal farms.

After six days of travel, they reached the bustling Is'antul harbor at last, where oceangoing ships from the four corners of the world crowded the deep pocket of still water. Here they gathered to sell their cargoes of fine wood and useful metals, spices and carpets, tools and cloth, and everything else imaginable, from the commonplace to the unheard-of. And here the ships would take on their new cargoes of woven astil, glass shards, rare dried fruits, and the whole collection of Aeyrie inventions which had made the lowlands famous across the known world. Here also the fishing fleets, with their precious cargoes of caricha, would come to port in noisy seaside towns where sailors, fishers and farmers, tradespeople and factory workers, artisans and moneychangers, all rubbed elbows and fought for customers and space on the same crowded streets.

From her vantage overhead, Bet smelled the stink and heard the noise, and watched the feverish activity as the day turned toward evening and the people struggled to close one last deal before dark. Their wide-winged shadows skimmed across streets and marketplaces now; but not one head lifted to see what was passing by overhead. That night, they landed on a tile rooftop in one of the quieter districts of a quieter town, where rich traders' villas occupied the shoreline or nestled among the hills. The landing required Bet to set foot on the rooftop lightly and precisely so that she neither broke the tiles nor ended up in the courtyard below. She did it alone, with no one to admire how well she had done. Immediately, she had to move the Wing aside to make room for the others in the small space.

This was the end of the journey for Arman and the other Aeyries who had flown with Bet all the way from t'Cwa. Tomorrow they would load her Wing into a baggage kite and carry it home again, to make all the many adjustments and improvements they had dreamed up during the journey. And she would have to rely on her own two feet like every other Walker.

A door on the rooftop gave access to the unheard-of second floor of the building. Eia jangled a bell rope, and eventually a stout Walker female opened the door to let them in. "Master Eia," she said, somewhat inaccurately. She could not think of any words

at all with which to greet the rest of the Aeyries and
onfrits who crowded the rooftop. Upon Bet she cast
a single disbelieving glance, but quickly smoothed her
features into an expression of professional indifference. She led the way down a polished hallway to a
plush suite, where the usual stools provided for Aeyries had been delicately carved with wooden vines,
and padded with expensive brocade, and where cabinets intricately made of a dark, fine-grained wood
held a collection of fragile painted porcelain. Through
the two open doorways, Bet saw three beds covered
with the same fine brocade.

The Walker fussed nervously about where they
would all sleep and how she would feed all of them,
unwilling to accept that most of them would simply
sleep on the floor, and plain food would be fine with
them. She did not seem too happy about the crowd of
onfrits either. Her anxiety and her strained deference
distressed Bet. She had forgotten what it was like to
live in a society where people were treated in accord-
ance with their rank.

After the innkeeper had left, Arman started another
of ids lengthy, technical discussions on the subject of
the Walker Wing. Soon all of them except Eia and
Delan, who retreated into one of the bedrooms, clustered around a scrap of paper on the tabletops as
Arman, expostulating tirelessly, used the fountain pen
id always clipped to ids flightsuit to draw one tiny
diagram after another. Bet went into the other bedroom to change out of the flightsuit and stand at the
open window for a while, as twilight fell over the tile
rooftops of the town. In the street below, a streetseller
pushing a handcart full of black bread sauntered past,
as his busy assistant raced from doorway to doorway,
delivering bread by the armload.

Bet had grown up on a community farm no different
from the many she had overflown recently. Occasional
trips to a nearby town, much more modest than this
one, had been a wonderful and awesome occasion.
Bet had traveled far since then; she had been transported vast distances in mere moments via the Void.

She had lived as a slave in the remote wilderness of
the mountains, as a patient and guest in idyllic Triad,
and as the only Walker in an Aeyrie Ula. She had
been violated and injured in ways which would never
heal; and she had recovered in ways no one had ever
imagined. She had worked magic, she had seduced an
Aeyrie, she had killed a mage; and now she had
become the first Walker to fly. Somehow, this fine
town, with its civilized quiet and clean streets, did not
impress her nearly as much as it once would have.

She went back into the common room when she
heard the door open. The innkeeper, leading a proces-
sion of tray-bearing servants, had returned. Even a
small stablegirl, recently washed and brushed, had
been recruited to lug in an armload of blankets and
towels. The Aeyries baffled the servants by bowing to
them and thanking them carefully in their own language, as they had been taught was proper. To teach
an Aeyrie to be polite only to those of equal or greater
rank than theirs was a hopeless task. Out of a perverse
sense of humor, Bet bowed to the servants, too. When
they left, they carried most of the porcelain with them,
evidence of the innkeeper's unspoken worry about the
number and variety of her guests.

Bet slipped into the other bedroom after she had
eaten. There, Delan sat at a desk with ids sketchbook
open under the bright flame of an air lamp, drawing
with one hand and eating a piece of fruit with the
other. The sounds of the street below entered through
the open window: the sweet music of a harp, the trilling of laughter, the banging of pans in the inn kitchen,
the rumble of wagon wheels on stone. Bet walked
softly to the bed and lay down on it.

Delan rubbed the paper with a fingertip, wrote a
few words, then turned to see who had entered the
room. "Well, are you sick and tired of flying?"

"I never thought I'd say this, but I think I'm going
to miss the Wing."

"Why don't you ask Arman to let you have it?"

Bet had leaned her head on the crook of her arm,

but now she lifted it in surprise. "Arman would never give me ids invention!"

"Can you think of anyone who deserves it more?"

"But what would I do with it?"

"Whatever you want. Disassembled, it will be easy enough to transport; it is so light. And soon you will have other baggage anyway, since Eia is sending you out shopping in the morning. Ask Arman for the Wing, Bet."

Bet got up to look at Delan's sketchbook. Delan had drawn her in flight, recording forever those brief moments before she landed, when she controlled her own wings, her direction, her destiny. Bet studied the drawing wistfully. "I'll never belong in the air. You make me look at home there, but I never will be."

"Considering that most Walkers are so afraid of heights that they can't bring themselves to climb a flight of stairs. . . ."

"Well—"

Delan turned the page and began to sketch again. This time, the Is'antul harbor began to take form under ids pencil. Bet went out into the common room, where the onfrits were licking the trays clean, and asked Arman to give her the Wing. To her surprise, Arman readily agreed, seeming delighted that she had asked.

"Well, the Wing is mine," Bet said, when she entered the bedroom again.

Frowning with concentration, Delan drew a ship from an Aeyrie's overhead vantage point: a strange vessel, all deck and sails. Bet lay on the bed again and watched id's work. Bet had more in common with Delan than she had with most Aeyries. Both of them had been hatched in a Walker community and raised by sharemothers; both of them had realized very young that they did not and could never fit into their community. Both of them had been blessed or cursed with mage gifts, though in Bet her talents had been destroyed, only to partially regenerate many years later. They even had Laril, Bet's lover and Delan's child, in common. Sometimes Delan seemed very like

a Walker, though other times, like now, id was pure
Aeyrie: concentrated, remote, secretive, troubled.

Bet said, "Delan—what about the fire painting?"

Delan set down ids pencil and turned on the stool.
The light shining through ids wings illuminated its delicate tracing of red blood veins. "I think about the
painting day and night. But I see only small, shattered
images: A lone Mer, traveling far out of sea. An
Aeyrie in a dark place, where water runs. Is'antul's
streets, chaotic with a bloody riot. Do these images
make any sense to you?"

"Not really."

"Then I guess we will know the future when it
comes and lands in our laps."

Arman and the rest of Bet's escort, including all the
onfrits, left at first light. Soon the innkeeper herself
knocked at the door of the suite: she had come to
take Bet shopping. Bet did not return to the inn again
until midday, when she entered the suite to find a
young servant unwrapping all the parcels which had
been delivered, and carefully repacking them into a
small trunk. Bet had been prepared to spend the
morning fighting against the purchase of overly sophis-
ticated and ornate clothing, but instead now found
herself the owner of an astonishingly expensive, surprisingly severe wardrobe in which the primary colors
were black and silver. She had also spent an amazing
amount of time and money at a hairdressers, but the
results were equally stark: a plain, blunt haircut which
emphasized her strong chin and ungenerous mouth.
No one who looked at Bet would doubt that she was
in Is'antul on serious business.

Delan and Eia emerged from the bedroom, having
donned Walker style clothing over their smooth brushed
fur. The inn servants took their baggage, including the
disassembled Walker Wing wrapped and tied in heavy
canvas, to a handcart waiting below. The three of
them followed soon after, to traipse through the inevitable assault of stares and whispers generated by their
passage, down the crowded street to the dock. By the

time they arrived, the servants had already hired a suitable boat, loaded it with their baggage, and stood self-importantly by to help Bet and the Aeyries board the small vessel.

Bet, who had yet to see any money change hands, whispered to Delan, "Who pays for all this?"

"In this case, the innkeeper—Eia has an account with her, managed by the Triad accountant. Most of Eia's expenses are billed to Triad, and eventually covered by the Ulas, which are supposed to send Eia a portion of their trade profits, an obligation they only occasionally neglect. They have no idea what a bargain they are getting—Eia has never asked for a salary, and, being Aeyries, it never occurs to them to pay idre. Of course, id could make a fine living on Walker bribes."

Their scarlet- and blue-painted high-sided boat had a scarlet sail which the crew of two hoisted as soon as the Aeyries and Bet had seated themselves on cushioned benches. They cast off from the dock under a brisk afternoon wind, leaving the bustle of the harbor town swiftly behind them. Delan opened ids sketchbook. Dodging sculls, sailing ships, and flocks of other water taxis like their own, the boat scudded northward across the crowded harbor.

Scarcely had they left the congestion behind than they entered it anew: this time, though, it was frail pleasure boats which had embarked from the capital city, and slow-moving barges laden with goods and supplies. The female crewmember, her bare torso burnt nearly black by the sun, came back to offer them tea and cakes and a commentary on the passing sights. She explained to them that in Is'antul no commerce was permitted, and so all of its goods were purchased in other cities and imported. Eia thanked her, and asked her pointedly to leave them alone.

The three of them sat in silence for the rest of the journey, as the pleasure crafts, crewed by brightly and expensively dressed young people, many of whom stared openly at the two Aeyries, slipped past them, and as they in turn passed the slow-moving, heavily laden barges.

Along the shore, the clutter of docks and warehouses gave way to beautiful parklands, through which quiet streams meandered and lush meadows grew. Then the pure white of the walls of Is'antul came into sight, blindingly bright in the sunshine. "How beautiful it is!" said Bet.

But as they drew closer, she began to smell the stink. Trash and sewage floated in the water, and soon the barges and pleasure boats gave way to another kind of boat: slow-moving, leaky tubs that hugged the shore, their sails patched and their wood rotting, occupied by whole families, who bathed in and ate from the same putrefying water they used as a sewer.

As their taxi passed the docks, where an army of hunched figures scuttled over a barge, unloading it and hurrying its contents into the city, they came to a pair of docks marked by pennants, where under white walls a canal opened into the sea. Here many other water taxis and pleasure boats bobbed on the waves, their sails loose and flapping, using oars and boathooks to fend off the docks and other boats. The taxi crew dropped their sail and drew up to the side of another taxi, where they exchanged clever insults with the other crew.

"We're waiting to get into the canal," said Eia. "We could have entered the Inner City on foot, but it's much faster this way."

Bet sat in silence, haunted by the thin faces of the frantic workers of the docks. Nearby, in the fouled water, a crowd of children splashed, diving for coins thrown for them by bored pleasure boaters waiting for access to the canal. A wine jar was handed from boat to boat. They listening to the bored drawls and inane giggles of the overdressed nobles in a nearby boat, as, one by one, ragged workers who crowded the docks caught the ropes thrown to them from the boats below, looped them over their shoulders, and dragged the boats and their passengers into the canal.

Soon it was their turn, and the two crewmembers

tossed their ropes onto the docks. With four sweating dock workers dragging at the lines, the boat began to slip past the dock. The boat haulers' feet slapped hollowly onto the wooden dock, then fell silent as they stepped onto the crowded white stone walkway which edged either side of the canal.

The walls of Is'antul's Inner City loomed overhead now. Occasionally, they passed a small window in the wall, or saw someone walking along its top, but otherwise there was only the pure, white expanse of stone, and the stinking crowd of haulers walking the narrow way below, where drains poured their effluvia into the sea. As Delan sketched one of the haulers bent into his rope, Eia stared grimly forward, wings folded tightly, long-fingered hands clasped across a slender knee.

I need my own kind, thought Bet ironically to herself. Certainly, she could see nothing here to make her proud to be a Walker. She supposed that the people who lived out their lives in Is'antul became blind to the poverty and exploitation of the Outer City. She had already seen more of it than she could stand.

The haulers delivered them to a pristine dock. The taxi crew tossed them some coins and then, at a gesture from Eia, tossed them some more. They disembarked under the watchful gaze of a crisply uniformed armed guard, who glanced at the pass Eia showed him and waved them on. Already, white-dressed porters with handcarts had materialized to transport their baggage to their lodgings. Thrice more Eia showed ids pass, as they climbed a stairway, walked through a broad courtyard, and at last passed through a pair of rod gates which guarded a narrow passageway through the wall. Bird-filled trees, manicured gardens, clean white walkways, and the perfume of flowers greeted them. They had entered the Inner City.

Chapter 6

Against buildings and walkways of precious white isanstone, under a sky blue enough to have been dipped in a dyer's pot, the flowers of late summer exploded with color. Wall-climbing vines swathed the buildings in gaudy robes of red and vermillion. From the edge of the broad walkway to the pillared and friezed walls of the A'lan Hall, a field of vivid blue and brilliant orange shivered in a faint breeze. A covered litter, painted as if to match the flowers, floated on the shoulders of its trotting bearers, preceded by a bell-ringing boy, self-important in his red-fringed tunic. Eia tucked ids hand into the crook of Delan's elbow. "There goes the Lan of Sa."

For Bet's sake, Eia pointed out the sights. The Inner City of Is'antul was divided into eight sections, one for each Lanhall and its attendant buildings. But the gardens were allotted space in equal measure. A vast lawn surrounded the central meeting place of the city, the A'lan Hall. Beyond it could be seen the crisp walls and soaring minarets of the Forbidden Palace, with more flowers abutting its walls on the west. The three of them turned aside, to cross the crowded courtyard of the Lanhall of Derksai, bordered by formal columns and delicate sculptures, and brooded over by the Lanhall itself; a vast, imposing building heavily decorated with priceless wooden carvings and screens.

Soon the adjunct buildings of the Derksai Quarter gave way to a view of the artificial woodland which

76

swept along most of the western wall of the Inner City. With a shining brook running amid close-clustered trees, and here and there a slender forest creature slipping among the shadows, it could almost have passed for a natural wood; if one could ignore the white wall rising behind it, and the occasional gardener hurrying here and there, carrying a shovel, or pushing a cart full of debris.

The Yard of Trade faced this woodland. There, overdressed petitioners paced, sweating in the hot sun, shadowed by slightly less well-dressed assistants, who carried heavy chests and finely carved wooden boxes, priceless containers for priceless gifts with which they hoped to win equally priceless favors from the Lan. Many of these could not restrain their curiosity and amazement as the Aeyries crossed the yard, but their expressions changed to ill-disguised hostility when Eia's presence instantly captured the attention of one of the harassed functionaries at the doorway of the Hall. Within moments a white-dressed servant had been summoned to escort them to the guest house, where their baggage had miraculously already arrived and been unpacked.

Eia sighed heavily when the door finally closed behind them. "So what do you think, Bet, is this a terrifying place?"

Bet sank into a plush chair that was so comfortable it made her want to shut her eyes and go to sleep. "It is so clean."

"And outside the walls, so indescribably awful. There are some things about Walker society that I will never understand."

"Just don't ask me to explain it to you."

Soon, a tap on the door announced the arrival of a Walker female, dressed as severely and expensively as Bet, accompanied by two white-dressed servants bearing armloads of boxes, packages, and messages in crisp white envelopes. Eia greeted her warmly, and introduced her to Bet. "This is Peline, who acts as my secretary when I am in the city."

"Pleased to make your acquaintance. Delan," she bowed stiffly.

"When will they believe that I don't accept gifts?"

Bet accepted the task of writing polite notes declining the gifts, while Delan declined the many social invitations. Eia paced the floor restlessly, discussing with Peline the rest of the correspondence: the requests for interviews, the offers, the lengthy philosophical discourses. Peline proved to be a perceptive, if somewhat embittered, scrutinizer of the political activities of the lowlands. Bet doubted that much happened which escaped her attention.

"Well, the newsmongers are unusually efficient today," she commented, when the housekeeper knocked on the door to deliver the first handful of fresh correspondence. "There must be less going on than usual." She sorted through the handful of envelopes, then paused fractionally, her eyes narrowing. "Yes, the town is full of bored people with nothing to do."

She handed Bet three of the envelopes. "I suggest you decline these, unless you have a taste for rich food . . . or you enjoy feeling like a creature in a carnival show."

"They're addressed to me! But I'm a nobody."

"A curiosity in this city." With a gesture, Peline encompassed the whole self-serving, self-indulgent, disconnected lifestyle of the Inner City's inhabitants. "It is the people in black who run the country. Everyone else has too much time on their hands."

They ate supper in their rooms that night. Bet, wearied and dazed by this alien world in which she could find nothing comforting or familiar, went gladly to bed.

She awakened to the sweetest sound she had ever heard: a joyous trilling and yodeling which seemed to fill the four corners of the beautifully appointed room in which she had slept. The pale light of dawn illuminated faintly the frail polished furniture of the bedroom. Bet stumbled groggily to the window, seeking the source of the sweet sound. Mist rose from the surface of the lake, and the perfectly groomed landscape lay still as a painting; almost too beautiful. Bet leaned out the window and looked into the face of the singer: a small, flat-bodied animal clinging with all six feet to the smooth surface of the exterior wall. It gazed at her without seeming to see her; all of its attention focused on the marvelous song issuing from its ballooning, vibrating throat.

The sun rose over the top edge of the city wall, and a whole chorus of small singers greeted its appearance by bursting into a beautiful, disorganized cacophony of song. "What marvel!" they seemed to cry. "The sun rises once again! A new day!" From the walls of the guest house, a manicured lawn sloped down to the edge of the glassy lake, where water lilies bloomed in the shallows. At the far edge, a half dozen tiny, brightly-colored boats bobbed at dock. Three white, long-legged beasts crowned by curled horns waded slowly through the water, trailing bright wakes. Beyond the lake, sunrise trimmed the rooftops of the Forbidden Palace with gold. Along the wall's rim, solemn soldiers patrolled.

Someone tapped on the door. "Bet? Let's go for a walk."

Delan waited out in their common parlor. "I want to walk by the lake," said Bet.

Outside, the chorus of the small singers had begun to dissipate. In the narrow passageways between the clustered buildings of the Trade Quarter, servants trundled handcarts loaded with bread and fruit. With practiced professionalism, they rushed past Bet and Delan, avoiding colliding with them while never actually looking directly at them. Delan led the way out from the buildings to a stony walkway which meandered down to the water's edge. The morning flowers had come into bloom, filling the warming air with their sweet fragrance.

Catching a glimpse of the seer's silver fur and pale wings out of the corner of her eye, for a moment Bet's heart thought it was Laril, and her chest constricted

with a kind of weary sorrow. Why had she let idre
talk her into returning to t'Cwa one last time? How
long would she let their relationship drag on before
she finally ended it?

Delan did not speak, but frowned at the pretty
scene as if it offended idre. They paused in a cluster
of trees to watch the long-legged creatures wade restlessly through the shallows. "Maybe nothing will happen," Delan said, half to idreself. "Perhaps I am
simply mad. How strange it is, to walk through this
delicate artifice, knowing that at any moment something horrible could happen. And what can I do,
except wait? How absurd it seemed last night, writing
all those trivial letters, and knowing. . . ."

"It's hard to actually believe that anything is going
to happen."

"Why should anyone believe in something so inex-
act, so undefined, a painting of nothing, a kind of
explosion—what is there to believe? I don't believe it;
at least not with my intellect. But my body is full of
dread."

"I am no seer, I guess. My only dread is sadness
and uncertainty. I don't know where I am going to
go, after Is'antul. I don't know what to do with my
life."

"When an Aeyrie l'shil stands for the first time on
a flight platform, id has a thousand choices. But for
that first daring jump onto the back of the wind, there
are no guarantees. Id simply must jump. I think you
are still waiting for a guarantee, Ysbet. If you wait
long enough, maybe destiny will take you by the hand,
and drag you down a road you never wanted to follow.
Better to act as if you believe in something even
though your heart is an unconverted skeptic."

"How long? My whole life?"

Delan tucked a warm hand into the crook of Bet's
elbow, and they continued on down to the edge of the
water. The waders came over to examine them: slender, graceful, long-legged creatures festooned with
long fur that floated behind them like mist. But they

wandered away again, once they realized that Bet and Delan had brought them nothing to eat.

"What do you think is going to happen?" Bet asked.

"A catastrophe." Delan's fingers curled with tension against the astil of Bet's sleeve. "I know it is coming, and I can do nothing to avert it, except what I have already done—communicate with my fellow mages, begging them to keep watch. Now all I can hope to do is somehow shield Eia from harm."

"You must wonder what good it is to be a seer, if you can't do anything to prevent the disasters you foresee."

"The good comes with the bad. If I could not have nightmares, I could not have visions."

At the center of the Inner City, the bell tower on the A'lan Hall chimed the hour. On the other side of the walls of the Forbidden Palace, a bell also chimed, as if in echo. A lone guard paced the length of the wall, proud and erect in the morning sun. In silence, Delan and Bet walked part of the way around the lake, then turned around and came back again. When they returned to the guest house, they found Eia sitting at a tea table, flipping absently through the mail which had arrived during the night. A functionary for the Lan of Trade had already visited, and an interview with the Lan had been scheduled for later that morning. Eia, who spent most of ids time in Is'antul waiting for one or another Lan to fit idre into ids appointment schedule, found this promptness astonishing. The Lan had specifically asked to meet Bet.

Bet had an appalling thought. "Surely they aren't all absurdly fascinated with me because I've been an Aeyrie's lover?"

It was Peline, arriving soon after breakfast, carrying a bundle of broadsheets under her arm, who finally gave them the answer. Silently she held up one broadsheet after another. "Walkers can fly!" declared their headlines. "Flying Walker arrives in Is'antul! Aeyrie invention lifts one Walker's feet off the ground!"

Eia put ids head in ids hand and laughed helplessly. "Great Winds, Bet, you're an 'item'!"

After an emergency delivery of art supplies from the Outer City, Delan had begun work on an etching, using the sketch id had drawn of Bet in flight. Peline had left for the Outer City, where she was making arrangements for a publisher of one of the better broadsheets to interview Bet and view the Walker Wing. "The more publicity, the better leverage we have. Not only are the Aeyries the only ones who can manufacture the Wing, we're the only ones who can teach Walkers how to use them." Bet felt like a leaf caught in a h'lana. She had never even imagined that the eye of the public, perhaps of the entire known world, would someday be focused on her. And for so small a thing!

A black-dressed male, silent as a shadow, arrived to escort them through the Trade Quarter to a side door of the Lanhall, where an equally silent guard gave way to let them pass. Bet found herself walking down a cool, hushed hallway, dimly lit by air lamps, with a Lan's ransom in carpeting crushing under her feet. The walls stretched magnificently to the high, carved ceiling. In a strategic nook one of Delan's paintings, illuminated by its own collection of lamps, hung in splendor. Delan glanced at the painting and turned away, as if id did not want to remember it.

At a double doorway their guide conferred in a hushed voice with another like him, who then opened the door for them to enter another silent hallway, where a single servant knelt with a cloth, polishing the already glossy wood of a doorframe. Their guide showed them to one of the doors, and tapped on it lightly with the tips of his fingers. It was opened instantly by yet another proud and stiff functionary, the sole occupant of a plush foyer, with velvet walls and deep chairs, and a fireplace where, despite the weather outside, flames flickered. In this silent depth of stone, the heat of summer would never be felt.

Their guide left them here, and the other functionary slipped through a door, leaving them alone. Eia, dressed in black even more stark than Bet's, straddled a stool and settled down to wait. Delan became absorbed in a study of the artwork in the room, all of which seemed to Bet to be dull, lifeless, and even colorless. She paced restlessly until the door opened once again, and the functionary intoned. "The Lan will see you."

From their cool, manicured city in the north of the lowlands, the eight governors of the Walkers, ruled over by the benevolent emperor, the A'lan, oversaw every aspect of their subjects' lives. Once, the Lans had merely been advisors, appointed by the A'lan to assist in ruling the lowlands. But, over time, the Lan position had become hereditary, unlike the A'lan, who was chosen by lot, and each of them wielded significant power.

The Lans of Sa, Hamsdrin, and Derksai controlled agriculture, commerce, and lawmaking in their respective lowlands. The Lans of the Northern and Southern Seas controlled trade, commerce, transportation, and foreign relations in all the known world. The Lan of Invisible Wealth controlled knowledge, magic, and the development of new ideas. It was he who authorized the printing of books and newspapers, licensed sorcerers, and administered the schools and Universities. The Lan of Peace controlled the militia and all aspects of law enforcement, both at home and abroad. And the Lan of the Trade Road, whom they were about to meet, controlled the major transportation routes and movement of trade goods within the lowlands, including the communication networks and transportation.

Bet, accustomed to the near anarchy of an Aeyrie Ula, puzzled over the overpowering control exerted by the Walker governors. Of course, the Walkers did not inhabit self-contained, discreet communities like the Aeyries did. They could not all sit together to eat dinner every evening, with their leader among them, and make all their decisions only after endless discussion. But even the Aeyries had now found it necessary to combine the economic power of all the Ulas into

one entity, administered by Eia, to give them greater
leverage and prevent destructive competition. Someday perhaps they, too, would have a central government, as more and more of the decisions were
entrusted to one person, leaving the Ulas with fewer
and fewer choices.

But it would never be like this, she thought, as they
walked down yet another hallway, through yet another
heavy, polished doorway, into yet another foyer,
where yet another functionary waited to open that last
door for them. Aeyries, being a flying people, could
not insulate themselves from each other without cutting off their own view of the sky. And without the
sky, they would go mad, as Raulyn had done.

The functionary swung open the double doors and
announced, "Malal Tefan Eia, Ambassador from the
Aeyrie people. Ishta Mairli Delan, Taiseoch of Triad.
Ysbet ib Canilton ib t'Cwa."

In the room beyond, a dozen Walkers, resplendent
in their bejeweled costumes, ranged about, seated in
chairs, standing along the walls, and conversing. The
older male, who separated himself from one such conversation and came forward to greet them, seemed
scarcely different from the rest of them: puffy from
too much rich food, ostentatiously dressed in red and
lavender astil, holding out to greet them a six-fingered
hand with a ring on each finger. "Eia, what a delight
to see you again. And Delan, such an honor for you
to visit us. And this must be Ysbet."

Bet found herself grasped by both shoulders. "I am
astonished," said the Lan, "by your bravery."

Bet wanted nothing more than to tell him what she
thought of his ridiculous outfit, but she refrained,
reminding herself of the power he wielded. "Thank
you," she murmured vaguely, wishing he would let go
of her.

"You must sit beside me and tell me all about this
Wing, and how you fly it." Calling for refreshments,
the Lan crossed the room, towing Bet behind him.
He seated her firmly in a chair. Her heart pounded;
something in him reminded her too much of Raulyn.

She opened her hand toward Eia, gesturing: I am in trouble.

Eia made a smooth circuit of the room, greeting everyone by name. One of them had already engaged Delan in conversation, but Eia gracefully avoided getting snagged, and casually drew up a stool beside Bet. "We would hate to waste your time telling you what you already know," id said.

The Lan did not seem altogether pleased that Eia had avoided all the traps set to prevent idre from joining this conversation. "Why, I know very little, naturally. Is it true, Ysbet, that you flew the entire distance from Triad to Is'antul?"

"I flew from t'Cwa to Triad as well. But you must understand that I made the journey with a large number of Aeyries who kept me airborne—without them I would have just glided to the ground."

The Lan waved this comment aside. "Of course, of course. But that you could bear to be in the air for—how long? Twenty-five days?"

"Fifteen, with two additional days of rest," said Eia. "That is how long such a journey would usually take, given friendly winds."

A tray of wine and cakes arrived. Rather than decline the cup of wine which the Lan handed her, Bet only pretended to sip it, then nodded appreciatively when the Lan seemed to expect a reaction. The cake she ate reluctantly; it was too sweet for her.

"And this wonderful invention, the Walker Wing you are calling it, was it made in t'Cwa?"

Caught with her mouth full, Bet could not reply, but Eia said, "It is Arman's work, of course."

"Id has been working on it for over a year," Bet began. As she narrated the events of the last year for the Lan, she gradually became aware that all other conversation in the room had ceased. She told how she and the Aeyrie inventors had worked together, first with miniature models and later with prototypes; how they had first floated the Wing with a dummy harnessed into it, and later how Bet had taken her first, brief flight down the gradual slope of a hillside.

She told about the journey, and what it had been like to view the world from above, and she spoke, lovingly, of her many landings.

But when the Lan began asking about the construction of the Wing, and exactly what techniques she used to fly it, Eia said mildly, "Bet would never bore you with such details. Of course, Arman and ids crew are making modifications now, and it will be some time before we have any Walker Wings to sell. . . ."

The Lan chuckled into his wine cup. "Ah, Eia, I know you well. When you think you have your hands on something worth selling . . ."

"Then you are free to decide if it is worth buying. I don't care one way or the other; the Walkers who want to fly can always just negotiate with us directly. There do seem to be a few of them."

"It is quite a novelty, of course, but I can't imagine that many Walkers will have the courage of your Ysbet."

Eia shrugged, ids folded wings whispering in the still air. "Of course, Bet is completely unique."

The Lan looked at Bet speculatively. She touched the wine cup to her lips again, wondering what he was seeing. Her name revealed her to have been destined to be just another farm community hatchling . . . who had somehow been sidetracked into t'Cwa. Perhaps the Lan saw a pawn, carefully and thoroughly trained by the Aeyries to make flying look easy. Perhaps the Lan saw a fool. And perhaps the Lan himself was no fool, and could read, from Bet's face or demeanor, that Eia had spoken, not a phrase to merely make it clear that this would be no easy negotiation, but the truth: Bet was indeed unique.

"Well," the Lan finally said, "tell me what it is you want."

So some of the Lan's advisors drew around, and the negotiations began. Eia told the Lan that the Wing would be included as part of the five-year trade agreement that the Lan had rejected on Eia's last visit to Is'antul. The Lan told Eia that the guarantees that Eia was demanding in the trade agreement were ridiculous; they amounted to highway robbery. Eia pointed out that the lowlands were reselling Aeyrie inventions for three times what they paid for them, and the Ulas were not seeing any of that profit. The Lan reminded Eia that the lowlands were providing the port and shipping facilities which made it possible for the Aeyrie inventions to be exported; and so the Aeyries had to take what they could get. On and on the discussion went, and much of it had to be ground which had been covered many times before.

Bet listened intently, but in the back of her mind she wondered what Eia had intended her to do when id first came to t'Cwa to fetch her to Is'antul. A catalyst, id had said. But she did not see how she could be a catalyst in this discussion, unless she had been a catalyst already, simply by virtue of her wings. Of course it was entirely possible that Eia had planned it that way; that the fortuitous passion of Walkers for wings had been no accident, that the journey, the broadsheet articles, even the timing had all been exhaustively planned. Eia was a master manipulator, a ruthless player in the cutthroat game of politics. Ids equally ruthless honesty and integrity must have proved to be quite inconvenient from time to time.

How disconcerted id must have been, when id accidentally provided the catalyst for Bet to leave t'Cwa, not for a brief time, but forever. Bet hid her smile in her wine cup. It had been a wonderful journey; how could she be angry?

And then something was terribly wrong. Something with the air lamps, which seemed to dim strangely; and a sound in Bet's ears, like a roaring of wind. Magic, she thought, starting to her feet, seeing Eia staring at her oddly, seeing Delan seem to fly across the room, wings spread, all expression blanked out of ids face, seeing the Lan's wine cup float into the air and land, slowly, spewing wine onto the priceless carpet. And Delan, grasping Eia and throwing id physically aside, throwing idreself on top of idre, spreading ids bright, bright wings to cover id, like a parent protecting a young child from the cold wind. And the

Lan, a horrible, hoarse scream gutting out of his mouth, twisting in a weird dance across the delicate designs of the carpet, screaming and screaming, clawing mindlessly at his body, as if he wanted to jerk out his very bones.

His bones were on fire. How strange, thought Bet, how very strange. And she could see a thin thread of fire, which ran from the Lan, through the ceiling, and into the sky. How strange, thought Bet, that she could see through the ceiling like that. And where did the thread go? She tried to follow it, but she could not fly without her Wing. So she started across the room toward the Lan instead, who continued his maddened, screaming dance, past his shocked and paralyzed advisors, past the servant who had frozen with the cakes sliding slowly off the tray and onto the floor. If she could cut the thread, she thought. . . .

In a spray of guts and hot blood and fried flesh and shattered bone, the Lan's body exploded.

Chapter 7

Delan, Eia, and Bet huddled together as the door was shut, and locked, and locked once again, and barred, and the bar locked. High overhead, grated windows sprayed broken sunlight across the stone ceiling. Water puddled on the stone floor. A heavy wooden bench, chained to the floor, stood along one wall. Eia finally sat on it. Bet abandoned her futile effort to wipe away the blood, flesh, and bone which spattered her clothing, and sat down beside idre. What else was there to do, except wait? But Delan began pacing up and down the length of the cell.

"You understand what happened back there?" Eia finally said.

Delan shook ids head. "I have no idea."

Preoccupied as Delan had been with Eia's safety, id could not have observed much. Bet began, "There was a thread of fire that came down out of the sky. His bones were glowing." But then she found she could not continue. She did not want to remember.

"Sorcery."

Water splashed beneath Delan's cleata-skin shoes. Ids wings whispered against the cold stone wall as id turned to pace back in the other direction. "It was *like* sorcery."

"You can wager your life that Aeyrie technology or Aeyrie magic will be blamed for it, regardless of the truth."

"Naturally. Indeed, here we are—there were fifteen or more people in that room, but it was the Aeyries

and the Aeyrie-friend who were arrested." Delan
paused, grim-faced. "I protected you too well, Eia. If
I had been less successful, then you and I would not
be the only ones who know that the attack was
directed against you as well."

"I thank you for my life, Del . . . not that it's worth
much at the moment."

Eia seemed to fade into the shadows and become
one with them, while the dim light caught in and
reflected in Delan's fur and wings like phosphores-
cence. Delan's fur and wings only grew brighter as the
day aged and the scattered patches of sunlight began
to fade. A morning and an afternoon had passed, and
still, in the corridor outside their secured door, no
sound could be heard. They had been taken prisoner
by the private military force of the Lan of Trade,
under the orders of the Lan's surviving advisors. To
Eia's outraged objections they had only replied, "You
were closest to the Lan."

When Delan ceased ids pacing at last, Eia instantly
raised ids heavy head. "What are you thinking?"

"I can unlock the doors, if that's what you want.
And Bet, as I recall, can make herself invisible. But
how advisable would it be to escape—especially with
the use of magic—under these circumstances?"

"You mean that our escape will be taken as proof
of our guilt."

"No doubt it will."

"But is there anything left for us here, or have we
lost everything anyway?" Darkness shadowed Eia's
grim features. Black against the shadows, only the
gray in ids mane could still be seen clearly. "In the
minds of many Walkers, the fact that we were incar-
cerated will be considered proof enough of our guilt.
Certainly, the Lans will hesitate to champion us.
Except for the Lan of Invisible Wealth, I have never
known a one of them to take a stand on a moral issue.
Perhaps our credibility has been completely destroyed.
Perhaps we have . . . lost everything, including all
hope for peace."

A shimmering ghost in the shadows, Delan brushed

a hand down the stone wall, as if to measure its sturdiness. Vaguely puzzled, id said, "I thought I had prepared myself for this possibility."

Eia leapt to ids feet, angry energy trapped in ids wings and limbs like firewood about to explode. But id could only pace the small cell, a caged shadow. "Now there will be a vicious power struggle over the Lanship of Trade. It will go on for months, before a new Lan is chosen. Only then will the person even exist who has the authority to release us. I can't just wait here for the outcome!"

"What about Peline? Don't you think that most capable female can get us out?"

"Peline is—profoundly self-interested. I do not know that she has any genuine loyalty to me at all."

Delan snorted. "Other than being in love with you."

Eia shrugged, holding ids hands out in a helpless gesture. "Well, then. You see that she is a mystery to me."

"I wouldn't underestimate her."

Bet's back had begun to ache from sitting on the low bench. But she felt detached from the pain, just as she felt detached from the dank basement cell where both Aeyries paced, paused, and paced again, in an erratic, tense dance. Was it just shock? Ever since the lights in the Lan's salon first seemed to dim, the strangeness had been upon her: the sensation of a strong wind blowing, of tightly closed doors suddenly slamming ajar.

Delan said suddenly, "If we do decide to escape, the most effective way to do it would be to contact Laril and have idre come get us through the Void."

"How would we ever contact Laril?" Bet asked. But then she saw the gleam of polished glass in Delan's hand. Though the soldiers who fruitlessly searched them for the weapon which killed the Lan would never have recognized the scrying glass for what it was, Delan certainly had conjured up a way to hide the glass from discovery. Some mages could scry anything: stone, water, flame, even the wind. But glass always provided the greatest verity and clarity. Even Walker sorcerers used mirrors. This Bet had been taught when she first attempted scrying at t'Cwa. Of course, she could not do it at all, not in any medium.

Delan settled onto the bench, the scrying glass cupped in ids delicate fingers. Frowning with concentration, Eia paced relentlessly, ids usually light feet thumping dully onto the stones. Watching idre, Bet could almost observe the pace, if not the content, of ids desperate thoughts. Time and again, id explored one or another possible solution, only to be drawn up short by an insurmountable reality. With each dead-end avenue down which id turned, the shadows hovering over idre seemed darker, bleaker, and more foreboding. The end of all hope for peace. The end of all hope for the survival of the Aeyrie people.

Delan drew in ids breath sharply. Eia, distracted from ids bleak quest for a solution, left off pacing and crossed the narrow cell to lay a hand on Delan's shoulder. "Del?"

Delan bowed under the weight of ids hand, as if exhausted. "I spoke with the Triad Mers. They are very distraught. They know that there is a new power loose in the world. It reminds them of something that happened—something in the past—which is terribly important. But none of them can truly remember it. I spoke with Orgulanthgrnm—nothing strange has happened at Triad that he knows of. Then I spoke with S'lin of t'Fon." Delan opened ids eyes, but darkness haunted them.

The silence dropped its net over Eia's body. "What news of my l'frer?" id said, but ids voice had become as flat as still water.

Delan said with dull surprise, "Hana is dead."

Eia's eyes flinched shut. "Not dead. How could id be—"

Delan continued inexorably, "And C'la of t'Han is also dead."

Only then did the jagged knife of fear and grief cut into Bet's own belly. Hana had been taiseoch of t'Fon,

and C'la taiseoch of t'Han. The taiseoch of t'Cwa
was—

"Not Laril!" she protested. Not with youth in ids
wings, not with ids life scarcely begun, not with so
much left unfinished between them. Not that wild
beauty. It was not the right time for death; not the
right time at all.

"A terrible storm is raging at t'Cwa. Scrying can't
even penetrate it. If Laril is alive or dead, we have
no way of knowing."

Only the sound of the bolts being turned finally dis-
turbed their stupified paralysis. "Hana," Eia breathed,
with all the pain of grief's jagged knife, raw and
unmasked in ids voice. Ids eyes stared at a nightmare
vision of ids beloved sibling's body exploding in a hor-
rific fountain, as the Lan's had done. And then, as the
door opened, id took in a deep breath, and pleated
up ids sagging wings, and turned a solemn, politely
questioning face toward the Trade Guard who stood
there, his face contorted with hatred. Eia's eyes narrowed: the expression of a Quai-du master about to
enter the arena. But then the soldier was shoved
roughly aside, and Peline, shaking with rage, strode
into the cell.

She snatched Eia's hand up into both of hers.
"Have you been hurt? Samil Infatil ordered your
release, with your apologies that she could not get to
it sooner. . . ."

"Samil has no power," Eia protested. "She is just
the heir. Peline!" Eia took her by the shoulder in a
grip that made her flinch. "What happened to the Lan
of Invisible Wealth?"

"They haven't told you?" Furious, she turned on
the soldier once again. "What were you going to do,
keep them here until they rotted, for a crime they
couldn't possibly have done?"

"How many of the Lans are dead?" asked Eia
softly, making Peline wince again under ids grip.

"All of them."

Eia's wings lifted involuntarily, then folded again.
"And the A'lan?"

"A crowd of officials entered the Forbidden Palace in a panic, and found her taking a bath, unharmed. Rumor, but a good source."

Eia let go of her at last. "Great Winds! Del, what does it mean?"

Delan got heavily to ids feet. "It means we get out while we have the chance."

They followed Peline out of the basement prison, into the Lanhall, where a chaos of servants and functionaries rushed through the once silent hallways, and outside into the cool evening. Every single resident of the Inner City seemed to have gathered in the vivid light of the setting sun. In small groups they clustered, asking each other questions which could only be answered by more questions. Or they stood alone, staring at the Lanhall's exterior, their faces blank with despair or disbelief. How many promising careers had been wrecked this day, how many fortunes lost? Some turned to watch the two Aeyries and the two Walkers pass, their faces ugly with anger and outrage.

"You couldn't possibly have killed all the Lans! Everyone agrees that you were pinned on the floor when it happened. You could not even have killed the Lan who was in the room with you, much less one who was in the far corner of the city! But it doesn't matter. Everyone has decided it must be your fault. You can see it in their faces." Peline shook her head in disbelief. "What good could it possibly do you to kill all the Lans? You have devoted your entire life to peace. You have written two books about peace. It just makes no sense for them to . . ."

Eia had scarcely seemed to be listening to her, but now id spoke, voice empty of expression, "There is no sense in any of this."

"You must leave Is'antul. The sooner the better."

Eia's thick, silver streaked mane had escaped its bindings and now partially obscured ids dark eyes, but Bet could see their unsettling, fixed shine; the look of a fighter who has taken a fatal blow but will not cease to fight. Her respect and love for Eia came to life, and she reached out through the cataclysm of her own fear to touch ids elbow. "I'm sorry." Everyone knew how much Eia loved ids wild-hearted, intractible l'frer. And the destruction of Eia's entire life work— how suddenly and horribly it had come to pass!

In the guest house, their unfinished projects mocked them: the etching for publication in the broadsheets, the invitations they had yet to answer, the letters half written. They stood in the salon like drafs bewildered by a sudden storm. Eia, passing a hand over ids eyes, turned to Delan. "We've always had a plan, you and I. We've always known what to do next."

"Leave!" cried Peline. "They'll blame you, they'll frame you—"

Looking somberly into Eia's face, Delan slipped ids arm around ids waist and stood hip to hip, wide wings whispering, shaggy manes obscuring their narrow, triangular faces. Never had they looked more alien to Bet: more remote, more closed in, more obscured behind layer upon layer of incomprehensible secrets. She gestured to Peline with her head, and led her into Bet's bedroom, where they sat in silence, or looked out the balcony window, or chatted vaguely about their lives. The sun set, but in Is'antul the walkways seethed restlessly and occasionally a shout or a cry could be heard from beyond the walls of the Inner City.

They pretended not to know that in the next bedroom, the Aeyries were making love. Bet could almost feel the passion and grief all tangled together in that joining. Over the span of thirty years, from the day of Delan's winging to this desperate day, the stormtamer and the seer had come together and come apart again, taken other lovers, lived nearly separate lives joined only by their children, only to discover each other again. Their friendship had survived and endured, even when their romance waxed and waned as unpredictably as the tides. Together they had struggled to create a new world. Now they were telling each other good-bye.

The shadows lay deep and dark throughout the

apartment when Eia appeared at Bet's doorway with
an air lamp in ids hand, dressed only in ids recently
groomed fur, even ids mane brushed smooth and tied
back. "I will remain in Is'antul."

Peline had been lounging on the bed, staring
morosely into the shadows. Now she leapt to her feet,
and Bet heard the joy that ruthlessly shadowed her
horror. "They'll kill you if you stay!"

"Yes. Will you continue to work with me, Peline?"

"What else can I do?"

Eia took her hand and held it for a moment, and
her face melted like ice on a stove. What a torture it
must have been, for Peline to have been forced to
listen as Eia made love to Delan in the next room.
Bet wanted to warn her: Do not love an Aeyrie, she
wanted to say. Not unless you also love the fey wind
which at any moment can carry them away from you.

Delan leaned in the doorway, dressed in a flightsuit,
with a knife strapped to ids thigh. At ids appearance,
Peline's face flushed with shame, but Delan politely
failed to take notice of Peline's passion. "Bet, I don't
know how far I can tow you and your Wing. Do you
think we'll make it out of the city in the air? After
that, we can walk. You can buy food for us along the
way—I've got money."

"We'll make it out of the city," Bet said. How she
could say this so confidently she did not know. Arman
had already worked out on paper that it would take
a minimum of six Aeyries to keep Bet in the air, and
another six if she needed to be lifted from the ground.

"It's a still night; not much light for the moons.
I'll have to fly by s'oleil, and we'll have to land in
darkness."

Aeyries avoided dark landings whenever they could
help it; most flight injuries occurred then. But on this
strange day, the chance of an injury seemed a small
thing, scarcely worth being concerned about. Bet
began to change her clothes, as Eia and Delan discussed communications, finances, the security of Triad,
and what help to offer the Ulas which had been so
suddenly bereft of their leaders.

"I'll go to Samil Infatil tonight, as soon as you have left," said Eia. "But she may not be able to give me sanctuary. These will be unstable political times, and my friendship will not be an asset to her. If I have to, I will find lodging in the Outer City."

Bet took the burlap-wrapped Wing out of the closet. It felt lighter even than she remembered, an insubstantial concoction of light and air. She shivered with eagerness: she had never thought she would get to fly again so soon. "Where will we launch?"

"Not the city wall," said Peline after a moment. "The city guards will never let you go up there tonight."

"The roof?" Eia looked worriedly at the bundle in Bet's arms. "How will Delan lift you enough to fly over the wall, starting from so close to the ground?"

"It will work out," Bet said, "Don't worry."

Delan, whose sharp gaze had been resting steadily on Bet for some time, stepped forward suddenly, to delicately touch a fingertip to the bundle under her arm. Id drew ids hand back slowly, forehead creased. "What has happened to you?"

Bet looked into Delan's face in silence. She had no answer.

Delan turned to Eia. "The roof."

Full darkness had extinguished the bright flowers and white walkways of the Inner City, but the voices of the gathered people could still be heard: a confused murmur of anxiety, anger, and fear. Delan and Eia walked ahead of Bet, with their wings slightly spread to expose their sensing hairs to the air. Peline led the way around the back of the guest house. In the stretch of grass and trees which sloped from the guest house to the lake, Bet could see no motion. She gripped her arm tightly around her bundled Wing. The sticky day had given way to a sticky night, and in her padded flight clothes her skin slicked with sweat.

A cluster of trees appeared ahead of them, their smooth trunks sloping gracefully, their gnarled limbs spreading a broad umbrella over the guest house's

tiled roof. Here Peline paused at the base of the trees.
Eia slipped past her, to lay ids hands on the tree trunk
and then, easily as an onfrit, began to climb it. As id
slipped among some thick branches, and then swung
up onto a limb which overhung the rooftop, ids wings
opened and shut like a fan. Then id swung idreself
down, to hang briefly by ids hands from the limb, and
let go, wings breaking ids fall, to land silently on the
sloped tile roof.

Bet gave her Wing to Delan and approached the
tree, feeling large and clumsy as a draf. With help
from Peline on the ground, she achieved the limb, but
from there she crawled painfully along the creaking
branch, until at last she swung herself down and hung,
arm sockets popping, wondering how much it would
hurt if she tumbled off the roof to the ground. Eia
gripped her by the legs, and when she let go, id let
her down slowly, until her feet rested firmly on the
tiles. "Not bad, for a Walker," murmured Eia.

They hauled up Bet's Wing with a rope. By the time
Delan had climbed the tree, Bet had spread the frame
and begun checking its joints and connections, as she
had watched the inventors do many times before.
The Wing felt alive and eager under her hands. She
checked everything, and checked it once again, then
she strapped herself into the harness. Delan and Eia
separated from their embrace, and Delan spread ids
wings, using ids sensing hairs and membranes to test
the night air. "Are you ready?" id asked.

The Wing quivered. Bet could almost feel the soft
breeze, scarcely detectable against her skin, brushing
against the stretched astil. "Yes."

Eia's fingers stroked down the taut cloth of Bet's
wing. She shivered, the way an Aeyrie would if someone touched ids wing like that. "What about the tow-
line?"

"I don't think Bet needs our help anymore," said
Delan.

The air thrummed against Bet's Wing. She set her
feet carefully against the uneven, slippery tile. By the
third stride, before she had even reached the edge of

the roof, she was airborne. The wings bellied out as if under the pressure of a strong wind. Lightly as a leaf, that wind lifted her up—no sudden gale blowing in from the ocean, but a mage-wind, blowing through the open doors of Bet's own heart. Over the rooftops she lifted herself. The lake, the clustered trees, and even the imposing wall of the Inner City dropped swifly away from her. She dove toward the stars.

The Outer City of Is'antul seethed beneath her. Like water in a flooded river the people crowded the narrow streets of the city, and even from her great height Bet could hear the roar of their voices. She spotted a building burning.

Dclan appcarcd ncarby, ghostlikc in thc starlight. Bet felt ids hand touch her Wing lightly in greeting. With a gesture id took in the simmering city below: the city of ids nightmare vision. "There it is," id seemed to be saying. "Our future."

Chapter 8

In a lush garden of redleaf and caricha, where lacy blue and lavender flags waved above coral towers, Ara made her haven. Here, bright waterwyths and isas and almenas swam, winding along watery avenues or taking shelter in the tumbled architecture of the coral metropolis. Among the thin, single-threaded thoughts of these simple sea creatures, Ara hung suspended in the warm water, rocking slowly back and forth with the motion of the waves.

Her eyes were open, but she did not see the sea. The voices of the water sang and chortled in her ears, but she did not hear them. She held herself like a canyon in which a river flowed, but the river was Tsal: She saw through Tsal's eyes; she heard with id's ears, she thought with id's reconstructed mind.

Tsal, wings held tightly closed, slipped between standing slabs of shattered stone, into a cool darkness where water dripped and trickled. In places, faint daylight still found its way among the racks of tumbled stone, but as Tsal set ids feet cautiously forward upon the rough ground, the darkness deepened and the light faded, until only darkness remained. With fingertips and the sensitive bottoms of ids feet Tsal felt through the darkness, scraping ids tender wings painfully on the rough stone.

How will I find my way out again? id wondered.

I will remember, said Ara.

Through narrow passageways the Aeyrie edged ids narrow form and then dragged ids wide wings. Once, the passageway widened enough so Tsal could spread ids wings, and for the first time Ara experienced s'oleil. So a Mer swims through a dark sea, singing and listening for the sound of ids own voice to echo back again. But for Tsal, it was the pressure of the air which created for idre an image of the lightless maze in which id traveled. The restless earth had riven this cleft through the rock and spread it open like the jaws of a clam. Behind them it wended, a narrow and twisting passageway. Above them it stretched into lightless darkness, and before them it also continued.

Tsal's wings felt a breath of air, a motion so faint it almost seemed an illusion.

There is an opening ahead, id said to Ara.

She held herself curled like a waterwyth in a secret corner of ids mind. She sent her response like a whisper: *Something is there.*

I must know what it is.

Ah, Tsal, she wanted to say. There is so much that you must know. In the storm of your curiosity, caution is just a passing breeze.

But she did not speak these words in Tsal's mind, for she was just a visitor there. Tsal stepped forward, and she stepped forward with id. Curiosity thrummed in the Aeyrie's blood like a sudden passion; and she felt it in her own blood: the heat, the excitement, the eagerness. Soon, they would know.

It is getting lighter.

Tsal hurried forward. First, a faint, frail suggestion of light, scarcely more than an illusion. And then, a length of stone, edged by light, standing in the darkness in harsh relief. And at last, the opening ahead of them, a narrow crack in the midst of tumbled stone, where blazed the fierce light of the sun.

Tsal squeezed through, shading ids eyes against a blinding blaze of light and heat, into a spherical bubble of white glass. The light, pouring down from the sun through a surprisingly narrow opening at the top of the spherical bowl, swirled and coalesced here, reflecting and rebounding in visible streaks of motion, flickering like lightning in the bright sunlight. Tsal had come out near the lowest point of the sphere, where just a few paces away ran the river they sought, flowing in a narrow, deep channel.

Awed by the remarkable geological formation, dizzied by the heat and the motion of the light, Tsal reached out to support idreself against the smooth, curved slope of the glass, only to snatch ids hand away. The glass had seemed to tingle and burn under ids palm. Even Ara, coiled as she remained in that small corner of Tsal's mind, could sense the raw energy stored in that glass.

I have never seen or heard of anything like this, said Tsal, amazed and drunk with discovery. Id stared fearlessly at the flickering lightning, never considering what might happen if one of those bolts should strike idre. As they watched, the lightning seemed to pause in midair and coil in upon itself until it became a kind of a pulsing, flickering ball of light. From that collection of energy emitted something which left Ara stunned with amazement.

It was thought.

It is alive?

Yes, she said to Tsal.

Can we communicate with it? Can you?

She began to uncoil herself from the small corner where she had been watching and waiting. She had never joined with Tsal in the way she joined with her own kind, so completely that her existence was obliterated. She had not dared, for she feared that when she disengaged from that separation, she would take part of Tsal with her; and part of her personality would remain within Tsal. She would cease to be a Mer, and id would cease to be an Aeyrie. Both of them would become . . . something else.

But now she had to try. Or she would never know the answer she had been sent out to find.

Tsal was afraid, but once again curiosity had more power. Id gave way before her, allowing the full liquid force of her mind to enter his, mixing water and air into a heady liquor. Cautiously, she opened themself to the presence of the fire, holding themself out like a hand to catch the rain of thoughts falling down.

There was the energy, and the motion, and the hunger.

Then it noticed them. All the other moving lights in that hot, bright place also came to a halt in the shimmering air, and coalesced into a full dozen of the pulsing, bodiless beings.

And then Tsal was torn away; all the intertwinings of their two personalities rent apart, and Tsal was gone, the river in which they joined was gone, and Ara was falling, flying, swirling in a vortex of water and air which deposited her at last where she had begun. In the quiet pool where the fans of coral waved, she sank to the sandy bottom and lay there, stunned.

After a while, she needed to breathe. She swam groggily to the surface of the sea, and stared out at the hot, mysterious sun and, far away, the jagged shoreline of Ara's Field.

Tsal was gone. Anywhere in the world, no matter how far away or remote, she knew she could find the Aeyrie, for id's orderly logic and surprising passions had become to her a bright beacon of unique personality. But Tsal had ceased to exist. And there were no answers, only questions beyond questions.

For a thousand, thousand years, the Mers had swum north in the early spring, and south in the late summer. Never, in all the accumulated memories of all those ancient, timeless seasons, had a Mer swum north in the late summer before Ara did so. She wondered: was it the swimming of the Mers which turned the direction of the currents? Would she alter the seasons of the world and the migration patterns of her people forever, by swimming northward like this, against the current, against her instinct, against her judgment, against the massive accumulation of tradition? She swam northward, day after day, pausing only after dark to eat what food she could find: the redleaf past its summer prime, a few late blooming caricha. From sunrise to sunset, and even in her dreams, she searched the world for Tsal.

This was the other terrible thing: no Mer had ever searched like this. To scan the immediate area of the herd for intruders, this was done all the time. But to abandon the limits of wisdom, and scan the world?

She found some wonderful things there, and she found some things that made her wish she had never even begun her search. But she could not find Tsal.

She journeyed until the shoreline became strange to her. The moons in the sky shrank and swelled and shrank once again. One dark night a thought came to her, awakening her from her sleep on the back of the rising and falling tide: *Do not love an Aeyrie, unless you also love the wind.*

She swam to the glassy smooth surface of the sea, where beneath the clustered moons the nearby cliffs glimmered, and stars glittered in the velvet sky. Amid black water and starlight she slid through the swells. Dodging razor-edged rocks which edged the cliff-riven shoreline, she paddled slowly inland, following a warm inlet of the sea. Here the water plants still bloomed; and here, she realized suddenly, a herd of Mers had recently passed.

She saw the lone figure at last; a two-legged person, pacing restlessly among the broken rocks against which muscled into the sea. It was a solitary person, like herself detached from her own kind, and like herself worrying over the unknown fate of a winged one. Despite the danger that the nearby herd of Mers might detect her and attack her, Ara sent out a quiet, tentative greeting.

The person on shore paused at once, to stare out to sea, until she spotted Ara, riding the swells. Ara cautiously captured some of the Walker's thoughts. The Walker wondered why a Mer was swimming dangerous waters in the darkness like this. She had recently completed an extraordinary journey, punctuated by wonder and horror and fear. Tonight, though she was physically and emotionally exhausted, she could not sleep. Thoughts of her beloved Aeyrie kept

her awake: fear for ids safety, and guilt that she had
not loved idre enough.

Everything is so much simpler in the herd.

I, too, love an Aeyrie who is missing, she told the
Walker. And she gave her just a little, a small piece
of the whole of all that had happened, but even this
small amount was enough to make a coldness come
into the Walker's mind, and an intensity so focused
that Ara found it frightening.

*You must stay with us. You know something which
is very, very important. It is something we need to
know. You must tell us everything that has happened.*

From the images in the Walker's mind, Ara understood much more than her words. She understood that
the danger already was, at least partly, known; that
the Walker was somehow associated with a group of
Walkers, Aeyries, and Mers, all of whom had come
together to form a kind of a herd. And she understood
that somehow this herd had taken on the responsibility
for the survival of all the known peoples of the world,
the people of the air, of the land, and of the sea.

There is another kind of people, Ara told the
Walker. *They are the people of fire.*

The Walker had seated herself on a rock, and
leaned her head into her hand. She seemed weary. To
continue to communicate like this, to tolerate Ara in
her thoughts, and to accept the entry of Ara's thoughts
into her mind exhausted her. There were others, who
could communicate with Mers far more easily than
she. She wanted Ara to wait while she fetched one of
these others, who slept nearby.

Promise me you will not leave!

The other Mers may come and chase me away.

*They may come, but do not be afraid of them. Many
of them were once strangers like yourself.*

So Ara waited, as the Walker began a weary climb
up the cliffs. But the rocking swells and the warm
water lulled her, for she was tired and hungry after
her hopeless journey. She dozed off among the rocks.
When she opened her eyes, she thought that she was
in her herd again, and all that had happened had been

only a dream. Except that these Mers which surrounded her were like her; a crowd of individuals,
with individual thoughts and individual memories.
They had no gestalt.

The sleek furred bodies of many Mers brushed by
hers, and their sweet voices sang in the warm water.
They welcomed her, and they used her name. This is
how Ara knew the herd itself was a dream, for Mers
know nothing of names. They warned her of the
sharp-edged rocks against which she threatened to
drift as she slept, and they offered to guide her to a
still, warm pool where she could rest with them.

She protested that the Walker had begged her to
wait here, and so they waited all together, males and
females and calves, all twisting together in the warm,
restless water. At last one of them opened himself up
before her, like the parting of water before a strong
wind. Because this was a dream, she dove into that
opening of his mind, and into the clear pool of a
strange gestalt.

She joined with the Mer, who joined with a male
Walker, and together they looked through his eyes
upon the confines of a small, cluttered dark space in
which a single candle burned. Here, a weary Aeyrie,
recently awakened from ids needed rest, sat folded
over a steaming cup, holding it with both ids hands.
A creature which the other Mer identified as an
Orchth lay nearby on the floor. The Walker female
with whom Ara had communicated earlier also sat
there, running her fingers through her snarled hair.

"We are joined," the Mers/Walker said. Ara had
never spoken before; and in that moment the whole
concept of language was made clear to her. The sound
represented an idea. It put a kind of a box around the
idea, but the box was too small. Yet it sufficed to
convey meaning, or at least part of meaning, in an
inaccurate kind of way. It was how those who could
not convey their thoughts directly were forced to
communicate.

"Is the visiting Mer included in the joining?" asked
the Aeyrie.

"Yes. Her name is Ara."

"I am Delan; this is Bet and Orgulanthgrnm. We understand that Ara was purposefully separated from her herd for the sake of exploring a dangerous mystery, and now her friend, an Aeyrie, is in danger. We hope that we will be able to help her, but we need to know everything that has happened."

The Walker, who seemed as familiar with Mer mindways as the Mer seemed to be familiar with Walker mindways, helped Ara to tell what had happened. Once again, they put a box around something, this time her memory of the event, so that they could learn about what had happened, rather than directly sharing the memory itself. Much was lost in this way. Therefore, when Ara had told all she could, there were many questions.

She answered them as well as she could. She told them she had not been mistaken when she detected thought coming from the fire people. As for what they were thinking, she told them again: it was a kind of emptiness, a hollowness, a ravening hunger. She did not know what had happened to Tsal: id had disappeared. Was id dead? At that question she paused; it had not even occurred to her as a possibility. But of course, a solitary individual's memory and personality disappeared completely in death.

The Walker Bet said to Delan, "So we have found the culprit."

The Aeyrie's head rested heavily in ids hand. "But who they are, or why they are trying to destroy our civilization, or how, or why we have never heard of them before, or where they have come from. . . ."

"Why do you suppose Ara escaped, when Tsal did not?" asked Bet.

Ara's Walker host responded with another question. "Did the fire people even realize that Ara and Tsal were two people joined together? Or was it something about Ara, that made it impossible for them to hurt her?"

"We need answers, not more questions."

"Ara does not know," said the Walker. "She is

young, she has little experience of the world. She cannot speculate."

He continued, "When the fire people first took action, to attack all of our leaders, the Mers knew at once that something had taken place. They knew that there was an important memory: they knew that something like this had happened before. But our Mers came to us from several different herds, and each of them carried a different piece of the ancient memory. Their pieces did not fit together.

"But Ara has a complete memory of that time. She remembers that the world was full of chaos, and then it became silent. That the water of the ocean became poisonous, and many of the sea people died."

"Why do the people of the land and the air not remember those times?" asked Delan.

Ara said, "I understand now that Walkers and Aeyries must speak in order to share a memory. Perhaps no one wanted to speak about it. So the children grew without knowledge, the elders died, and the memory was forgotten."

"The Aeyries do talk about the Forgotten Times," said Bet. "They just have nothing to say."

"But no one knows what made the times Forgotten."

Bet swirled her drink, which had long since ceased to steam, in its cup. "I don't think anyone is even asking why the times are Forgotten. When I lived in t'Cwa, I couldn't get anyone to discuss it. Not the scholars, not the the teachers at the University—and these are the people who live to discuss questions."

Delan unfolded idreself suddenly: slender limbs, muscular, triangular torso, huge wings. There was a fire in the depth of ids haunted eyes. "Then they must know, or at least suspect what happened. Otherwise, why be afraid to discuss it? Great Winds, if we could just get a message through to t'Cwa!"

"Then we would know," said Bet heavily. "There is so much that we could know."

Chapter 9

Bet dreamed of cool water and soft light, of swaying sea forests and a thousand particles of life blazing with the reflected light of the distant sun. Below the mercurial surface of the sea, she swam in a Mer herd, twining amid the slender stalks of the sea plants, blending her voice with their chorus. They sang of water: of storms that churned the ocean's surface into a tumbling froth, of currents that swept them past monoliths of stone and coral, of the rich, warm summer shallows where redleaf flourished and caricha bloomed. The waves lifted them forward and carried them back, and the entire Universe moved with them: the fronds and stalks of the plants, the galaxy of tiny stars burning overhead, the feathered tips of the coral. Bet broke free of the herd and dove for the sky, shattered through the water's surface, spreading her wings . . .

. . . And awoke in a strange bed, snarled among the bedsheets, with a band of sunlight blazing in her eyes.

Bet kept her mind locked shut like a steel strongbox, for she had been stolen from herself once. But when the Mer Ara came calling for her, she had cracked open that box enough to allow the Mer's thoughts to enter. Now, Ara had learned to use words, which somehow made it easier. *I have found Tsal,* she told Bet, dropping the words one by one through the crack of the box, like leaves from a tree. *I felt id's presence for the time it takes a drop of water to fly through the air and land in the sea. Then id disappeared again. So I know that id is neither alive nor dead. Id is missing.*

Bet spoke out loud to the stuffy air of the empty bedroom. "In that moment of contact, what did you learn?"

I learned that without idre, my mind is an emptied shell. I must return to find Tsal.

Though the Mer had learned to use words, some of her emotion leaked around the boundaries of language, telling Bet that argument would be a waste of time in the face of this resolve. Better to focus energy on giving Ara's mission a chance of success.

"I have an idea." Bet offered it through the slender opening of her steel box, and watched it sink softly into the deep pool of the Mer's mind.

Then the Mer's response came: *I am leaving at once.*

The community house creaked and whispered around Bet's room, as the people of Triad went about the everyday business of working the farm, raising the children, caring for the sick in the hospital, and running the printing press. Bet and Delan had outflown the terrible news of events in Is'antul, but arrived at Triad to find that Orgulanthgrnm and Feili had already increased the community guard and begun discussing the possibility of an all-out war. When the local Walker farmers and fishers learned of the massacre of the Lans, would they turn mindlessly against the strangers in their midst, the people of the Triad community? Or would they remember that the people of Triad had been good neighbors to them, turning out in force when help was needed, opening to them the doors of the hospital, sharing the food supply in bad years and sharing the celebrations in good.

And what would happen to the Aeyries in their Ulas?

Bet sat up in bed at last, trying to clear her head so she could remember the little she had been taught about Aeyrie history. In truth, there was little to know.

Over five hundred years ago, the Aeyries had domi-

nated the known world. This was the time they called
the Age of Balance: the time before the coming of
the Walkers, when Aeyrie Ulas, each a scant day's
flight from the next, filled the glasslands. Few artifacts
had survived from that age: a few mechanical drawings, a handful of rusting machines the use of which
had been forgotten, the art of Quai-du, a few traditional songs and fragments of a play. And, of course,
the ruins of a hundred Ulas, each one little more than
a hollow mountain with the wind whistling through it.

The historians did know that the Aeyrie population
had dropped from thousands to mere hundreds in the
course of a very short time. Everything the Acyric
people knew had been lost and destroyed. Not one
book had survived; even in the extensive library at
t'Cwa, the oldest book, many times reprinted, was
four hundred years old. The Aeyries had reverted to
a level as primitive as that of the Orchths, beginning
their history all over again.

The Aeyries blamed their decline on the Walkers,
of course. And while it was true that the burgeoning
Walker population had taken control of all the fertile
lands, it was also true that the Walker people had only
expanded to fill a void. According to Walker history
books, the Walker people, who had not even set foot
on lowland soil until after the Forgotten Times, were
recent arrivals by comparison to the Aeyries. They
had settled first in Sa, and a hundred years passed
before they even realized they were sharing the land
with the Aeyries.

So for what exactly did the Aeyries blame the Walkers? And what was it that they had so thoroughly,
deliberately forgotten? Why, although they had recre-
ated at least a portion of their lost and destroyed culture, had their population remained practically stagnant?
Because, Eia had said, implying once again that it was
the fault of the Walkers, they could not believe in the
future. But was it really the future they were missing?

Bet got out of bed, pulled a shirt and a pair of pants
over her stiff, aching body, and climbed the stairs to
Delan's room. "I think Ara is right," she said.

Delan lay in bed, reluctantly awake, with ids youngest child, Isa, wrestling furiously with one of ids legs. In the day and two nights which had passed since their arrival at Is'antul, id had scarcely rested. Worn thin as an old workshirt, to raise ids head to acknowledge Bet's presence seemed too much effort.

"I think something terrible did happen to the Aeyries: something so horrible and shameful that the Aeyries did everything they could to prevent their children from ever knowing what it was. They destroyed all their books, all their records, everything. And since the children didn't know, they couldn't tell their children when they were hatched, and so the entire history of the Aeyrie people was forgotten. There is a void where there should be a history. I think that the Aeyrie people cannot believe in the future because they have no past."

Delan silently reached out a hand to stroke ids wriggling child's thick fur.

"I'll bring you some breakfast," Bet said belatedly. "Bread and tea?"

Delan's voice, hoarse with sleep, apprehended Bet in the doorway. "What could be so horrible and shameful that it made us destroy our own past so that we would not remember it?"

Bet wondered if she should answer, and then she wondered if the problem all along, for five hundred long years, had been that no one would say the obvious out loud. She leaned on the doorway with a sigh. "If you were any other Aeyrie, I would never tell you what I think. It would destroy our friendship. You would decide that I am just like all the other Walkers: an Aeyrie hater, refusing to take blame for my part in what has happened to your people."

Delan smiled wearily. "And the Aeyries like to claim that we are without prejudice! Never mind, Bet. I know you are no Aeyrie hater."

"I think the shameful thing that happened during the Forgotten Times is that the Aeyrie people massacred themselves. They could even have created terrible weapons—like the moonbane weapon—and used them on each other. You Aeyries are a clever people . . . but that can be for good or for evil. Now are we still friends?"

"We destroyed ourselves?" Delan tucked ids wiggling child close to ids chest. "It makes almost too much sense. But what reason could we possibly have?"

"The fire people. They created a reason, just like they are doing for the Walkers."

Bet went downstairs to lay out a tray of rolls and jam and a pot of tea. When she returned, Delan stood at the ancient scrying stone called Calan'a'fa, which occupied a binewood stand in the corner of the room, gazing with a creased forehead into its depths. Bet rescued the squeaking child from Delan's arms—a soft, fat, wiggling armload of incoherent energy—and fed idre bread and jam with her fingers. At five years old, Walker children were considered old enough to go to school and be responsible for chores. But Aeyrie children were still babies: getting into everything, and only just learning to talk.

Delan murmured, "Bet, come here."

Reluctantly, Bet set Isa on the floor with a roll in ids hand. She would not be able to see anything in the glass, but she did not want to distract Delan with argument. The frosted edges of the block of glass seemed to contain a piece of faded blue sky, as if the color had leached out of it over the centuries. If Delan were to seek history's truth in its depth, would the glass be able to answer? Scrying stones did not necessarily tell only the present.

Delan's hand clasped Bet's. "Now look."

She looked into the glass, and saw there—Laril. With ids face drawn, ids charcoal eyes burning and ids mane in wild, twisted disarray, seated at the binewood chair in which the t'Cwa taiseochs had always sat, with ids knees drawn up almost to ids chin. And all of Bet's anger and loneliness came back to her, and she wanted to take idre by the shoulders and shake idre.

"The first onfrit got through a break in the storm

at around midnight," id was saying. "I spent the rest of the night hoping that the onfrit's message was some kind of bad joke. I can't tell you how relieved I am that you at least escaped harm. And Eia?"

Delan spoke out loud, so that Bet could hear. "I was able to protect idre. One of the ids old friends is now Lan of Internal Peace, so id is still safe for now, though Is'antul is like a pile of fuel just waiting for a tinderstick. Id says to warn you, by the way, that anything could happen . . . even war between Aeyrie and Walker. You should be prepared."

"Not war again." Laril sighed, rubbing reddened eyes with fingers tipped by broken nails. "Eia remained in Is'antul? Why?"

"Id could not fly away from ids lifework."

Laril unclasped ids hands then, and Bet glimpsed briefly the brand on the inside of ids wrist, so recent that it appeared raw and unhealed. So id had been named a Quai-du master at last. But the most extraordinary ability to fight and to dance and keep one's balance would not make a difference in this war.

"I can't believe that Hana . . . and C'la . . . what am I going to do without them to teach me? By the mountains, Delan, you warned all of us to beware!"

"You know Hana. Id never did have patience with precaution. And C'la did have a mage with idre, but it happened too fast."

"What are they going to do now? Hana's eldest child is not winged, and C'la's heir is younger than I."

"Neither Ula will name a taiseoch for several years, I think. For now, until we know how to protect ourselves, they are running by committee so that the fire people—if it is them—won't have a clear target. Perhaps you should step down, my dear, so that t'Cwa can be run by a committee as well."

"I can't tell you how attractive that sounds. I've scarcely slept in five days. It's been a hell of a storm. For a while we thought the entire Ula was going to fall off the mountain. I'm glad I didn't know it was just the beginning."

Id paused then, ids unguarded face sagging with tiredness and shadowed with wistfulness, or loneliness, or grief. "What about Bet?" id asked, almost hopelessly.

"She is standing beside me. She can see and hear you, I think."

To Bet's surprise, Laril's face did not instantly slam shut. Id gave a faint, ironic smile that overlay the rest of ids expressions without disturbing them. "So how goes your search for happiness, Bet?"

She had the advantage of being able to hide her face, for without a scrying glass Laril could see nothing. "It's more of a search to find out what I'm searching for. I don't think it's something as simple as happiness."

"I would settle for happiness right now."

"You always were easy to satisfy."

Laril made a graceful gesture with one hand, the motion with which a Quai-du dancer concedes defeat. Bet felt like a heel. What had Laril done to her, that she had to take every opportunity to insult idre? What had id done, except have ids life at risk, so that Bet had to spend the long, terrible days and nights wondering if id lived or died? "I'm glad you were not hurt," she said, too late. Laril made no response.

After a moment, Delan, pretending that id had not witnessed an interchange that should have been carried out in private, said to Laril, "You haven't been aware of anything strange at all? A sense of danger, an alien power?"

"Nothing," said Laril.

"Well, if lightning affects our ability to scry . . ."

Bet interrupted. "Laril, did you get some rain?"

Laril grimaced. "Buckets. Sheets. Floods. We'll be mopping up for days. We lost parts of our roof."

Delan turned to Bet, and the image of Laril immediately began to fade from the scrying glass. "Water!"

"Ara was in the sea, Laril in the rain, and even the A'lan was taking a bath."

"What?" said Laril patiently.

"The fire people attacked the Aeyrie Tsal, but not the Mer Ara who was also present. They attacked all the taiseochs except for you, and all the Lans except the A'lan. What the three of you have in common is water."

With Delan's attention focused on idre once again, the image of Laril brightened. "You mean I owe my life to this lousy storm?" Id shifted restlessly on the chair. Parts of ids fur were matted with water. Id must have been inspecting the storm damage when Delan came calling. "The Aeyrie who has disappeared, is that Arman's child Tsal, the one who has been at the Triad Hospital for most of this last year?"

"I'm afraid so."

Laril sighed. "What will I tell Arman? When Tsal was first hurt, id locked idreself up in a room and would not come out until we learned that Tsal would survive. Tsal is such a wanderer, I doubt id has been in t'Cwa for ten years. Delan, this is just too much at once."

"I don't think anyone knows what to do."

"I want to know more about the fire people. I want to know why they have never been encountered until now. I want to know why they are trying to destroy the world like this."

"If they are," said Delan.

"It has to be them!"

"I do not doubt that they are the ones who killed the Lans and the taiseochs. But to assume that they are trying to destroy the world, that is quite a leap of logic. We do not know what their motives are. I suspect a connection between what happened in the Forgotten Times and what is happening now, but I do not know what the connection is. The scholars of t'Cwa . . ."

"No one knows what happened during the Forgotten Times."

"What if we do not know what happened because we are afraid of the answer?"

"If I put it to the scholars like that, they will take it as a challenge, and perhaps they will turn something up." Laril spoke absently. Id's face seemed narrower; ids gaze focused onto a point in a remote space. It was a dangerous look, for Laril, one which had become extinct when the responsibilities of being taiseoch first burdened down Laril's flight.

"Just don't be an idiot," said Bet sharply.

Laril blinked, then smiled suddenly, sweetly, a smile like a razor. "Ysbet, my dear, what do I have to lose?"

Delan covered the scrying glass with an embroidered cloth, as Bet, glad to have something to distract her from her unhappy confusion over Laril, picked up the soggy mess of crumbs that little Isa had spread around the room. She dragged the child out from under the bed to brush the dust and hunterworm webs out of ids fur. Flat on ids face across her knees, the child fell asleep under the stroking of the furbrush. Bet, carefully avoiding with her brush the sensitive wing buds, thought about the wonder of Aeyrie transformation, from this fat, ungainly, awkward child to a magnificent, wild-hearted flyer. By the time Bet lay the sleeping child in the bed, Delan had finished eating, and sat in a chair at the open window, teacup in hand, viewing the activity in the fields below, where the grain was being harvested.

"I had a talk with Ara this morning," said Bet. "She thinks she contacted Tsal briefly. She decided to go back to Ara's Field and try to rescue idre. She has probably already left."

"What can a Mer do on her own? The water alone will kill her."

"I told her I would go with her. I'd like to bring Orgulanthgrnm, too. If there's a chance Tsal is still alive . . . who knows what id can tell us?"

Delan slipped from ids teacup. So gentle and mild mannered id always seemed, except for that spark of passion in ids charcoal eyes. "Take whatever you need from the stores. The Orchth will eat three times the food you eat—be sure to bring plenty of nuts. You should see," id added, "the expression on your face. Did you expect me to prevent you from choosing your own wind?"

"I guess I did."

"You are a flyer now, Ysbet. To choose is your right."

She went to Orgulanthgrnm's house and awakened him from his deep sleep to ask him to travel with her. "If we are able to rescue Tsal, we need a way to carry id back to Triad. Any Orchth could do it; but yours is the company I prefer."

The Orchth chuckled deeply, patting Bet sleepily with his padded forehands. "What company is it, for you to fly by daylight, and me to run at night?"

"I can see well enough in the dark to travel at night, like you do. The nights are still shorter than the days, but Ara will be hard put to keep up with us anyway."

"Good, good. Long years have passed since last I journeyed, and mine are a journeying people."

"I will put lots of nuts in a pack for you to carry, and meet you at sunset."

"Do not forget a bottle for water," rumbled the Orchth.

Besides food and a water container, there was little else Bet needed to pack. By mid-morning she had gone back to bed, and though she doubted she would, she immediately fell asleep and did not awaken again until mid afternoon. She went to the healers for some salve for the raw sores that the Wing's harness had rubbed into her flesh. Out of the last twenty-five days, she had already spent perhaps twenty of them in the air.

Soon after sunset, Orgulanthgrnm, lightly laden with all of their supplies, started north along the seacliffs. Bet, self-conscious before her fascinated audience, launched herself from the flight tower.

As her mage-wind lifted her lightly into the darkening sky, and Triad's buildings and fields dropped behind her, she wondered again how she could have made the transition so easily from being baggage to, as Delan put it, a flyer. The wind felt like no outside force under her control. She found its source within, a thing no more unfamiliar or mysterious than any other part of her personality. The wind had always

been within her, she just had never before known it
for what it was. And had Arman not given her the
opportunity, and necessity given her the reason, she
never would have realized what she could do.

The ache of her body where the straps of the harness dug into her flesh had not even begun to abate
after her last long journey, which had ended only two
days before.

But, despite the pain, her heart lifted as she winged
into the stars.

For the fastest foot traveler, the journey would normally have taken twenty days. But Bet, near dawn of
the eighth day, landed in Ara's Field. Orgulanthgrnm
had easily kept pace with her, for the Orchths are
tireless runners. Ara and the other Triad Mers who
had accompanied her, aided by a strong current which
carried them firmly southward even when they slept,
were less than half a day behind.

Bet and Orgulanthgrnm ate breakfast together before
sunrise, and by the time the first red sliver of the sun
had appeared on the flat ocean horizon, Orgulanthgrnm, curled in a cleft riven into shattered gray
stone, slept with his head tucked under his foreleg.
Bet lay beside him, but as soon as the sun rose, the
heat began to blast off the bare rock. In her padded
suit, she felt like bread baking in an oven. Sticky and
irritable, she got up and wandered to the edge of the
water.

It was not much cooler there. Far out at sea, a
fishing boat sailed on wind-ruffled water. Closer to
shore, when occasionally the ripples and swells became
still, Bet could see the waving fronds of the greenleaf
seaweed, just under the water's surface.

Ara's greeting startled her. *You are still awake.*

"It is miserably hot here. How close are you?"

A sleek body leapt out of the water in reply, spray-
ing a veil of sparkling water behind her.

"I'm going to swim out to visit you."

Come.

Bet gladly abandoned her padded suit on the rocks.

The cool water shocked against her hot skin. She waded carefully through the shallow water, but unlike most of the lowland shoreline, here there were no knife-edged chunks of glass breaking through the sand, only the gray, coarse-surfaced stone. Soon, seaweed scratched softly against her skin. She slid forward through a breaking wave and began to swim.

Where the Wing's harness had chafed her skin raw, the salt water stung fiercely. But she stretched the aches out of her muscles as she swam, and the sea rocked her playfully in its waves. When she began to tire, she floated with the hot sun burning here and there on her skin, and the seaweed tickling along her back. Then she swam onward, until at last the Mers surfaced around her, their hands full of seaweed, gazing at her with their dark, wet eyes.

"Greetings," she gasped.

In her mind there was a feeling which if translated into sound would have been laughter. *You are the only one in the world who can walk, fly, and swim. Which one is your home?*

"How could I choose? I love them all."

She swam with the Mers as she had in her dream, with their sleek, soft fur pressed against her bare skin. They twined around her, filling her thoughts with their laughter. When she could swim no more, they carried her to shore, buoying her up in their arms, and setting her down softly in shallow water.

We cannot go any closer to the bad water, they told her as they left her. *Tomorrow, Ara goes on alone.*

"Orgulanthgrnm and I will try to find Tsal's baggage kite. Good luck, Ara."

How easy to love the Mers, with their sweet voices and gentle hearts. Bet lay down beside Orgulanthgrnm on a bed made of her own clothes, and stared at the dull blue sky. And at daybreak the next day, Ara began the terrible last leg of the journey, which she herself knew she could not survive, alone.

When at first she entered the poisoned water, Ara did not think she could go on. The foul smell and taste nauseated her, but the way it felt on her skin panicked her. Though water was cool, it burned. And soon her lungs burned, and her eyes. The sound of her singing voice grew thin and strange, and she swam through dead and rotting tangles of seaweed where once crisp, sweet forests had swayed.

On the second day she reached the river, which poured its poisons into the sea through a broken dam of rock and glass. She slipped through, and then the struggle against the current began. Between narrow walls of stone the river muscled its way into the sea. In total darkness, Ara fought her way against the silent torrent. Her voice could not help her here, for the rush of water distorted the echo. She could only be certain that she made any progress at all when she made her way to the water's surface to take a breath of air. Here her voice carried; sometimes in small spaces and sometimes in large; sometimes with the area between the water's surface so narrow that she could scarcely get her nose above the water to take a breath.

If it had been winter, and the water had been at its highest level, she would have drowned.

Without the sun, she could not measure time. She could not stop or rest, or the current would have carried her out to sea once again. She grew weary, and weak, and still she swam, as the burning in her skin and her lungs increased to a terrible pain, and her determination and resolve burned away before it. Still she swam, though it seemed she made no progress at all.

Then there was light, glowing faintly on the billions of particles which filled the water, and at last she saw the blaze of the sun. When she came up for air, she had entered the polished sphere of the fire people, which she last saw through Tsal's eyes. They hovered over her head, quiescent in the heat of the noonday sun. Ara watched them, seeing how the sun, captured and reflected in the white, polished stone, fed them with its heat and light. She saw the byproduct of their digestion floating down like dust to pollute the river below.

Her vision blurred, her eyes burning. She wanted to ask them about their hunger, but she could not risk alerting them to her presence here. She continued upriver, swimming with her head above the surface, until she spotted Tsal.

Id lay as id had fallen, wings awry, one arm beneath ids body and the other stretched loosely across the stone. How long had id lain like this? Fifteen days, or twenty? Ids flesh looked shrunken against ids bones, ids wing membranes withered in the heat.

Ara made herself very small. Like a coral folding its long feathers up into the tiniest of bundles and slipping into an invisibly small hole, so Ara shrank her mind, and covered it over with a hard, impermeable shell. Under the protection of this invisible fortress, she swam up to the edge of the river, and hitched herself onto shore.

The fire people did not notice her. We are nothing to them, she thought. If they cannot perceive our thoughts, then we do not exist.

She was not like Bet, to transplant herself casually from water to land. Her sleek, sinuous body felt heavy and flaccid on the rocks, and its weight pressed down upon her lungs, so she could scarcely breathe. She hitched herself painfully across the jagged rocks. At birthing time the females must come ashore like this, but they choose a soft, sandy beach, and do not go much farther onshore than the tideline, and do not stay for much longer than it takes their cub to draw a first breath. The Mers are not meant for land.

At last her hand touched the one which Tsal stretched across the rock. She grasped it as tightly as she could, and began to hitch herself backward. Tsal felt as light as a dried flake of wood. Though Ara's hand had never lifted anything heavier than a handful of seaweed, the Aeyrie followed her easily, dragging behind her down the slope once again, and into the water, where id slipped from her grasp, and sank like a stone.

She found idre on the river's deep bottom, id's wide wings drifting like leaves on the current, id's thick fur flowing like seagrass. Weak and weary, she swam up to grasp idre by the waist. Should she not let the river carry id slowly out to sea? The bright spirit which had once inhabited this frail frame had long since departed.

Then something flashed in her awareness, like the sun rising suddenly over the sea, and Tsal opened ids eyes. Wide, startled, even panicked, id stared at her, ids cheeks puffing with ids last breath of air. With a stroke of her strong tail fin Ara brought them both to the water's surface, and Tsal gasped, and gasped again, desperately sucking air into id's lungs.

The current rapidly carried them toward the narrow underwater opening through which they would have to pass. Ara clutched Tsal, stroking desperately with her tail to keep them both afloat. *Trust me, you must—or we both will drown!*

Tsal took another gasping breath, and then a brief, wry smile crossed ids face. "We meet at last," id said out loud.

Hold your breath. We're going under water again.

Tsal took in a last deep gasp of air, and Ara let them both sink into the grip of the current, to the narrow opening where the water battered them ruthlessly against stone before spewing them through, into the pale water where the glowing particles floated, and on into darkness. Ara felt Tsal's heart thundering against her body, and she lifted them to the surface again. Tsal brought up ids arms, to fend off the low-hanging surface of the invisible ceiling. "How far?" id gasped.

Ara felt ids panic: a desperate horror of deep water, making ids heart thunder and ids muscles spasm under her grasp. She slid herself into Tsal's mind like a newly sharpened knife, and cut the link to Tsal's primitive instincts which gave idre such a horror of water.

Tsal took a deeper, calmer breath. "You Mers," id said mildly. "Always fooling around with other people's brains."

The fire people cannot touch you through the water. This was the only way to bring you to safety.

Tsal fended away a spur of rock which jutted from the ceiling into the water. "Well, you know what my parent always used to say? Out of the storm, into the hellwind. Not that it means anything to you; it's sort of an ironic saying. . . . Never mind. Do Mers have nightmares?"

The terrible journey seemed to have no end. They clung to each other, sinking under water when they had to, never certain when they might find the water's surface again. Ara's strength began to fail. Her buoyancy was not quite enough to counter Tsal's density, and she had to keep swimming to keep them both afloat. Tsal's chatter became a mindless babble. When she probed ids mind, she found only a disordered chaos.

She had to sink below the surface to give herself a rest, but in ids delirium Tsal forgot to hold ids breath. She thought she had lost idre, but after some desperate coughing id was able to breathe again. "What next?" id asked wildly of the darkness.

The current seemed to be gaining force. Ara struggled against the water, struggled to lift them above the surface one last time, for one last breath of air. And then they crashed into stone, Tsal was torn out of her arms, and she washed out of the river into the cool light of the stars.

Tsal floated away from her, a beacon of chaotic intelligence and renewed terror, and then suddenly blinked out. In the darkness and the depth of the sea she could not find idre. She circled desperately, singing wildly into the swirling water. Id was dead, id had to be dead; how much more would it have taken to kill a being so fragile, scarcely more substantial than a leaf of sea lettuce? So when she found idre at last she had no hope left in her, and it was only because a creature of the air should die in the air that she dragged ids limp body in out of the sea and into the shallows where Bet and Orgulanthgrnm waited for her.

She lay on the ragged rocks beside idre, and wanted only to close her eyes and sleep. When Bet rolled Tsal onto ids side and forced the water out of ids lungs and breathed into ids mouth until id began to breathe on ids own once again, Ara did not know. She did not know when they lifted the Aeyrie onto the Orchth's back, or when Bet, grunting with effort, lifted Ara herself up in her arms and began to carry her, stumbling under her weight, along the jagged shore. Not until almost dawn, when Bet set her down heavily, did Ara regain consciousness again. The salty water of an unpolluted wave, shot through with the energy of an incoming tide, washed over her. Ara lifted her head weakly out of the water and peered up at Bet, who had tipped her head back to breathe cool air into her lungs. Bet was naked. Her smooth, hairless skin shone with sweat.

Thank you for bringing me home to the sweet water.

Bet dropped to her knees beside her then. "Your friend is still alive."

Tell id that I am sorry.

Bet waited with her, holding her head above the water so she would not drown, until the rest of the Mers came in with the tide, to take Ara out to sea with them.

Chapter 10

Twenty days' journey north of Ara's Field, Bet awoke late one afternoon to discover that Tsal had disappeared.

Many times during that difficult journey she had feared for the Aeyrie's life. Normally, Aeyrie illnesses tended toward the dramatic: severe, but quickly resolved by either death or recovery. But Tsal had passed from delirium to torpor and back to delirium once again, alternately burning with fever and shivering with cold, never capable of speaking a sensible word, too weak to stand, to care for idreself, to eat solid food. Using the cooking gear and food supplies in the baggage kite, Bet cooked rich broths for idre. Orgulanthgrnm, whose strength alone proved an incomparable asset, fed the Aeyrie one spoonful at a time, carried idre on his back, and sometimes dipped idre into the sea to cool ids fever or to rinse the filth out of ids fur. Already shrunken and dehydrated from imprisonment by the fire people, Tsal survived from crisis to crisis, sometimes worsening, sometimes seeming to improve, and demonstrating with each passing day how much less frail the Aeyries are than they seem.

And now id was gone.

Orgulanthgrnm slept with a black cloth over his head. Bet eased away from his furry side, against which she habitually curled, got to her knees, and breathed a sigh of relief. At least no nightmare of blood and flesh spattered the nook in which they slept.

On her knees she crawled through the hollow, her sticky hair falling forward to blind her, and out into the cool sea wind and the sound of crashing waves.

While they bore the desperately ill Aeyrie homeward, the winds of autumn had begun to blow. Once, when Tsal became too weak to even ride on the Orchth's back, they had holed up for two days in a rickety shed in an abandoned corner of a farm. From afar, Bet watched the farmers bringing in the harvest. She remembered the harvests of her childhood: the red stockings and red kerchief so she would be visible in the head-high grain, the sweet smell of cut corn, the swish and hum of the scythes and the rhythmic harvest songs. And, after all the work was finished, the feasting, the harvest parties, the autumn masques, the last, sensual days of food and pleasure before the blood slowed in the veins and she wanted only to sleep the winter away.

At one of these feasts, sated with pies and cakes, puddings and dancing, Bet had seduced her first lover. Throughout the sweet-scented, warm night she lay with him in the fresh-cut hay. But she was already restless, and he could not hold her for long. Perhaps a child of hers was, at that very moment, harvesting the grain of Canilton. She could not know for certain, as the farm communities kept no records of whose egg hatched what child, and Walker farm children were always raised by sharemothers.

Tsal had grown stronger, and they left their rickety shelter and continued the journey.

Now she saw idre, huddled atop a rock, buffeted by the wind, thin as a shriveled leaf, sitting watching the sea. Ids golden fur, tarnished by grime, gleamed dully in the sunlight. Scarred, metal-patched wings the color of kipsbutter hung limp like rags from a line. But as Bet picked her way among the jagged rocks and drew up to idre, id turned to her a bright gaze, burning with intelligence, restless with pain. "I do not even know your name," the Aeyrie said, speaking the Walker tongue with a delicate accent. Bet leaned her weight into the rock. She had exchanged the pain of the flight harness for the pain of sore feet. She did not judge it a fair trade.

"Ysbet ib Canilton ib t'Cwa. Friends call me Bet."

"Of course. I have heard of you. A friend of the people." Tsal frowned down at ids hands, which were painstakingly working through the matted fur of one thigh. "But how did I come to be with you? The last I remember, Ara—"

"You've been very ill."

"This much I had guessed. Perhaps the water is not poisonous only to Mers." Wind blew open the Aeyrie's metal-patched wings, and the sun shining through the membranes briefly highlighted their multitude of scars.

"I had been in Is'antul with Eia and Delan. At lot has happened in the world—it's hard to know where to begin. Delan and I returned to Triad, and Ara arrived there the same night. Perhaps she knew from you that she could find help there, or perhaps it was just chance. Orgulanthgrnm and I traveled to Ara's Field so we could pull you out of the water and carry you back to Triad . . . but it was Ara who brought you to us. We found your baggage kite, too."

"Yes, I saw. Thank you for that. Some of my mapmaking instruments would be difficult to replace. And thank you sincerely for your help. But why did Ara expose herself to the water? I went exploring on her behalf so that she would not have to risk her life like that."

"Because we could not rescue you any other way, and she chose to do it. It seems water is the fire people's only barrier."

Tsal's gaze focused on the sea. "Her voice has gone silent. Where did she go after she delivered me to you? What happened to her?"

"Some Triad Mers had made the journey with us, and they carried her out to sea with them. I have not seen them for twenty days. I think they are trying to get her to Triad, but they are swimming against the current. Tsal . . ." The Aeyrie turned ids golden eyes to hers. She hated to have to say this to idre, and, being a stranger, she could not guess what ids reaction would be. But there was no one else to tell id the truth. "She may be dead," she said. "She already seemed extremely ill when I saw her. I had to carry her upshore to the clean water, for she was too weak to swim."

"I know," Tsal said. "I know she may be dead. Why sacrifice herself for me? Because the herd will remember her and I have no herd?"

She brought idre dried fruit and travelbread and a cake of soap. On tottering legs id stood, supporting idreself against the side of the rock, while she sluiced ids fur with pots of water scooped out of the sea. As she worked the soap through ids thick fur, she discovered more scars where a knife-edged mountainside had cruelly gashed. Perhaps, Bet reflected, she should not have been surprised that Tsal had survived the poison water and the fire people. This assault must have seemed relatively mild, compared to what id had already survived.

Behind the wind-shelter of a boulder, they sat together in the warm sun and Bet brushed the mats out of Tsal's fur as it dried. The setting sun brought out the red overtones in the gold. Once, Bet thought, Tsal had been a spectacular beauty: the kind who could command any Aeyrie's attention, under any circumstances. And then, as id leaned forward to peer around the rock and look once again out to sea, with the metal patches in ids wings flashing in the sunlight, Bet's vision cleared. There was no tragedy of lost beauty here, only a new beauty growing out of an old.

Two nights later, under the light of five full moons, Walker, Aeyrie, and Orchth walked up to Triad from the sea. The Orchth sentries, having recognized their scents from afar, did not challenge them. In the Triad fields, Orchths loaded wagons with harvested roots. It smelled like harvest time: of earth and plants, of herbs hanging in the drying shed.

Someone brought Delan word of their arrival, and id joined them in the big kitchen, where Orgulanthgrnm brewed tea with an expert hand, Bet grilled bread over the stove's open flame, and Tsal, having already eaten a bowl of cold stew, presided over the jam pot, eating three of every four slices of toast idreself. "I see you are on the mend," said Delan.

Here in the warm kitchen, with onfrit nests in the rafters and rag rugs on the floor, crocks of pickles and bins of flour lining the wall, and the knife-scarred work tables gleaming with oil, it had been easy to forget everything in the relief of coming home. But Delan, red-eyed and haggard with sleeplessness, was a sobering sight. Id sat heavily on the stool beside Tsal, refused bread but accepted a cup of tea, and lapsed into blank-eyed exhaustion as if it were idre, rather than they, who had just returned from a hard journey.

"Have the Mers returned?" asked Tsal. "Has Ara?"

"Not yet. The current will be slowing them down."

Tsal did not even look at the last tray of toasted harvest bread which Bet set before idre. She sat with Orgulanthgrnm near the stove, and cupped a hot pottery mug in her hands. The last leg of their journey had been made even more miserable by a damp, chill wind coming out of the sea. On the kitchen floor, they had piled the detritus of their completed journey: the collapsed baggage kite, Bet's Wing in its case, Tsal's maps and tools, journal and camping gear, Orgulanthgrnm's empty pack, with the flaps sagging open. Bet thought she would die of weariness if she had to lug any of it even one more step.

"Tell me what happened," said Delan.

After so much risk and effort, there was surprisingly little to tell. Delan could ill disguise ids impatience when Tsal could not answer ids questions. "The fire people are not like us. After encountering them, I can easily see why some scientists insist that the Aeyries, Walkers, Mers, and Orchths all have more in common than we have in difference. Strange as an encounter with a Walker or a Mer may be, at least I can describe it. But for the fire people . . . I don't have the words. I can't even begin."

"We'll have to ask the Mers to help, then."

Tsal, reaching absently for another piece of toast, froze mid-reach. "Why not?" id said, too softly. "My mind is just another common room after all. Let the whole world take a tour."

"I wouldn't ask if it wasn't so important," said Delan wearily.

"It didn't sound like a request to me."

"I guess I'm too tired and worried to bother with niceties. If there's anything you know that can help us. . . ."

"If it would keep the world from coming to an end, would you unhesitatingly lie down and have sex with someone you didn't love?"

This question, and the revelation it contained, seemed to silence Delan. Both Aeyries, Bet realized with a shock, were on the verge of tears. For Tsal, whose gaze kept so hopelessly turning toward the sea, the reason now seemed clear. But Delan. . . .

"I want my Mer," said Tsal.

"I'm sorry. Lack of sleep is making me behave like an idiot." Delan drew an unsteady breath. "If you can't do this, then what can you do?"

"Give me a day, Delan. Just one day, in a quiet place, with my journal. Then we'll talk about it again."

"All right."

The coals crackled in the stove. A half grown Orchth cub came in and offered to carry their gear away. "Later," said Orgulanthgrnm, and sent the youth away. "Delan," he rumbled, "What has happened to Eia?"

Delan breathed into the steam from ids teacup. "Well, as you know, Eia has been given refuge at the Lanhall of Invisible Wealth. The day after you left, a male named Tor Kates was named Lan of Peace, having assassinated all four of the rivals who stood in his way."

Bet snorted. "The irony of that title has always amused me. Why can't we speak the truth, and call him the Lan of Violence, or the Lan of Death?"

"In the end, no one dared make a stand against Tor

Kates. Even Samil Infatil found it politic to cast her vote for him, though she detests him and everything he stands for. His first official act was to order Samil to hold Eia under house arrest. He said that if she would not do it, then he would. So Eia has spent the last—what, nearly thirty days now—in a single room at the Lanhall of Internal Peace, writing ids memoirs. But Tor Kates hates Eia—hates all Aeyries—has always believed that for the Walkers to trade peacefully with the Aeyries is tantamount to a heinous crime. We all know that it is only a matter of time before Tor Kates has consolidated enough power to challenge Samil directly, and take Eia away from her."

Both elbows on the table, Delan rested ids face in ids hands. The tangles of ids mane straggled through ids fingers like twisted silver threads. "Bet, I don't know how I can have the nerve to ask you for this. I want you to go back to Is'antul."

Bet, shocked out of her daydream of uninterrupted sleep in a straw ticking bed, cried, "You want me to what?"

"Any Triad Walker would be willing to go; you know that. But they would never get through the gates into the Inner City, if they made it that far. It has to be you, Bet. You're the only one that I know can do it."

The last moon had set, but only the faintest tinge of light on the horizon promised the dawn. The sky blazed with stars, a thousand whitefires in the velvet darkness. Between earth and sky, a lone traveler across the spinning world flew on spread wings, carried by the wind of her own heart. She landed, stumbling, on a gentle hillside where grasses bowed their heavy seedheads. The stars had begun to disappear. Weary to the bone, she dismantled her Wing by touch, and packed it away into its travel-stained canvas bag.

For what remained of that one night, she had slept in a bed. Now, four more days and nights had passed, and she no longer cared where she slept.

She heard the sound of a stream trickling nearby. She followed the sound to an overhanging tree, which would shelter her from the morning sun. There she lay down on the bare ground and pillowed her head on the bundled Wing. Had she found happiness yet? she asked herself. But she knew that in all her long journeying she had left herself behind. Whatever she had hoped to do with her life had been swallowed up by the land's desperate need for peacemakers.

She awoke to the sound of a wagon passing, and the shimmering voices of excited children. The sun, slipping between the yellowing leaves of the tree, burned into her eyes. She sat up, grunting with pain. Instantly, her stomach rumbled.

The wagon, bedecked with heads of grain and harvest ribbons, rumbled down the nearby wagontrack toward a distant farm. There, among the barns and outbuildings, a dozen other wagons had already parked, and in swirls of color and motion the local farmers milled, coalescing and separating in a complex dance of greeting.

Bet stripped off her stinking flightsuit, and washed herself as well as she could in the frigid water of the stream. She dressed in clothing brought from Triad: a farmworker's trousers and smock, knotted at the waist by a coarse braided belt. The canvas bundle she tied onto her back. Barefoot, she walked down the wagontrack to the farm, where, refusing her money, they gave her bread fresh from the oven and urged her to stay for the harvest feast. She had to repeatedly decline the invitation, for the males seemed to substantially outnumber the females, and to spend harvest night alone was to become an object of ridicule or pity.

One offered her a ride to the crossroad in his wagon, no doubt hoping to convince her, as they traveled, to change her mind. He entertained her well enough until he ventured his opinions on the subject of the murder of the Lans. He said that everyone knew that the Aeyries were responsible, and even if

Eia could not have actually committed the murders, then id had been instrumental in planning them. What other Aeyrie had unchallenged access to Is'antul's Inner City? "The Aeyries mean no good," he concluded. "They never have been anything but trouble to us. I think we should just go clean them out of their dirty towns."

The male glanced at Bet, expecting her now to compliment him on the profundity of his opinions. She picked up her bundle, hopped out of the moving wagon, and started briskly across a harvested field, leaving him shouting in surprise and outrage behind her. She found the crossroads on her own, and by dark she had reached the merchanter's town of Maner on the shores of the Is'antul harbor.

"Save your money," suggested the innkeeper when she tried to rent a room for the night. "No one will bother you if you sleep on the street, so long as you choose the right street. You'll be needing your money to see you through the winter, for there're no jobs to be found this late in the year. And with all the troubles—I suppose you're not too old to go into the army."

Too tired to find another inn, she hired a room from him anyway.

The voice of a dawn vendor woke her. She slept in rented blankets that had been rented out a few times too often, and she was happy to throw them aside and stumble over to wash her face in a bowl of cold water. In the chill morning air of autumn, her breath steamed before her face. Her body thrummed like a strung harp; her fertile time was coming. She dressed in her plain clothes, picked up her bundle, and left the inn just as the first light of the sun paled the sky. Another restless night's sleep, another long day's journey ahead; weariness overlaid weariness like a hundred coats of paint on a rotten barn door. Footsore, she stumbled down the street, just another exhausted farmhand at harvest end.

A dawn vendor sold her some bread and dried fruit, and told her where the drafbuses would be loading their day's passengers. Busy people already crowded the street: sweeps and loaders, people pulling handcarts and people carrying baskets of laundry, a few half-naked, wailing children sitting on the curb. Near a crowded market where farmers spread their wares on bright, woven blankets, a drafbus waited. From wagonboard to wagonboard, people and their children and their many bundles and boxes and small animals in cages crammed the bus. Yet the driver took Bet's money and hauled her aboard, and she found a narrow spot to perch on the end of a hard wooden bench. Three more people came on board and pushed and shoved their way to a place to sit, before the driver tapped her long stick on the backs of the drafts. They started off with a jerk, dumping Bet and several others whose seats were precarious at best, to the floorboards.

The wagon swayed and jerked over the road's uneven paving stones. They creaked and rumbled out of the town and along a road overlooking the harbor, where late-season tradeships clustered, past a gathering of thin and worn children, dressed in ragged clothing and carrying small bundles in their hands, through the outskirts of another town, where people lived in crowded, ramshackle shacks, with a stinking, open trench running through the center of their community. From there they followed a circuitous route along the edge of a busy trading district, where fat merchanters strutted, followed by entourages of servants and assistants and handcarts laden with purchases. When one of the drafs pulling the wagon let fall some dung, the driver had to immediately stop and clean it up, lest she be fined.

The children in the drafbus fretted, whined, laughed, and slept, while the adults mostly stared blankly forward. They all seemed to Bet to be exhausted, or overwhelmed by the sheer challenge of trying to survive without land.

In town after town, the wagon paused to allow passengers to disembark and to load fresh passengers. Bet worked herself into a more comfortable spot on the bench, and then gave it away to an elderly female who sat down with a groan, shut her eyes, and did not open them again throughout the rest of the journey. The noon sun beat down on Bet's neck and shoulders, and then it began to slip down the side of the sky. Bet could not imagine how much farther they had yet to go to reach Is'antul. The journey seemed interminable.

The beautiful park which she remembered seeing from the water taxi spread out to her left, though a formidable fence prevented users of the road from violating its pristine lawns and woods. To her right, the harbor swelled and sighed, its gold sand beaches littered with trash and debris that had washed ashore. The white walls and flowing banners of Is'antul finally appeared, with the Outer City spreading like a shattered shadow from the walls to the sea.

It was still daylight when, stiff and tired and hungry, Bet disembarked. She found a disreputable bathhouse where she could wash the dust from her face and use the outhouse for a price, but she had to search for a street vendor whose food would not pose too much of a danger to her health. The Outer City's racket inundated her: children, who seemed to have neither caretaker nor home, screamed incessantly. Vendors and hawkers and brokers, who preyed upon the poor with as much energy as the merchanters preyed upon the rich, shouted their wares without pause.

Many had made their homes upon the street, and snarled at Bet when she accidentally trespassed upon their invisible boundaries. The pungent scent of crich and the deceptively sweet scent of 'achea filled the streets. Crich smokers lay in peaceful oblivion on every corner, and on the edge of every walkway, smiling in their sleep. The 'achea smokers were almost as easy to spot; with their sprightly walks and loud laughs and interested, uncomfortably intense gazes. Bet avoided them as soon as she spotted them, for 'achea smokers, despite their appearance of warmhearted good cheer, were prone to sudden fits of violence.

She asked her way several times before she finally

found herself on a straight, wide boulevard, patrolled by uniformed guards who kept the squatters and the dealers from setting up shop along its perimeter, and who urged the loiterers to pick up their pace. Their gruff cries of "Get along there—this is the Lans' Road" echoed at every corner. Bet matched her pace to that of the others: purposeful but not too brisk, and followed this boulevard through the remainder of the Outer City and right up to the white walls of the Inner City.

Though the sun had dropped almost to the horizon, the gates hung open, allowing a steady stream of weary, white-dressed servants to exit. Most of them seemed to live in the tiny houses which clustered at the edge of the boulevard, so close together that there was scarcely a passageway between them. Harassed by beggars who clustered at the gateway, they made their way quickly to their houses, and shut the doors firmly on the stink and noise of the city.

Though the guards allowed the servants to leave the city, not one person did they allow to enter. As Bet watched, they turned three people away: well-dressed people, who had presented passes, and stalked away fuming. Soon it would be sunset, and all the gates to the Inner City would be locked and barred. One of the guards who patrolled the street had noticed Bet; she had stood still for too long. She shook her head as if baffled, turned around, and let the flow of white-dressed servants surround her.

Then she disappeared.

Chapter 11

Bet had not ceased to exist to herself; but no one else could hear, see, or smell her. The boulevard guard who had been watching her so intently now looked right through her. The people crowding the street made room for her without seeming to know they were doing it.

She did not think that she had actually become invisible. Rather, she had become so inconspicuous and uninteresting that she was literally beneath notice. The gate guards gazed past her, as another unfortunate traveler approached them with his pass in his hand. Bet walked between the guards, unnoticed and unchallenged. The evening horns called sweetly, and the gate clanged shut as she hurried down the walkway.

She had entered the Inner City through the Sa Gate. A lush, exotic garden, fragrant with its last summer bloom, crossed by delicate walkways, spread to her right. In the Sa Quarter, with its clusters of white, tile-roofed buildings trimmed in fine wood and hung with banners, servants and supplicants still hurried busily down the walkways.

Spending all day sitting in a wagon in the hot sun had given Bet a headache. The difficulty of negotiating the Outer City and the strain of disappearing had increased her pain to agony. She paused in a small garden where a fountain trickled, to splash some cool water on her face. She squatted among the damp plants to catch her breath and consider what to do next. She would find Peline, if she knew where to look. According to Delan, Peline lived with an extended family in the Outer City, but actually spent most of her time in one or another Inner City guest house. The Lan of Trade had usually housed her, as a courtesy to Eia, but now she could be anywhere. Delan did not think she even had an employer anymore.

Bet's head throbbed. She shut her eyes, pressing them with her fingertips. Her blood thrummed in her ears.

"That's quite a trick."

A Walker male, dressed in somber black, stood at the garden entrance. He frowned slightly as she stepped aside, but his gaze continued to track her. "I saw you in the boulevard in the Outer City. I watched you disappear. It was one of the strangest things I have ever seen," he added, as Bet glanced around herself, considering which bush would best shield her escape. "You don't remember me, do you? Ellin ib Duanden? I am also known as Ellin a'Tal."

A wallet of black-stained cleata-skin, decorated with silver beads, hung at his waist. His double-breasted tunic buttoned up the front with silver buttons. Except for a ruff of bangs, his hair was tied back with a silver cord, and silver studs pierced his ears. But he had broad, strong hands like hers; farmer's hands. It was his arrival which had distracted the guards at the gate as she slipped between them. Apparently, his pass was of sufficient authority that he had been allowed to enter even at this late hour. Bet could not see a weapon; she could probably outrun him. He gave a faint smile. "I feel like I'm talking to empty air, but I know you're here. I studied at t'Cwa four years ago. Then, I wore brown and green, University colors."

He had been studying history, Bet remembered, often occupying a corner table of the t'Cwa library, half-hidden behind a mound of books. Like the unclenching of a hand, she let herself become visible, sighing as the pain in her head eased. Ellin, too,

seemed relieved. "I thought I had lost you several
times," he said. "You were very difficult to follow."

"That someone I knew would just happen to be
watching. . . ."

"I spotted you on the street and was coming over
to greet you. How did you disappear like that?"

"What are you doing in Is'antul? I thought you were
going to teach at one of the Walker Universities."

"We could make an agreement. I won't answer all
of your questions, and you won't answer all of mine.
Try this: are you in Is'antul to liberate Eia from the
Lan of Peace?"

Bet put her hand involuntarily to her head once
again as the pain suddenly intensified. "The Lan of
Peace has id in custody now?"

"Yesterday he finally forced Samil to hand id over.
Are you?"

"It's one possibility."

"If you need any help—"

She stared at him in astonishment.

"My employer wants Eia safe," he said.

"No doubt you'll refuse to tell me who your
employer is."

"No doubt. Will you have supper with me?"

"You don't think it will look a little funny, you
eating supper with a barefoot farmer?"

"Why? I was a barefoot farmer once myself. But
we'll eat in my rooms, of course. And I've got a feeling no one will see you go in."

"I've got a feeling you're right."

Ellin knew at once how Bet could get a message to
Peline. Soon, Bet's city clothes, carried by an uncom-
prehending servant, arrived at Ellin's door. But Peline
herself did not appear until after Bet, bathed and
changed and dosed with a potion for her headache,
sat down to eat a late supper. Ellin meanwhile had
engaged in his own mysterious business, which in-
volved several back door visitors whom Bet never saw.
He eventually joined Bet at the table. A bottle of

wine sat among the food unopened. Both of them drank water.

Peline arrived, dressed in rumpled and slept-in clothes. Beneath the shallow surface of her brisk self-confidence lurked anxiety and tension. From the doorway, as Ellin admitted her, she gave Bet a hard look, as if to ask her if she knew what she was doing. Ellin promptly gathered up his plate and cup, and excused himself into the next room, firmly closing the door as if to emphasize his intention to respect their privacy. But Peline studied the closed door suspiciously and sat down reluctantly at the table, saying that she already had eaten. Bet dug in eagerly, too hungry to care that the food long ago had begun to cool.

"Are you mad?" hissed Peline. "Do you know who he is?"

"We've met before, at the Ula. Then he was a history student. What is he now?"

"He's a spy for the Lan of Peace!"

"He said his employer wants Eia set free."

"Well, that was a clever way to get you to trust him, wasn't it?"

"I never had much choice except to trust him. He hasn't offered me any harm." At this, Peline hissed even more energetically, but Bet, uncaring, continued to eat. "So you will come stay with me, of course," Peline concluded.

"Don't you think that will be a little obvious? Besides, I won't be in Is'antul very long."

"What are you planning to do?"

"Set Eia free and fly out of here as soon as I possibly can."

"Yes, yes," said Peline impatiently. "But how? Especially now that you've all but told the Lan of Peace what you're planning?"

"Well, I guess it's impossible, isn't it?" Bet stabbed at the remains of the meal on her plate. "I should just go back to Triad again!" She felt an absurd urge to slap Peline, as if that would somehow bring her back to her senses. "Or maybe we'll just have to trust Ellin not to tell anyone."

"Now you are being ridiculous."

"How do you know he's a spy for the Lan of Peace, anyway?"

"Everyone knows he works for the Lan of Peace. He has a peace pass."

"You mean to tell me a pass has never been forged before?" Now Peline looked as if she wanted to slap Bet, but Bet continued, "And how effective could he be, with everyone knowing who he is and who he works for? And why would he let me send for you, when he should have known perfectly well that you would tell me everything about him?"

"So he could listen to our conversation," said Peline, looking pointedly at the shut door once again.

Bet had never imagined that she and Peline could end up at cross-purposes, for didn't they both want Eia freed and safely out of Is'antul? But she hadn't included Peline's need to be in control in any of her plans. "Why don't you tell me what you have in mind."

"If you had just gotten here a little more promptly—"

"Delan told me Eia would probably refuse to escape so long as id was Samil's prisoner—id would not want to damage her credibility. So I think my timing is about right."

"Well, of course Delan knows everything about Eia."

Bet held her tongue. Peline's passion, however misguided, was far preferable to indifference. Perhaps Pelline had expended every moment of Eia's imprisonment in careful, deliberate planning for her personal rescue. Perhaps she had dreamed that she would thereby earn id's love and unending gratitude. Now Eia had been moved to more dangerous quarters and far closer guard, and Bet had arrived, to steal away all of Peline's thunder. So love and desperation was making Peline foolish; a malady to which Bet herself was not wholly immune.

She leaned forward, offering Peline the sweet tray. "Between the two of us, we'll work something out.

Right now, I need a place to stay—not here, obviously, and not with you. Do you have any other ideas?"

"I'm sure Samil would give you a place, but . . ." Absently, Peline accepted a sweet from the tray. "Everything she does is closely watched. Tor Kates has labeled her subversive because she refuses to treat him as if he were the A'lan herself. What the A'lan thinks of all this, I can only wonder."

What the A'lan thought of this autumn's political crisis was scarcely relevant. A benevolent, powerful, mystical ruler in the eyes of people; the A'lan was, in fact, a powerless figurehead whose actual duties included only two things: affixing her seal and signature to laws and proclamations written by the Lans, and making an occasional, highly ritualized public appearance. The only purpose of her existence, according to Eia, seemed to be to lull the Walker people into believing that someone in their government had their own best interests at heart.

Peline continued, "But I can find you a place at a guest house in the Southern Seas Quarter. It will take money, though."

Bet produced the heavy purse she had carried with her from Triad, and Peline left to make the arrangements. Bet shut the door quietly behind her. Peline, like Ellin, could be a good friend or a dangerous opponent, and Bet still did not know for certain which either of these would be.

Bet slipped across the salon and suddenly opened the door behind which Ellin had disappeared. She found him seated at the far end of the room, beside an open window, his empty supper plate pushed aside, a document spread out before him and a pen in his hand. "Please come in," he said politely oblivious to Bet's peculiar behavior. "Is your friend gone?"

"She'll be back."

He nodded neutrally.

"She tells me you're a spy for the Lan of Peace."

"Everyone is a spy for the Lan of Peace," he said lightly.

"You have a peace pass."

"That I do."

"I suppose it's forged?"

"No. It's stolen. Look, I know you have no reason to trust me. I won't insult you by trying to convince you to do so. I think that the best help I can give you is to get out of your way, so I intend to do so." Ellin dipped his pen into the ink once again, and wrote a few more words onto the sheet of paper, before handing it to her. "I thought you might be able to use one of these."

It was a floor map of a huge, unidentified basement. Part of the basement was used for document and supply storage. The other part was a well-equipped dungeon, complete with guards, holding cells, and torture chambers. Each of the guard stations were neatly marked, and across one of the holding cells Ellin had written, "Eia." There was a guard at the door of that cell.

"How do you know?" asked Bet.

"I ran into you on my way home from visiting one of the Peace Guards, with whom I have an understanding. I know things . . . that he would have kept secret. It's a sleazy business, I know."

"You were planning to go after Eia yourself?"

"I was exploring the possibility, but I had pretty much decided it was hopeless. There's a good reason why no one has ever escaped alive from the Lan of Peace."

Bet folded the map and stuck it inside her shirt. "It's looking pretty hopeless to me, too. Sure, I can get in. But how am I supposed to get Eia out?"

"You have plenty to think about. Don't let me distract you."

When Peline came to guide Bet to her new lodging, Ellin did not even attempt to find out where she would be staying. Having given her the map, he seemed to have lost interest in her or her project. He would tell his mysterious employer that he had done what he could to help Eia. He had dispensed with this duty. Now, obviously, there were other matters on his mind.

Either that, or he was doing a very good job of disarming her suspicions.

Peline and Bet walked together to the Southern Seas Quarter, where a disreputable guest house pressed up against the city wall, hemmed in on all sides by other buildings. No clean, brisk servant greeted them at the door to show Bet to her room. Except for a single lamp, the hallways were dark. Unperturbed, Peline showed Bet down a dusty corridor to a shabby, windowless room. "The Lan of the Southern Seas used to put up his unwanted guests here," she explained, after the door had been closed behind them. "He liked to insult people. But now that there is a new Lan, the building isn't being used anymore. The housekeeper will deny any knowledge of your presence here."

Bet set her Wing and the trunk of clothes she had carried there on her shoulders onto the floor. Peline lit the air lamp, which at least worked, though it burned dimly. Bet said, "Tell me what is going to happen with lowland government. Have all the new Lans been named?"

Peline sat in the one creaky chair, so Bet sat on the edge of the dusty bed. "Well, yes, for what it's worth. But with the exception of Tor Kates and Samil Infatil, none of the Lans has any genuine support in their jurisdiction. You see, this is what happened: the city has been rife with rumors that it was the Lan of Peace who engineered the executions of all the Lans. Those rumors worked so well to his advantage that I suspect he planted them himself. The obvious candidates to replace the executed Lans declined the position in favor of others, who also in turn declined. At last only the most obscure candidates remained, and they, scarcely able to believe their good fortune, accepted the positions. But they struck deals with Tor Kates first, agreeing to support him without question, in exchange for his assurance that his assassins will leave them alone. So the government of the lowlands is now effectively in the complete control of . . . a very dangerous man."

"I expected things to stay pretty chaotic. Usually, when a Lan dies . . ."

"Usually, there are accusations and counter accusations, repeated assassination attempts, an incredible amount of favor currying and secret negotiations. It goes on and on for months. But not this time."

They discussed at length how to go about rescuing Eia. Peline thought that bribing the captain of the Peace Guard was the solution. She named a staggering sum, which Bet supposed Delan could come up with, given time. They parted at last, much more amicably than Bet might have expected, and Bet lay down on the bed and fell asleep.

The sound of a bell tower chiming the hour awoke her. She sat up in bed, instantly awake, counting the hours as the tower tolled them. Four hours till sunrise. Her heart thundering in her throat, Bet got out of bed. Four hours.

She did not remember even making her decision. It was clear to her that if she were to succeed, then she had to act immediately, without anyone's help.

She dressed in black, strapped the Wing in its bag onto her back, and slipped into the deserted hallway.

Chapter 12

Autumn, Day 10

Somehow, I knew that I was being held a prisoner. I was not conscious, and yet I did possess a kind of awareness. It was like knowing in a dream that it was no dream.

Every aspect of my body and my mind was tethered so tightly that the very concepts of control and motion were incomprehensible to me. Time became very strange: in jumps and starts, it was light, and then dark, and then light again. Thirty days passed, and it seemed like no time at all. And yet each moment seemed to last forever.

I survived that long without food or water, which is impossible.

I remember—something very strange. While I was nothing, a spark that could neither burn nor be extinguished, I yet retained something. If I had been physically tethered, it would have been as if every part of my body was so tightly tied I could not move at all, and yet by some oversight, a hand had been left free. So it was with me. There was almost nothing I could do, and yet I retained a small shred of awareness, a small shred of will. Enough to know that the fire people were rummaging through my being, uncovering and examining everything I knew, or was. All those shattered pieces which the Mers had so carefully, painstakingly glued back together again, the fire people examined.

And this is the strange thing: they did not know that I could see them. I watched them for an eternity, and *a realization came to me (slowly, since so little of my intellect remained under my control). I realized that there is no taking without giving—every time they comprehended some small part of myself, I could in turn comprehend a small part of them. There is no such thing as mental contact which flows in only one direction.*

Out of anger, I began to take everything which flowed in my direction, and I packed it into that small space where I still remained myself and in control of my destiny. I could not understand what I collected, nor could I do anything with it. My sole act of will during the entire time I was prisoner was to collect and pack away.

Now I must see what I have gathered.

First, just as I find it difficult to think of these fiery beings as people at all, so it is with them in relationship to us. They are energy. They can go anywhere in a mere moment; they are not limited by the constrictions of time or space. To them, we seem to be trapped because our spirits are contained in bodies of flesh and bone. They do not realize that our imaginations are free. They have no imagination. We are so slow-moving compared to them, and so alien that they do not even consider us to be alive.

We are like livestock herds to them, or pieces in a game, or rocks with which a house is built.

Second, they are a lost people. They come from a place so remote in time and place that they scarcely remember it. Thousands, millions of years ago, they abandoned their home: a land where the seas were full of fire and flames exploded far into the sky, which was filled constantly with the flicker of lightning. It was when their land began to cool, the flames to settle, the molten seas to harden, that they first became hungry.

That is the third thing: they are slowly starving to death. These ten or twelve beings are the last survivors of their race. They have learned to subsist on what heat and energy they are able to find: the heat of our sun, for example, reflecting off the white glass of the chamber they created for themselves. But it is never enough.

And then they discovered us.

This is how we, the intelligent beings of the world, appear to them: we are like weak, slow-moving flames in the frozen night. Our warmth is too tiny to ease the cold; our light is too faint to challenge the darkness. But they have learned that when they manipulate us in certain ways, we emit a kind of explosion of energy which they can then consume. If enough of us can be manipulated in this way, then the fire people can, for a little while, have enough to eat.

In order to manipulate us in the ways which work, the fire people need information. This is where I fit into the picture, I realize. They collected my information—as well as they could, considering that they are incapable of truly understanding me—and will use it to make their manipulations more effective. They have collected such information from many other such people, all the rest of whom, I must assume, had no Mer to rescue them.

As for what they are doing to create these explosions of energy which they crave so much, I can only point to the obvious. Strong emotion is what they are trying to create: fear, intense anger, violent rage. What they need to do is incite a war.

This is the fourth thing: the fire people have been here before. Perhaps they have been here many times before—who can say how old they are? They left (by what means I do not know) and now have returned, hundreds of years later. We are like a field in which they graze until they have eaten us down to bare ground. And then they leave, only to return when we have regrown and rebuilt, to consume us once again.

Delan, when I presented id with a copy of this journal entry, became very solemn as id read what I had written. Id sought me out later to ask me some thoughtful questions: *Are the fire people traveling through the Void? Are they completely invulnerable, or is there anything which they fear or dread? Do they experience anything comparable to the emotions we (Walker, Aeyrie, Mer, and Orchth) all have in common with*

*each other? To the third question I could tentatively
reply in the negative; but for the first two I could only
offer speculations.*

*Of course it is possible that the fire people travel
through the Void. It might be even more likely that
their experience of space and time is so dramatically
different from ours (for these very concepts are dependent upon the possession of a physical body) that the
Void would not exist for them. Or rather, that the Universe as they experience it is so similar to the Void, that
it is our Universe, the slow-moving, material one,
which does not really exist to them.*

*As for their vulnerability, I do not know. I suppose
their hunger makes them vulnerable (of course it also
makes them dangerous). And we now know for certain
that water is an absolute barrier to them. We know that
it is relatively easy to come physically close to them,
undetected (once again, evidence that they do not perceive the physical world as we do), so long as we do
not attract their attention by unusual mental activity.*

*These speculations tire me. My fur is still full of salt.
I want a bath.*

Autumn, Day 11

*Waiting to learn what has happened to Ara is making
me mad with impatience and worry. Staring out to sea
or straining to send my thoughts out on winds they
cannot fly will not make the Mers travel any faster. If
I were not still too weak to do so, I would have flown
off in search of her days ago.*

*In desperation I have come up with a project with
which to distract myself: a detailed map of Triad and
environs, a charming project really, complete with
drawings of each individual building, and even some
Mers out at sea. As for topography it is not much of
a challenge (except for the shoreline, with its rugged
cliffs), but the accuracy required to place each tree in
its spot . . . well, it has kept me pleasantly occupied all
afternoon. It felt good just to hold my compass in my
hand.*

I actually taught a handful of youngsters how to tri-

angulate and how to estimate the height of something on the basis of its shadow. I remember the first time my parent showed me how logic and mathematics made it possible to measure the world. I suppose Arman wishes I had become an inventor, too, but I have no interest in creating what is not. I want only to discover what is.

Autumn, Day 12

In the dead of night Delan came to my room. "The Mers are coming home," id said. "My eldest child, who is a Merfriend, just awakened from sleep and told me so."

"What happened to Ara?" I did not want to know, and yet it is better to have an answer than to wonder any longer.

"She is extremely ill, but she is still alive. The rest of the herd is swimming out to sea to help carry her in—they should be back by daybreak."

I went with Delan to awaken the healers, so they could prepare for Ara's arrival. This is the time of year that the hospital begins to empty out—those who are going to die do so, and those who were injured during the activity of the warm seasons have recovered enough to return home. The healers were all asleep in their beds, but they are accustomed enough to having their rest interrupted.

Gein, Delan's old friend and a sh'man among healers, a couple of other healers (one of them a Walker) who have among them a great deal of experience in working with Mers, and I climbed down the steep, difficult path into the Gap, a deep crack in the shoreline into which the sea washes. Here they have built a new boathouse where the old one used to stand, before it was washed away in the terrible storm five years ago. Within it are several shallow pools which can be filled with sea water warmed by being pumped along the length of a hot stovepipe. There was no wind with which to pump the water, so I and Orgulanthgrnm, who had guided us down the path through the darkness, turned the pump by hand.

*He was still there when they brought Ara to shore,
just before dawn. He waded into the water to lift her out
of the arms of her exhausted caretakers, and carry her
out of the water, into the shelter, and lay her into the
warm pool. I wanted nothing more than to see her, to
lay a hand upon her and know she still lived, but I stood
back. She hung limp in the Orchth's arms, and even
in the darkness I could see how small she had become.*

*Now day has arrived, and Orgulanthgrnm has re-
turned to his dark house. Soon after daybreak, a contingent from Triad appeared, with food and supplies,
and for me a small table and stool, my unfinished map,
and my journal. So I am sitting at the table now, with
Ara nearby. They have suspended her in a kind of
sling, so that her head can stay above water, and they
have plunged their needles into her limbs. She is still
unconscious, they say. The other Mers come and go
through an underwater tunnel—she is never without one
of her own kind to support her.*

*Everyone seems to expect me to remain here. But
she does not need me.*

Later

*I knelt for a long time beside Ara's pool, touching
her small, membraned, strangely jointed hand, and
thinking about how similar in construction her hand is
to my wing. She is too weak to communicate with me,
but she did open her eyes once, and perhaps she was
able to see me. Perhaps the other Mers told her that I
was near.*

*There is nothing to do now except to wait. The heal-
ers will not even try to predict what will happen. They
know that in the past, the Mers who were exposed to
the poisons (the waste from the fire people's living
processes?) died. But until Triad, the Mer herds always
abandoned their sick, making their death inevitable.
And in the past, there were more of the fire people—
many, many more. Perhaps on this visit, the water is
not so deadly.*

I guess I need to believe that there is hope.

For Ara at least there is hope.

Later

Ara is neither better nor worse, the healers say. She merely continues to survive. The water in her pool is being constantly replaced by fresh water—the healers hope this will help her. When there is no wind, I run the pump by hand. Orgulanthgrnm spends every night down here, keeping watch and running the pump so that I and the healers can sleep. Any of the Orchths could do this, but he says his heart is tied to Ara, too. The Orchths are not a neutral people: they cannot make a choice without also making a commitment. If the Aeyries are the intellect of this world, and the Walkers are the hands, then surely the Orchths are the hearts. And the Mers? They are the ones who remember.

Delan came down in the afternoon. Id looks completely exhausted; I do not think id is sleeping at night. We sat together for a long time, saying nothing. We are bonded together by helplessness and desperation, the mage and I. For all ids gifts and talents, id cannot rescue ids lover. And I, for all my restlessness and ability to survive, cannot make Ara survive. We wait together, watching the Universe turn. We cannot turn it faster. We cannot change its direction. All we can do is wait.

Later

I sat at my table, working on my map. It is turning out to be quite a work of art. I was drawing a tree when I felt something: a touch, a question. I turned my head, and Ara was looking at me.

Autumn, Day 13

I sit on the edge of her pool, with my legs in the water and my wings crushed painfully on the floor, and I hold her. I hold her in my arms, and I hold her in my mind. She is liquid and soft, she is simple, and she is very, very complex. She is ancient as the sea. She remembers the dawn of time. And she is a child, an infant, who in the course of half a season has been born, been assigned the duty of saving the world, and consigned herself to mortal danger to save a friend.

Perhaps I have led a frivolous life. I have loved every Aeyrie who would have me. I have flown every wind that blew my way. I have never asked myself what this or that decision would cost me.

And no one has ever needed me before.

It puts a heaviness on my heart. It pins me to earth. It scares me. Still, I hold her.

Autumn, Day 15

Yesterday evening, Delan came to us, with Orgulanthgrnm at ids side. "Do you never sleep?" I cried, and sat idre down on my stool, and put food in front of idre and urged idre to eat. My heart is full lately; I am not usually so solicitous, not even of my friends.

Delan let me distract idre for a while, but once id began to talk, the food never did get eaten. "I have been thinking," id began. And certainly, id has been.

Delan thinks that the fire people killed all the leaders of the Aeyries and the Walkers to destabilize civilization; making war, not just between the peoples, but among ourselves as well, much more likely. Then id said a terrible thing.

"Eventually, we are supposed to destroy ourselves, just as we did in the Forgotten Times."

"No one knows what happened in the Forgotten Times," I said, perhaps too firmly. For, in a deep place in my gut, I knew that Delan had said something which I already knew to be true. Five hundred years ago, Aeyrie killed Aeyrie until all but a few were dead. And Aeyries destroyed their own civilization—deliberately, thoroughly, absolutely, until almost nothing remained. That is how it had to have happened. There is no culprit but ourselves. There is no enemy . . . but ourselves.

I understood something that no Aeyrie on earth has ever been willing to understand. We are still a dying race because we are dying of shame. How proud we are, in our isolated Ulas, so superior to the Walkers.

How proud; and yet we will not hatch enough children to even replace the dead. So long as we could blame the Walkers, we survived. But now that we are at peace with the Walkers, and have no one to blame but ourselves, we are dying of shame.

It was a hard, horrible truth. For a long time I could not listen to anything other than the thoughts in my own head. I tried, with all my will, not to weep. And then I realized the most terrible thing of all: that if it was the fire people who caused the death of our people, then we have lived, every day for five hundred years, with a guilt we never deserved.

"But this is what I really want to know," Delan was saying when I began to pay attention once again. "I want to know why the fire people destroyed the Lans and the taiseochs, but left the sorcerers and the mages unharmed. Is it possible that they are blind to the power of magic?"

"What they are doing is so similar to what the Walker sorcerers do—" I began, and then stopped again. Of course not all Walker sorcerers practice the magic which depends upon another's anguish and pain for a source of power. I have not always known this, and it is too easy to fall back on my old prejudices rather than depending upon my newer, deeper understandings. But what truly stopped me was another question, one which perhaps will never be answered: is it possible that the Walkers learned their cruel magic from the fire people?

"Walker sorcery is similar in some aspects," Delan agreed. "But that is not the kind of magic I mean. Why did the fire folk ignore me, for example? Or Bet, who is turning out to be one of their most effective enemies, or any of the other mages? For we are the ones who can oppose them."

"Maybe magic is something new since their last—visit," I suggested.

"Or maybe they just aren't capable of understanding that a nothing, a person of matter, is capable of transcendence."

Delan's mane stood on end, so many times had id ran ids fingers through it. "I am going to call a convocation of mages," id said. "Se'ans and em'ans, Mers and Merfriends, mages and sorcerers, Orchth throat singers . . . I want to call all of them together."

"It's never been done before," I said.

"Then we'd better do it now. Soon it will be too late."

Chapter 13

Hard on the heels of the decision came the terror.

Shivering more with fear than with cold, Bet paused on the decaying doorstep of the guest house. Within the Inner City, all lay in starlit stillness. The white walls lay like crouched, leviathan ghosts. The flowers, carpets of starlight, nodded rhythmically in a soft breeze. Across a black stretch of lawn scattered with sentinel trees, the water of a brook glimmered in the darkness, a ribbon of silver across the velvet shadows.

Bet heard no voice speaking to her; sensed no remote attention focused on her as she stepped onto the pathway. But even if Delan did gaze upon her in the scrying stone, what could id do to help her?

The cold paving stones chilled Bet's bare feet. She padded down a narrow walkway between stark white walls. A window hung open despite the autumn chill, and a curtain swelled and flapped overhead like a wind banner. Here a lamp glimmered, where someone could not or chose not to sleep. Someone slipped past ahead of her, along another walkway, softly as a shadow, and disappeared in the darkness. Other than this, all the inhabitants of Is'antul seemed asleep.

The Lan of Peace could not afford to allow Eia to live for long. Once the blood heat had eased off a little, and cooler heads began to realize that Eia could have killed the Lans no more than Tor Kates himself could have done it, then it would be too late. To execute Eia then would work to his disadvantage. To do it now would be to become known for decisiveness,

while giving public opinion little option except to
agree with the act which would fold history thirty
years back upon itself.

Tor Kates would have to act now.

Urgency overwhelmed Bet's fear, and she began to
run. The Lanhall of the Southern Seas, with its exotic
sculptures and frieze of gold, slipped past on her right.
In the courtyard an exhausted servant, condemned to
spend the night scrubbing the paving stones, lay huddled on the bare ground. He did not lift his head as
Bet hurried past. She was only a silent shadow, a fig-
ment of his imagination, a wind-swept dream. She
loped through the knee-high flowers of an exotic garden, rousing up clouds of perfume in her wake. Then
she stumbled across a delicate pathway, winding like
fine embroidery among the carefully planted and
pruned trees. She smelled the rich scent of damp
earth, and swerved sharply to avoid running into a
still pool, where white blossoms floating on the surface
of the water seemed to glow in the starlight.

A silly, fantastically curved and ornately decorated
bridge spanned the narrow stream. Bet ignored it and
leapt across without breaking her stride. Through a
rock garden, where delicate mosses had been cultured
over hundreds of years, she set her heedless feet,
crushing fragile flowers and disturbing the careful living mosaic over which nameless servants had sweated.
And then she was in grass again, beginning to breathe
heavily now as she climbed up a gradual slope. The
Forbidden Palace suddenly appeared far to her left,
as delicate and ghostlike as the flowers in the pond,
with its minarets glimmering in starlight, and its white
walls patrolled by guards.

Bet felt a sudden, absurd rage at the A'lan who
slept so comfortably and safely there. She had been
chosen to guard the rights and welfare of the people,
and she did nothing. Could she not see that what
affected the Aeyries affected them all? If the clever
and innovative Aeyries could no longer survive in the
world, how could she have the arrogance to think that
anyone could survive?

Ahead of her loomed the Lanhall of Peace. Bet slowed to a walk to catch her breath. In the bushes nearby, an amorous insect crackled its discordant song. From the distance, the Lanhall seemed to be closed up on itself as tightly as a money box, with the doors locked and bolted, the windows barred. At one door, three heavily armed male guards kept guard. They did not talk with each other, but remained at stoic attention, their gazes sweeping the landscape.

Bet continued her circuit of the building. On the side of the building which faced the water gardens there was only one door, no different from the others. A light moved slowly from window to window, and the shutters rattled as a guard checked their security. As Bet slipped up to the door and laid her hand on the knob, the clock tower rang the half hour.

With her eyes closed, Bet examined the interior of the door. Three locked bolts secured it. Forged in fire and tempered with heat and cold, no saw could have cut through the bolts, and the locks had been made by the finest locksmith. Only three separate keys, which were distributed among three different people, could unlock them. But Bet had needed no keys the night she slipped past a Quai-du master's guard and unlocked the door where the moonbane weapons were kept, supposedly safe from sabotage. She needed no keys now. In her mind's eye, her hand, insubstantial as a shadow, held a fantastically formed key. She slipped her hand through the massive door; she turned the key in the locks, one by one, and slid the bolts in their tracks. When she opened her eyes, the door felt like stone under her hand, but it took only a gentle push to open it.

She shut and locked the door again behind her, and started down the hall after the guard, whose lantern light she could still see faintly.

He finished his slow, careful circuit of the building's exterior windows and doors, and then turned and led Bet down another austere hallway. He opened one of the tightly closed, dark doors, and stood in the doorway, his arms held stiffly at his sides, until a voice questioned him from within. "The building is secure," he replied.

Bet followed him once again, down one hallway and down another, until at last he paused and spoke at another door. Bet hurried forward, and when the door opened to admit him, she slipped in behind him. In the well-lit room, three other armed and armored males greeted the fouth. He passed the lantern to another, who promptly departed, Bet assumed, to make the rounds of the building once again, while this one took his place within the room. The room contained neither furniture, nor books; only another locked door. Bet pressed herself against the wall, and waited. Sooner or later, that door had to open.

The guards did not move or speak. If they felt bored or tired, they did not show it. Their muscles bulged ostentatiously, and in the massive hands with which they gripped their weapons, blood veins stood out, blue and red. Surely the Lan of Peace had gone through tremendous effort to have gathered this collection of monsters.

The door into the main hall opened suddenly. The guards, already standing at alert attention, stiffened into inhuman rigidity, gazing fixedly forward, as two more males entered the room. One of them, as heavily armed as they but more richly dressed, Bet assumed to be their captain. But the other, a slender, quick male dressed in astil and velvet, with a thin-lipped, harsh face, could only have been Tor Kates.

Bet stepped in behind the captain and the Lan, walking so closely to them that she could smell their sweat. One of the guards briskly opened the door, and closed it so quickly upon their heels that Bet had to skip hastily forward to prevent the bundle she carried on her back from being caught in the door. Down a narrow hallway scented with mildew she followed the captain and the Lan, as she heard the sound of the door being locked and bolted behind her, and then down a steep flight of stairs. The air cooled. The lamp in the captain's hand cast only a dim light. Bet slowed down to keep from tripping on the stairs, and soon the two she followed had moved far ahead of her. At the bottom of the stairs, in a hallway once again, she ran to catch up with them, past metal clad doors with barred windows. She heard the faint, weary sound of someone groaning in his sleep. Dark patches stained the floor, and a carrion stink emanated from more than one of the cells.

When she caught up with her prey, they had paused at another door watched over by three more monstrous guards, where the captain worked his key in the stiff lock and then stood back as the door swung open, laying his hand warningly on the long sword he carried at his side. Bet rushed up behind him, to slip through the door in front of the Lan, and hastily secreted herself in a corner of the cell within, breathing heavily with exertion and fear.

Eia stood very still in the center of the cell. Compared to the five Walker males confronting idre, id seemed very small and frail. But Tor Kates at least seemed unlikely to make the foolish mistake of underestimating Eia. Even without a weapon, even secured by a short chain from ankle to floor, as Bet now saw Eia was, a Quai-du master was no enemy to take lightly. Tor Kates entered the cell, but he kept carefully out of Eia's reach, and the captain stood with his hand on his sword.

"Tor Kates," said Eia quietly.

"Have you decided?"

"It is not much of a choice you give me, sir, between a hard death and a harder one. And ultimately, I have only your honor to guarantee my payment, such as it is. What would you choose, in my circumstances?"

The Lan seemed amused. But at a wave of his finger, the captain stepped sharply forward and struck Eia in the face. "The Lan will ask, and you will answer!"

The captain stepped swiftly out of Eia's reach again. Perhaps he had noticed the effort of will by which Eia kept ids physical reaction in check.

After a moment, id lifted a hand to touch ids cheek,

which was already swollen from other, earlier blows.
This had been for Eia the longest of days. Weariness
shadowed ids face, and in ids eyes hopelessness had
dawned. Bet saw it in ids eyes: the weariness, the
dawning hopelessness.

"I am like everyone else," said Eia. "When I die,
I want to die quietly, in dignity and peace. But since
you deny me that choice, then at least I will die with
my integrity intact. No doubt this is the choice you
expected, even though you are unable to understand
it."

The captain started forward again, but Eia did not
even flinch as he raised his fist. This time he hit the
Aeyrie more than once, and Bet thought she heard
the sound of a fragile, hollow bone cracking. When
he stepped away, there was blood on his hand from
Eia's split lip.

The Lan watched impassively, his hands tucked into
his richly embroidered sash.

Eia spoke thickly. "I will not confess to a lie. The
Aeyries had nothing to do with the murder of the
Lans. Our taiseochs were murdered, too."

"So you say," sneered the captain.

"I will not sign the paper taking responsibility for
their deaths. If there is to be war, let it be on your
conscience, if you have one."

When the Lan and the captain had left, and the
door had been bolted and locked, Eia continued to
stand stiffly, facing the door. Bet edged along the wall
until she could see what Eia gazed at. It was one of
the guards, staring impassively through the grate.

He could not stand there forever, thought Bet.

But as time crawled slowly past, she began to wonder if she were wrong. The guard's face left the grate,
only to be replaced at once by another. Eia continued
to stand, the side of ids face swelling quickly, the
blood drying in ids fur. The sound of the bell tower
could not be heard in this place, but dawn had to be
drawing near. Soon the Lan's torturers would come,
and Eia's signature on the paper would be obtained,

one way or another, even if it was written in blood.
Soon it would be too late.

Still, the guard stared into the cell.

With nothing else to do, Bet watched Eia's face. So
it was that she saw the change in ids expression, subtle
as a change in the wind, and she saw ids lips move.
Delan, id would have said, had id been free to speak.
So Bet knew that Delan was wakeful this terrible
night, and that they were being scried in ids pale blue
stone.

She saw Eia's eyes narrow slightly. Casually, id
glanced to the left of the door, where Bet had squatted with her back against the wall, out of the guard's
line of vision. For the briefest of moments she let
herself go, let herself exist in this place. Eia's expression did not change, but she saw ids fingers move
in an abbreviated gesture of greeting. Then another
gesture, disguised as an absentminded brush of the
hand against fur: *Be ready.*

The guard gave a startled jerk, and turned his face
sharply away from the door, as if at a strange and
threatening sound. Bet leapt forward. In a moment
she had snapped open the lock that secured Eia's
chain. Eia slipped ids foot free, and Bet grasped ids
hand.

By the time the guard's head turned back to look
once again through the grate, Eia had disappeared.

"It was a very peculiar noise," the guard insisted.
"A sort of a howling—" he turned pleadingly to the
other two stoically indifferent guards. "You must have
heard the sound!"

The guard captain peered once more through the
door grate. Though Eia and Bet stood poised to rush
through, neither the guards nor the captain had made
any move toward unlocking the door. "It looks as if
the chain just fell off its foot."

"I didn't even hear it happen, I swear—"

"It's sorcery."

The captain pushed past the anxious, hovering

guard. "Don't take your eyes off the cell. I don't care if all the winds of hell are screaming in your ears."

Then he was gone, and the guard, with a glimmer of sweat on his forehead, appeared at the grate to stare nervously inside. Beyond him, Bet heard a murmur of voices as the other guards repeated to each other the dreaded word: "Sorcery."

Eia rested ids shoulder heavily against the wall and shut ids eyes, as if there were nothing id wanted more than to simply go to sleep. But when, after some time had passed, the captain's voice once again spoke in the hall, Eia jerked sharply alert. Ids hand felt slick with sweat.

"Who is that with him?" whispered Bet.

"Tor Kates, for certain. . . ." Eia sighed, shoulders slumping. "And the sorcerer M'bala a'Thal. A most loyal servant to the previous Lan of Peace. I am surprised to see him here now—the new Lan has no place in his Universe for sorcery."

"A sorcerer will be able to see us."

"No doubt, my dear. No doubt."

The guard moved aside from the grate. Tor Kates first peered into the cell, his face white with anger. Then he stepped aside to give way to the aging sorcerer, whose rumpled hair testified to the fact that the decent hour for arising from bed had not yet arrived. The sorcerer gazed into the cell, his mouth set in a grim line. He looked directly at Bet and Eia where they huddled against the wall. He looked at them for a long time, the expression on his face never changing. Then he turned his face aside. "I wish to go into the cell."

"Do you confirm that no one is there?"

"The cell is empty."

"Then why do you want to go in?"

"Begging your pardon sir, I thought you might be interested in knowing how the escape was carried out."

With a hiss of frustration, Tor Kates motioned for the guards to open the door of the cell. The bolts creaked, the hinges squealed, and the bowed sorcerer

came in, followed by the Lan and the captain, as the
guards crowded in the doorway. Bet and Eia drew as
close to the door as possible, but could gain no passage through. The sorcerer went to Eia's abandoned
manacle, squatted, drew some signs in the air which
looked to Bet like nonsense, and held his cupped
hands over the manacle.

In a moment, a thin stream of white smoke appeared
from between his fingers and emanated into the cell.
"Stand back," said the sorcerer sharply. "The smoke
will show the route of escape."

The guards hastily gave way as the stream of smoke
meandered toward them. Bet and Eia, following after
the streamer, eased slowly out of the door, past the
heavily breathing Lan and the clustered guards, and
into the hallway beyond. The smoke continued down
the dim hallway, glowing faintly in the light of the
guards' lanterns. The captain and the guards followed
after it, with Bet and Eia walking beside them, up the
steep stairs, through the heavily guarded door, and
out of the guard room into the pristine corridors of
the Lanhall itself. There the smoke suddenly dispersed
like fog in the sunlight. With a curse, the Lan turned
on his cowering captain of the guard. "What nonsense
is this—" he began.

But Bet and Eia left him and his anger behind. In
the corridors of the Lanhall, early servants had
already begun their day's work. Bet and Eia slipped
among them, down the corridors and then out a door
which hung ajar, into the courtyard of the Lanhall of
Peace, where anxious supplicants had already begun
to converge. At the top of the stairs they paused, as
a half-dozen armed guards burst out the door behind
them and shot across the crowded courtyard like a
flight of arrows. North, south, east, and west they ran.
In moments, a second cluster of guards followed, each
of them carrying a crossbow. Eia said wearily, "The
gates are secured, the wall is shut off, and soon every
high place in the city will be closely watched. By nightfall, we can expect that Tor Kates will have searched

every room of every building in the city. What do we do now, Ysbet?"

Eia's eyes were stark with pain. Bet thought of the tidy, artificial woods which meandered through the city, but these would certainly be searched thoroughly; and she did not think either one of them could launch themselves from the branch of a tree. Even if they could find a flight platform which was not guarded, would Eia be able to fly? She did not think the Aeyrie had eaten in at least a day, maybe longer.

"At least, let's get to a quiet place where we can think," she said.

"Bet, I don't think I can go far."

She put her arm around Eia's waist and half carried, half dragged idre down the flight of steps. More guards appeared and began questioning the supplicants who crowded the yard. Among the nervously milling people sauntered a casual figure dressed in stark black, managing by skillful maneuvering to keep himself out of sight of the guards. Bet bent over to pick up a stone, nearly upsetting Eia in the process, and she lobbed it at the wandering male, striking his upper arm. He turned his head sharply, then his narrowed eyes told Bet he had spotted them. He sauntered casually over and muttered, "I'm an obvious scapegoat. Can you make me invisible, too?"

Bet grasped his arm with her other hand. "You're invisible."

Not until he studied the milling people and the guards working their harsh way through the crowd did Ellin relax, having realized that they indeed could not see him. "Are you badly hurt, Eia?"

"I'll live," said Eia thickly. "The Lan has peculiar tastes. I wish I could say the Aeyries are immune from such. I'm extremely surprised to see you here, Ellin a'Tal."

"Ah, well, you're the only ones who *can* see me at the moment. Come this way, my dears."

That Ellin had just happened to be hovering about in the Lan of Peace's courtyard had certainly been no accident, but he had made it clear that it was not his intention to turn them over to the Peace Guards. Eia's reaction to Ellin had offered Bet no enlightenment. To Eia, too, Ellin seemed to be an enigma. "Where to?" she asked suspiciously.

"To a secret place, where all will be revealed."

Bet wanted to slap him for his lightheartedness. At her questioning glance, Eia shrugged slightly. What choice did they have? "Let's go," said Bet.

Chapter 14

As casually as holiday strollers, they sauntered arm-in-arm through the Lake Garden. The morning's small singers had ceased their joyous serenade among the buildings, but here among the trees an occasional, piercingly sweet voice could still be heard. Standing atop the grassy slope, they watched a contingent of Peace Guards rush down the slope and run out to search the branches of the manicured trees that lined the lake. "Invisibility has its uses," said Ellin speculatively.

Eia's slight weight dragged against Bet's arm. Disoriented, disjointed, and indifferent with the weariness which had set into her bones like hardening concrete, she followed Ellin's lead passively. But at a picturesque ruin, where he led them among its tumbled columns toward a disguised locked door, she hung back. "You go first."

He produced a key, unlocked the door, and went in. The ruin proved to be nothing more than an elaborately disguised storage shed. Within its dusty interior, ladders, pruning shears, and shovels hung on the walls. Burlap sacks, spilling golden trails of grain, were piled in the center. Invisible rodents scuttled among the equipment. Bet shut the door, darkening the shed into dim twilight, for the only light came through a small dusty window.

"Surely they'll eventually search in here."

"Maybe, but not many people have the key." The shed was far larger than it at first seemed. They passed piled pots and more handtools, finally arriving among dark half-barrels full of sawdust—for storing bulbs, Bet guessed. At one of these Ellin paused, reached under it, and then with one hand slid it aside. Underneath the barrel, a narrow hole gaped.

Eia had been silent for so long that the sound of ids voice, hoarse with exhaustion, startled her. "I thought such things only existed in penny novels." Bet could not see ids face through the shadows, but ids voice sounded ironically amused.

"You'll have to move the barrel back again," Ellin told Bet before he lowered himself into the hole and began descending an invisible ladder into its depths. He disappeared in the darkness, though for a while Bet could still hear the sound of his shoulders brushing the sides of the tunnel. The weight of Eia leaning against Bet provided no comfort in the terrible solitude of waiting for some sound from below. Far below, a faint light flickered, and Ellin peered up, with a lantern in his hand. She could view the tunnel down which they had to climb: the walls had been reinforced with carefully cut stone, like the walls of a well. The rungs of the ladder were set into the stone with mortar.

Eia could scarcely fit through the narrow opening, even with ids wings tucked tightly against ids body. Bet, not sure she could trust her strength to last much longer, waited until id had reached the bottom of the hole before climbing in herself. Moving the barrel over to cover the hole once again was a simple enough endeavor: the barrel seemed to be on some kind of a track which made it slide easily, almost soundlessly, into place. But then it seemed to latch shut, and Bet, though she tried, could not figure out how to open it again.

At the bottom of the narrow well, a low, narrow, rubble-scattered tunnel, finished with stone but frequently shored up with wooden braces, stretched into darkness. The tunnel swallowed their voices into its ancient silence. "How old is this tunnel? It looks to be on the verge of collapse."

"Very old," said Ellin. "Older than the city." Here

in the tunnel, he seemed much more the sober history student Bet remembered from t'Cwa, having left his rapscallion lightheartedness above ground, like a discarded theater costume.

"Where are you taking us?"

In the narrow tunnel, Eia, no longer able to lean on Bet, walked with ids hands pressed against the walls for support. The light from the lantern Ellin carried cast grotesque shadows down the length of the tunnel. Eia turned to Bet and rasped, "He can't tell us. He already has taken risk enough."

Ellin turned his head as if he wanted to make Eia tell him what id knew, or guessed, or suspected. But he did not speak. His shoulders, and Eia's wings scraped against the narrow sides. The tunnel smelled of damp, and mold, and stone. Bet felt so tired she wanted to lie down and sleep on the damp earth.

She could not judge how far they had walked, when the tunnel took a turn, and ended abruptly at a heavy, iron-clad door. There was no lock or bolt, no doorknob, only a bell rope which Ellin pulled in a jerky rhythm. "We may have a bit of a wait," he said then.

Bet sat on the floor with a sigh, her bundled Wing digging into her back, and shut her eyes.

When she opened them again, Eia lay on the floor beside her, with ids head pillowed on her thigh. Ellin was rising from his squat beside the door, the lantern flame flickering. Metal scraped against metal, and suddenly the door jerked open to reveal an older Walker female, dressed in plain brown, her gray hair tied in a loose knot at the back of her head.

She examined Bet and Eia where they struggled groggily to their feet, her gaze lingering longer on Eia, who swayed on ids feet, wings drooping wearily. Bet put her arm around ids waist, though she was not in much better shape herself. Then the Walker at the door turned to Ellin, raising an eyebrow in response to his helplessly outspread hands. "Come this way," she said.

She led them through the door, into the dusty clut-

ter of an unused cellar, where ancient wine barrels
leaked vinegar onto the floor and hunterworm webs
hung from the beams in dusty, ghostly shrouds. Up a
steep flight of stairs, through a kitchen, where more
hunterworm webs hung where the hearthfire should
have burned, and dust lay thick on the tabletops, and
up another flight of stairs—the servant's stairs, thought
Bet—they followed her, until she opened a door and
waved them into a small, modest bedroom.

Bet put her hand to the door to prevent them from
closing it. "If we could have something to eat—"

"Of course," the woman said. "You are my guests."

Eia lay down on the bed and seemed to fall instantly
asleep. But Bet, having unstrapped her bundled Wing
from her shoulders and laid it on the floor, paced
restlessly through the room, checking the empty draw-
ers and closets, testing the door to be certain it was
not locked, and finally looking cautiously out the lav-
ender-tinted windows.

She saw a lush, overgrown garden watered by a
captive stream, a delicate minaret swooping skyward,
a smooth white wall covered with vines, their leaves
blushing red in the first autumn chill. "By all the
winds of hell," she whispered.

When Ellin tapped on the door, she let him in without a word. He carried a tray with steaming bowls of
thick soup, a pile of rolls and soft white kipscheese,
and a teapot. Bet brought Eia a bowl of soup where
id lay, but id got up stiffly and came to sit at the table.
Ellin also pulled up a chair, and poured himself a cup
of tea.

The soup tasted delicious, its deft flavoring with
herbs and sweet vegetables having obviously been
orchestrated by a professional. Bet had asked for food
more for Eia's sake than for her own, but now found
herself greedily gulping down the soup. Eia cautiously
maneuvered the spoon around ids battered mouth, ids
face so swollen that Bet could not guess which bone
had broken under the Peace Captain's fist. Ellin sat
casually, gazing mostly out the windows. None of
them even tried to make polite conversation.

Bet spread some cheese on a roll and poured Eia a cup of tea, sweetened with honey. "You've brought us to the Forbidden Palace."

Ellin nodded, swirling the dregs of his tea in the cup.

"It's not what I would have expected." Bet gestured vaguely at the genteel neglect of the garden.

"The A'lan could have anything she wants, so long as she remains safely within these walls. But she discovered over the years that she did not, in fact, want very much. She has only a few servants now, and only one wing of the palace is in use. She never has guests, except for the Lans, and even they don't realize that the money to run her household is being used for— other things."

"What do you do for her?"

"I am her eyes, her hands, outside of these walls. One of many."

"Were you working for her when you lived at t'Cwa?"

"Yes." Ellin turned to Eia, who used a spoon to drink ids tea. "She wanted to know more about the Aeyries. She knew that you wanted to meet with her. But she could no more arrange it than you could."

Eia nodded, but did not speak. Bet wondered if ids silence was only to avoid the pain of speaking. There was a broody look to ids eyes which worried her.

"Have the Peace Guards come here looking for us?" asked Bet.

"Even Tor Kates would not insult the A'lan by implying that she would knowingly house fugitives."

"I don't know about that," said Eia. "Except for custom, what is there to stop him?"

With a shrug, Ellin admitted the answer to Eia's question.

"Does the A'lan know what is really happening? That Tor Kates is methodically taking over the country?"

"She knows," said Ellin. "She knows. It is making all of us old before our time. She also knows that there is something she does not know. There have been too many sudden, urgent journeys, too many comings and goings from Triad.''

When Bet glanced at Eia for guidance, ids fingers told her to follow her own judgment. So she told Ellin about Ara and Tsal and the fire people, talked until she saw his eyes glaze over with wonder and shock, talked until at last he could listen no more and he left them.

Eia lay down and slept. Bet also lay down, but her body jangled with tension. She stared out the window, thinking about the lone woman, chosen by lot to serve out her lifetime in this palace, a veritable prisoner; servant of the people, powerless. She could have had anything she wanted: lovers, fine food, entertainment, leisure, comfort and luxury. Instead she had hired spies, to do with their eyes and ears the one thing she had first been mandated, and then been forbidden to do: to watch over her people.

To watch, and be able to do nothing.

When Ellin tapped once again on the door, Bet slipped out into the hallway to walk with him, through the abandoned wing of the building and out into the garden where the plants had so overgrown the paths that the two of them simply walked where they willed. The morning had aged into afternoon. In the last heat of autumn, the plants gave forth their sweet fragrance of crushed leaf and opened flower. In a tangle of twining vines that covered the wall, a lush plant bloomed, its huge white blossoms emitting a heady fragrance. Bet found herself longing for a pair of pruning shears.

"Why do we even have an A'lan?" she asked Ellin. "She does nothing; she has no power. . . ."

"Technically, she does have one power, and it is not an insignificant one. She has the seal."

"But I have never even heard of an A'lan refusing to seal a law or edict."

"It did happen once. He was young; an idealist. He was assassinated. All the A'lans since then have found it more judicious to do as the Lans dictate, not surprisingly."

"And this A'lan has never exercised her one power either."

"She never has. But at least she reads the laws and edicts before she seals them."

Bet snorted, unimpressed. "So why do we have an A'lan?"

"So that we will believe that we have one governor whose sole purpose is to serve the people rather than themselves."

"She is a symbol of something which does not really exist."

Ellin smiled stiffly. "You do have a succinct way of putting things."

"How can you serve someone who is willing for her entire life to be a deception like this?"

He sighed. "Of course, at one time I thought it would make a difference. Now I don't know what good it does, to be torturing the A'lan with knowledge she cannot use. Better for her to be indifferent and self-indulgent, perhaps, than to feel responsible for the things that one cannot change. But I have come to admire her. Yes, she lives a lie. She has no choice; she was chosen by lot. It could just as easily have been me, or you. But at least she does it with her eyes open."

"Did you tell her about the fire people?"

"I told her. Do you know, it was as I was telling her that it finally occurred to me how strange it is that the Aeyrie people do not know their own history. They could only have lost it so completely because of a concerted effort, as you have said. It must have been a horrendous time, for them to want to completely blot it out of memory like that."

They sat down together in an arbor, where they had to hold aside great drooping fronds in order to enter, and to brush many layers of moldering leaves from the stone seat before they could sit. In the privacy of that overgrown place, Bet suddenly realized that in her entire life she had never talked with a fellow Walker like this. The realization overwhelmed her with shyness, and for a long time Ellin chattered by himself, talking about the Aeyries and what it had been like to live among them for a year.

Bet all but interrupted him mid-sentence to ask, "Do you know a sorcerer named M'bala a'Thal?"

"The Peace Sorcerer," said Ellin, in a voice heavy with irony.

"He tricked Tor Kates into letting Eia and me go. He knew perfectly well that we were still in the cell, but he convinced them to unlock the door, and so we were able to escape. Why did he do that?"

Ellin did not reply immediately, but drummed his fingers on the mossy stone arm of the bench, frowning in thought. "Well, I would like to believe that the sorcerer has suddenly developed a conscience in his old age. More likely the Lan has offended him in some way—by implying that magic is little more than fancy illusion, for instance—and M'bala decided to retaliate."

"It seems such a childish thing—what good will it ever do M'bala, to have Eia go free?"

"Probably no good at all. But M'bala is a powerful man, intelligent, and in his own way loyal. Perhaps I should pay him a visit."

Bet stared unhappily into the green canopy. More than just the strangeness of being a guest of the A'lan herself, within the palace that no farmer's daughter had ever before entered, another idea haunted her. She tried to tell herself that it was just her over-wrought nerves, but the notion would not pass quietly away.

They had sat in silence for some time when Ellin said, "Tell me what you're thinking."

"Do you really want to know? Maybe you'll regret having asked." She saw motion among the vines of the wall: a sweet singer, stalking an insect. She rubbed her eyes with her fingers, only succeeding in further blurring her vision. "If I wanted to create extreme strife and violence among the Walker people, this is how I would go about doing it. First, I'd get rid of all the governors who have in the last thirty years done business with the Aeyrie people, and replace them with governors who either hate the Aeyries, or are willing to turn whichever way the wind blows. Then I would create a reason, however far-fetched, for the Aeyries to be blamed for something. I would take Eia, for instance, and imprison idre, and then give idre the opportunity to escape, so that by escaping id would declare idreself guilty for the supposed crime. I would make a point of doing all this in the autumn, after the harvest was in, during the fertile season when everyone's emotions are running at high tide."

"And how would this create strife and violence among the Walker people? It sounds like a dangerous situation more for the Aeyries."

"For the Aeyrie people? Do you think so?" said Bet. "Do you really think so?"

The sound of a bell chimed sweetly throughout the still garden. Ellin stiffened beside Bet. Once again, and then a third time, the bell rang.

"What does it mean?" asked Bet.

"One of the Lans is coming to visit the A'lan."

Despite Ellin's assurance that no one would come looking for them, Bet took the precaution of disappearing and standing guard down the hall from the door where Eia still slept. A long time passed before Ellin appeared, pale and grim, so preoccupied that he almost walked through Bet, before she reappeared herself.

Rest and food had effected in Eia a transformation no less startling for all that it was commonplace enough among the Aeyries. The swelling in ids face had gone down, ids split lip had completely healed, an even the pain of the broken bone had eased to the point that Eia seemed able to speak without much discomfort.

Ellin took them along a circuitous route, through many doorways and winding hallways, until they reached a wing of the palace where puffs of dust did not rise up from the carpets, and hunterworm webs did not adorn every corner and ledge. They saw several servants, who made a point of failing to see them. And then they stood at a huge double door, where

was depicted in a beautifully carved fresco the arrival
of the first Walkers to the lowlands.

Ellin opened the door without ceremony, and waved
them into the huge library which was revealed beyond
the doors. From floor to soaring ceiling, books were
ranged, with ladders on wheels to reach them, and
windows along the ceiling for light. Huge map racks
and stacks of atlases filled the center of the room. At
the far end, at a large and cluttered desk, sat the
female who had first opened the door to let them in
from the tunnel: still an aging, tired woman, though
no longer dressed in plain and faded brown. She wore
an undercoat of rich, shimmering astil. Slung casually
over the chair was the rest of her clothing: a heavy
robe, encrusted with jewels, lush with gold thread.
And there also lay the A'lan's mask, fantastically
adorned with jewels to ransom a nation, cast carelessly
aside.

Eia laid ids hands over ids breast, and bowed. But
Bet was too stunned for even this minimal acknowl-
edgment of the woman's obvious rank. The A'lan
waved them forward, saying firmly, "No nonsense.
You know and I know how meaningless my position
is." She came forward to take Eia's hand in hers.

"I have never met an Aeyrie before." She sounded
breathless—Bet remembered how her own first meeting with an Aeyrie had taken her that way. What magnificent, delicate, beautiful beings they are, with their
frail wings and wild manes and bright, intelligent eyes!

Eia laughed. "Madam, you need not be concerned.
I am the first Aeyrie most Walkers meet. I play the
role well, after so much rehearsal. This is Ysbet ib
Canilton ib t'Cwa, of whom you surely have
heard. . . ."

Bet stepped forward to be greeted in her turn. "I
do get the news here. I suppose I am too old to fly,"
said the A'lan wistfully, "even if I were allowed to
try."

She seated herself on the edge of the desk, crushing
papers and dislodging books. "The Lan of Peace has
just come to me with an edict for my seal, signed by

all the Lans. The edict declares all Aeyries to be enemies of the Walker people. It is a declaration of war.
Five armed guards escorted him. I gave the edict my
seal: I had no choice."

Eia lowered ids gaze then, and for a moment Bet
feared id would weep. But id said with stern dignity,
"Ellin told you of the threat which faces our world,
and yet you signed it? Lady, there is no one left but
you to stand in opposition to the fire people's manipulation of the Walkers. And now . . . you have sealed
the death sentence for your own people."

Chapter 15

Autumn, Day 16

Recently having awakened, I lay beside Ara's pool, trailing my arm in the warm water where she floated, with only her nostrils and occasionally her eyes showing above the surface of the water. Here in the boathouse I hear the constant sighing of the sea, and I am learning to know by the sound when it is high tide, when the wind is blowing, when the weather is still. But Ara knows by the feel of the water: by the strength and direction of its energy. She knows the water much as I know the wind—by a kind of s'oleil. It is the one thing we truly have in common with each other. I trailed my arm in the water, trying without much success to feel it as she feels it: not merely as wet and (to me) uncomfortable, but as a conduit similar to the air, rich in energy and meaning.

The boathouse door opened, but rather than Gein the healer, who usually visits first thing in the morning, it was to admit Delan. Ids hunched shoulders and dragging wings, reddened, too-bright eyes, pinched face and sharp bones, mane fraying away around ids face . . . all of these told me of ids ever increasing exhaustion. How many anguished nights had id paced the floor beside ids sleeping children, keeping an increasingly desperate watch over ids scrying glass?

But this time the watch had not been in vain. "It required the work of two mages and a sorcerer," id said, "But Eia is free."

I do not know how I have become a seer's confi-

179

dante. The world is full of Delan's friends—everyone who has seen one of ids paintings feels as if they know idre. And here at Triad there are a dozen or more people—Aeyrie, Walker, Mer, and Orchth, to whom id can turn for advice. But id is coming to me—because I, too, have nearly lost someone I love (interesting how my hand stutters over writing this word) to the troubles of the times? Or because I am all but a stranger, an independent wanderer, neither mage nor artist nor Triad-re, to whom Delan is neither obligated nor responsible?

The Orchths usually bring some food down each night, for Orgulanthgrnm to eat during his watch, and for myself to eat during the day. I set some of this in front of Delan, and made id sit down and eat, refusing to hear one more word until the plate was empty. Then Delan told me a wonderful tale, of how Bet made herself invisible and penetrated to the very cell where Eia was held prisoner, how Delan distracted the guard's attention so that Bet could free Eia from ids chains, and how unexpected and unsought-for assistance came from a Walker sorcerer who engineered their escape, and from another Walker of unknown affiliations, who took them to an underground tunnel where they would escape detection in the ensuing search. There they are now, with neither Bet nor Eia nor Delan certain of the trustworthiness of this Walker Ellin who has aided them.

In the midst of this tale, Gein came in. One look at Delan and id ordered idre to bed. "Do you think the whole world is spinning on your fingertips?" id scolded.

With a sigh, Delan said, "No, not the whole world. Just the fate of my lover and my children and my people—Walker and Aeyrie both."

Delan left to get some rest. But I myself am restless now, with Ara out of danger and my own strength returning. It is autumn; for Walker, Aeyrie, and Mer the fertile time of the year. The Mer males already are keeping their distance from Ara, as she would not survive a pregnancy in her condition. Last year should have been my egg year, but due to my injuries I never

*did become fertile. Perhaps I will be fertile this year,
and perhaps not—it could go either way. It would not
be important, if I did not find myself suddenly longing
for a pillowfriend. It has been a very long time.*

Autumn, Day 17

*I went up to Triad last night, after Orgulanthgrnm
had appeared to take over the watch. He plays his stone
flute for Ara, and she lies for hours with her head
propped on the edge of the pool, listening to him. Ara
tells me that the Orchths and Mers have much more in
common with each other than do Aeyries and Mers
or Walkers and Mers. Orchths and Mers both are a
migratory, food-gathering people with homogeneous
societies. The Walkers and the Aeyries have far more
complex societies, but I will not go so far as to say that
we are more advanced. The Mers and the Orchths
both, with their formal traditions of remembering and
passing on knowledge, have a far more cohesive sense
of history than we. And I envy Ara her perspective on
the Universe: her sense of participation in a complex
and ancient cycle of death and renewal. I will never be
half as at peace with myself as she is.*

*Up at Triad, the evening meal was nearly finished
when I arrived. I helped myself to a plate full of delicious herbed dumplings and roasted vegetables, and sat
at a table where Orchths, Aeyries, Walkers, and onfrits
all shared a bowl of autumn fruit. We talked pleasantly
enough while I kept an eye on the activities of the
room, trying to determine who was, as we Aeyries say,
a "floater." It used to be that I could home to an available Aeyrie like an onfrit to a friendly wind. After a
while I began to wonder if I had lost this talent, but
no, it was just that the many different customs mixed
together caused interference with each other. Before
long I had introduced myself to a lovely and clearly
available Aeyrie, and the whole pleasant, playful anticipation of courtship had begun.*

*Delan came in quite late, much more rested looking
than I have seen in some time, but with a new element
in ids demeanor. Id banged on a table for everyone's*

*attention and announced, without much preliminaries,
that the Lans of the Walkers had declared war against
the Aeyrie people.*

*Feili, who is the sh'man Quai-du here at Triad,
immediately doubled the watches and suggested that the
community prepare to evacuate. The defenders of Triad
have successfully beaten off many an assault over the
years, but never a concerted attack by a disciplined and
trained army such as the Lans have at their disposal.
In such a confrontation, Triad, burdened with children
and handicapped by a species which cannot bear the
light of day, could only lose.*

*I went up to Delan after the discussion had died
down, and asked, "What about Eia and Bet?"*

*"Eia left Is'antul tonight and is flying here," said
Delan. Id did not look greatly relieved at this knowledge: the skies certainly are no longer safe for Aeyrie
flyers.*

"And Bet?"

"She has decided to stay in Is'antul."

*This surprised me. Surely, of all Walkers, Bet has
thrown herself on the back of an Aeyrie wind. She
belongs here at Triad, if not at t'Cwa. What good could
she possibly do in Is'antul?*

Autumn, Day 18

*There is nothing to do but wait. My dalliance with
one of the Triad Aeyries—a wind-crafter, with whom I
at least have mathematics in common—has developed
into as sweet an alliance as I could have hoped for. I
find I am too worried to throw myself wholeheartedly
into the heady game. Nevertheless, the other Aeyrie and
I have kept Ara well entertained. Sex is comparatively
matter-of-fact among the Mers, I guess. I suppose this
is inevitable, especially within a gestalt, when no matter
who the identity of one's partner, it is essentially a matter of having sex with yourself.*

*Good thing we Aeyries are not nearly as modest and
private as the Walkers. I think Ara would have been
hurt had it even occurred to me to exclude her.*

The people of Triad are accustomed to living under

the threat of violence. Everyone (except the youngest children) is capable of wielding a weapon. Here, Quai-du is not an esoteric art form, but an unglorified, every-day skill. For the entire history of Triad, the commu-nity has been torn between ideal and reality. They truly believe, as I do, that violence only breeds more vio-lence. But in the position of facing an implacable enemy, for whom violence is the only language, what can they do except fight back? Their dilemma is typified in Eia idreself, an unrivaled Quai-du dancer who cer-tainly cannot claim to have no blood on ids hands, and the author of two books about peace which have changed the face of our world. For some questions there are no clean answers, however desperately we may wish for them.

At Triad, the children are being kept closely herded, and watchers have been posted as far away as the near-est Walker town. By day, there is always at least one Aeyrie watching from the air, and by night the Orchths range over tremendous distances, holding their sensitive noses to the wind. Even the Mers are keeping guard, using their unique mental powers to try to detect the advance of any hostile forces, by land or by sea. One species takes over where the other leaves off—I should think it would be all but impossible to launch a surprise attack on this community.

Autumn, Day 19

The warning has been delivered, but from the last expected source. I was in my Aeyrie friend's bed last night, when, shortly after the turn of the night I would guess, I heard a commotion in the hall and went out to find that an Orchth had come to awaken Delan. I and some other Aeyries who had also been awakened by the noise (most of us are sleeping lightly, lately) went with Delan down to the kitchen, where sat several of the farmers who moved to the area after the people of Triad had proven that this could be fertile soil. Delan sent the Orchth to awaken a couple of Walkers, just to make the visitors feel more comfortable, I think.

Then the farmer who had been designated their spokes-man told us the news.

He had been at a public house in the nearest town when a messenger on a racing draf rode into town with the news that war had been declared on the Aeyries. Some of the local rowdies were all for starting off at once for Triad too, but the messenger herself talked them out of it. "Everyone knows that a bunch of half-drunk farmers can't even get close to Triad," she said. "But wait a few hours—there's a unit of the army half a day behind me. You can go in with them to see the fun."

The farmer paused in his story then. He was con-fused, I think, by the calm with which his news was greeted. Delan finally told him gently, "We have our own means of getting information, and we already knew that war had been declared, so your news is not such a surprise. But that you went through such trouble to bring it to us—that is a surprise, and a happy one. I suppose we assumed that all Walkers would turn against us."

"Why should we turn against you?" asked the farmer, genuinely puzzled. "You have been good neighbors. Do you think we do not know that we owe all of our harvests to you?"

Delan looked as if id could have kissed the man.

"For the army to come after you like this, just because you're—well, not Walkers—it's just not right. Who are they going to come after next? You know what I'm saying? So we—" the farmer gestured, encom-passing not just the other grim-faced, hard-bitten farm-ers sitting so uncomfortably in the warm kitchen, but the land, and all of its inhabitants, "—we agreed that we will come and help in your defense."

I think Delan must live ids whole life for the sake of such moments of plain common decency. There was no passion or high poetry, there was nothing to solem-nize in a declaration; no high emotion to record in a fine painting, just some ordinary farmers who could not even conceive of doing anything other than what they had decided to do.

"*Thank you,*" *Delan said. What else was there to say?*

"*We would gladly accept your offer of help, but we have already decided that we will not try to fight the entire lowland army—it is a battle that we can only lose. We are going to have to leave instead; and I think it is best that we not tell you where we are going. But there is one thing you can do. Our barns are full of the harvest that was meant to carry us through the winter. Can you take it, and put it in your own barns, so that if we are able to return we at least will have something to eat?*"

So, in the dead of an unseasonably cold night, the farmers came with their wagons, bringing along their neighbors and their children who were old enough to help, and they emptied out the barns; and when that was done they divided up among themselves the precious equipment without which the work of Triad could not be accomplished: the wagons and plows, the shovels and scythes, even the drafs. They even took Delan's paintings, intending to bury the precious, damning canvases in the midst of their grain silos. It was a terrible, wonderful sight—with the addition of the Triad-re, there must have been a hundred people working frantically by lanternlight to fill the wagons, drive them away, and return them again for another load.

Shortly before dawn, I found Delan in the flight tower, with ids youngest child sleeping in ids arms, watching the last of the farmers drive away in their wagons. "This one night has given me a whole lifetime's worth of paintings to paint," said Delan.

I put my arm around idre; for once it did not seem a presumption. So we leaned wearily against each other, with the warm and limp-limbed child between us. Then Delan sighed and straightened. "The Mers tell us that the tide will turn at daybreak. If we leave now and walk in the sand, the water will cover up our tracks."

We climbed the stairs down to the yard, where the Orchths were waiting. Delan put id's child into Orgulanthgrnm's arms for him to carry to safety. What few

goods were to be brought with us had already been
brought to our haven over the last few days, so the
Orchths left, with the children of Triad riding on their
backs or in their arms. Those who could make the
journey on their own two feet followed after, two or
three at a time, walking carefully on the established
pathways so as to give no hint to the coming army as
to where we had gone. As we began to climb into the
Gap, the Orchths had already vanished from sight, for
they were racing against the sun. I looked longingly
toward the boathouse where I have spent most of my
time these last few days, but I knew that Ara was
already gone. The Mers found her a warm pool close
enough to the sea caves so that a healer could fly out
to her if necessary, but I knew I would not be allowed
to make so dangerous a flight just to hold my Mer's
hand.

A boardwalk had been constructed over the rough
stones of the Gap, but once we had passed the boathouse we had to find our way among the great, broken,
sharp-edged boulders in the darkness. The Walkers,
with their better night vision, helped the Aeyries as
much as they could, but nonetheless there were some
injuries. By the time we reached the edge of the ocean,
day had begun to dawn, and the cleata lizards came
swimming in out of the sea to spread themselves sleepily
on the rocks in anticipation of the sun. Fortunately,
there was no reason for anyone to come to the ocean
at dawn, at this time of year, and so there were no
fishing ships or early-morning seaweed gatherers to spot
us, trekking so wearily through the soft sand along the
water's edge.

By full daylight we had reached the sea caves, which
are bored into the cliffs halfway to the top, several times
the height of a tall Walker. Rope ladders had been
dropped for us—the infants had already been lifted in
baskets by the Orchths. We climbed the ladders and
found, deep within the caves, the children sleeping with
the Orchth cubs on top of a disordered pile of blankets,
and the Orchth females who were in milk patiently

nursing as many infants as they had teats, with no particular regard for species.

As I write these words I am sitting in a cave opening, watching the sea wrinkle and unwrinkle below me. Onfrit messengers carrying news of our plight have been dispatched to the seven corners of the world—to each of the Ulas, to Bet in Is'antul, and to search the likeliest ports along the coast of the lowlands for the Triad ship. These are cramped quarters, to say the least, and the novelty of the adventure is bound to quickly wear off the children. Certainly, this is a more secure place than the Triad buildings, but a persistent search will uncover us here. Yet there is nowhere else for us to go.

Autumn, Day 20

The onfrits, who can be all but invisible when they are convinced of the need, have been our eyes and ears in the town of Mondamin, where the army arrived early today. When the army scouts found nothing at Triad but abandoned buildings and empty barns, they immediately occupied our buildings, and are now methodically searching the countryside, just as I feared they would. Of course there are rumors that the local farmers helped us escape, but there are other rumors as well, just as impossible to substantiate.

The existence of these sea caves is no secret, though it would never occur to a Walker to seek haven in them. If the army does find us, we can survive a siege for some time—but not forever. There was some talk of separating, with the Aeyries heading for Ula t'Han, the Walkers spreading out into the countryside where they could be relatively anonymous, and the Orchths . . . well, they pose a problem. But, late this evening, one of the onfrit messengers who had been sent to Ula t'Han returned, to report that the Ula is surrounded by Walkers—not an organized force, but organized enough to make it difficult for a flyer to safely reach the town. So the Aeyries, while we can fly away from trouble, will have no safe place to land.

Out of curiosity and restlessness I have done some exploring. But all of the tunnels have been blocked off for fear of losing children—the caves dive deep into the earth, I am told, into a vast and impenetrable darkness. Over the years, the Orchths have explored as deep as they dare, and even they have gotten lost and feared they would never see the light of day again. I talked to some of the Orchths who have done the exploring, and they told me as well as they could about the marvelous things they saw: spires and waterfalls and columns of stone, caverns filled with crystals, deep, quiet pools of water undisturbed by life. Now I can think of nothing else except my desire to explore the caves. If I can make a map of a mountain range, surely I can make a map of these marvelous caverns! Someday.

Ara's passive presence within my mind is gradually becoming more active. Today she asked me to explain war to her. She doesn't understand the concept of hatred, and she doesn't understand why killing someone makes the killer morally in the right. After struggling for a while to explain it to her, I realized that the whole thing is indeed inexplicable nonsense. This, at least, was an answer she could accept.

Later

Delan has been holed up (literally) with ids scrying stone for most of the last day. This evening id came out in search of me. "Two days' flight north of here, where the ocean cuts deeply into land—do you know the place?"

"You must mean the Is'isre Inlet."

"Further in from the place called Is'isre, there is a place on the south shore, far inland, where the terrain is rough and mountainous. It is inhabited, I'm told, only by an ancient Walker sorcerer and her community of acolytes."

I dredged through the bits and pieces of knowledge that I have collected over the years—any Aeyrie wanderer who wants to survive must make a study of Walkers. "The Asasaran?"

"Do you know anything about her?"

*"I doubt I know any more than you. She is fiercely
independent, has refused to accept the rule of the Lan
of Invisible Wealth. She is feared because of her powers
and so she is pretty much left alone. As for who she is
or what she does—I don't know."*

"She has offered to host the convocation."

"Convocation?" For a moment I could not even
remember what Delan was talking about. I know that
only a few days have passed since Delan first mentioned
the possibility of a convocation to me, but so much has
happened since then! I said in astonishment, *"War has
been declared! What makes you think the Walker sorcerers will even be interested in meeting with Aeyrie
mages? And how are the Aeyries supposed to travel to
Is'isre, with the Ula flightways guarded by Walkers with
crossbows?"*

"They will travel through the Void," said Delan.
*"And the Asasaran has promised that some Walker
sorcerers will be there—and not just those who had
studied with her. But you and I must travel the hard
way, since I have no talent for the Void."*

"You and I?"

*"Of course you must come, Tsal. No one else can
tell what has happened to you and Ara."* Then Delan
gave me a hard, piercing look, which pinned me like
a Quai-du master's knife. *"You are famed for your
independence. But you must come."*

"Well, then," I said, as gracefully as I could, considering the circumstances, *"I suppose I have been draft-
ed into the war."*

I will not claim to be surprised. In a world as small
as ours, there can be no such thing as neutrality.

Autumn, Day 21

Delan and I were to leave at daybreak, but just as
id and I were about to launch ourselves from the mouth
of one of the caves, a slender, drawn, weary Aeyrie
landed on the beach. So Delan launched idreself onto
the beach instead, and I watched as id and Eia grasped
each other's hands. They did not embrace or speak.

After a moment they turned and walked toward the ladder I had dropped for them to climb.

The only words I heard Delan say to Eia were: "Orgulanthgrnm will tell you everything. I must leave at once."

But once we were in the air I glanced over at Delan, and saw that ids face was wet with tears.

Chapter 16

In one of the many sadly overgrown gardens of the Forbidden Palace, Bet hacked through the lush growth of a vine, holding back the tangle with one hand as she chopped at it with the pruning knife held in the other. The sweet, pungent scent of the plant's juices rose to her nostrils. Her hands were stained green and brown. Her fingernails had broken and chipped. Farmer's hands, she thought, looking at her thick, strong fingers. And what is a farmer doing here?

The minarets, which no Walker would ever voluntarily climb, pierced the overhand of clouds, fluffy as a soft woven blanket. At daybreak the clouds had come in from the sea. It was afternoon now, and still Bet had not seen the sun. Autumn weather, making her body as rambunctious and unmanageable as a draf in spring. A foreboding tension, much unlike the usual sensuous, self-indulgent holiday spirit of late autumn, thrummed in the air. The A'lan's servants, with whom she now ate her meals, spoke about the aftermath of the riots, in which several had died, and about the continuing violence in the Outer City. Many of the most successful merchants, whose fortunes had been made through the sale of Aeyrie ingenuity, now found their shops boycotted or burned, their ships confiscated.

The heavy knife stung in her hand as she hacked through the vine. Sweat dripped from her nose and her chin, and burned in her eyes. There was nothing here for her—nothing. Why had she stayed behind?

"Remind me not to make you angry with me," said

a light voice from the walkway. Ellin, who came and
went, had come once more. "You would make a dangerous opponent."

"Only if you were an overgrown vine," Bet said.
She sat back on her heels and watched him pick his
way amid the debris.

"You are wearing white now?"

She shrugged. "Why should I care? How long will
you stay this time?"

"As long as my lady needs me." Ellin squatted
among the prunings. He usually wore his hair loose
on his shoulders, but today he had braided it with
ribbons. For a moment, with his bright, alert gaze and
his slender frame, he looked like an Aeyrie. But the
lack of wings set his entire body out of balance. "Well,
as a whole, the Walker race isn't behaving particularly
impressively. What do you think, Bet, will we pass
muster?"

"I agree with Ela—when the A'lan sealed the declaration of war, she sealed the Walkers' death warrant."

"Well, then, if you were to return to an Aeyrie
community you would be much more likely to survive,
wouldn't you? So what are you doing here?"

"I don't know." Bet laid down her pruning knife
and rubbed her stinging palms on the grimy legs of
her trousers. "The garden is pretty badly neglected—
I don't know if it will recover or not. Maybe pruning
it will just kill it. But I never could walk away from
a garden that needed me."

Ellin looked around at the tangled garden, his eye-
brows raised in irony. "I never took you for an
idealist."

A single raindrop fell onto the top of Bet's head,
startlingly cold. "Sometimes, hope is just a kind of
desperation," she said. This was a ridiculous conversation.

Ellin, also struck by a cold raindrop, looked up at
the sky. "Well!" he said, as if offended that the heavy
clouds had finally decided to unload their burden. "I
hope the weather doesn't interfere with tonight's fes-
tivities. Bet, if you will come see the A'lan with me,

then I won't have to tell the news twice. I always hated repeating myself."

Bet slipped her arm through the pile of prunings, lifted them, and tucked them against her waist. "Give me a quarter hour."

As she dragged her load to add to the mountain of prunings that she had already accumulated in the last few days, she felt Ellin's gaze following her. But when she turned back, he was gone. In the garden, the sweet scent of the damp earth rose, succulent and lush with promise, as the rain began to fall.

She hung her sodden, muddy clothing to dry, and dressed again in black. The garden was a gray, blurred confusion of shapes beyond the rain-streaked window. Bet lit a lamp and drew the curtains closed. But gloom stalked down the hallways of the unused wing of the palace, following after her as she hurried to the A'lan's library.

There, Ellin was just pouring her a cup of tea. The A'lan pored over the map pinned to the table, where she used wooden markers to show the location of the army, and red flags to identify places where violence had flared. The red flags were spreading southward as the news of the war spread, but not one Aeyrie had yet been injured, or even attacked, as far as they had heard. Walkers were using the excuse of the war to attack other Walkers, whom they perceived, for one reason or another, to be sympathetic to the Aeyries. If they knew that the A'lan herself was one of those hated Aeyrie sympathizers, would it have made any difference?

Ellin handed Bet the cup of tea. A warm fire burned in the fireplace. She sat near it with a sigh, not really wanting to hear what Ellin had to say. "How is the garden?" the A'lan asked her. She answered vaguely, knowing that no one really cared, and scalded her tongue on the tea.

Ellin leaned over the A'lan's map. "There are more people surrounding t'Han now—perhaps three hundred. But so far not many have continued on toward t'Fon and t'Cwa—maybe a hundred, between the two Ulas. Of course, the Aeyries there have been sufficiently forewarned of their danger, and were prepared. What do you think the Aeyries will do, Bet?"

"Close their doors and wait it out."

"Not fight?"

"Why should they? The weather will do their fighting for them." Winter hit early and hard in t'Cwa and t'Fon. Almost overnight the cold winds would scour the suckerplants away from the mountainsides, leaving their pure, polished glass naked to the harsh winter sun. If not the cold and the lack of shelter, the agonizing glare of the glass burning into their sensitive eyes would quickly drive the attackers away. The Aeyrie population was too small for them to squander it on a battle that the weather and a little patience could win as easily.

Ellin tapped a finger hollowly on the map. "There have been riots—here, here, and here."

Her face gray with worry, the A'lan flagged the map.

"A division of the army has reached Triad, but there's no word—"

Bet's head had begun to ache. She pressed her fingers to her temples. Surely the Triad-re had not been taken by surprise. Orgulanthgrnm, Tsal, Delan, Delan's children . . . and soon Eia.

Ellin's voice droned heavily through the gloom, and finally dissipated into silence. A servant came in and began lighting more air lamps. Bet wondered if the Walker people would now throw away their Aeyrie-invented air lamps and return to using candles and torches, if they even remembered how to make them anymore. "Dinner will be served soon," the servant said. In this household, the division between the classes was an uncertain one.

"What would you do," asked Bet, "If you had the power to do it?"

The A'lan half frowned, half smiled at Bet's presumptive question. "I would start by rescinding the declaration of war."

"Do you think that would be enough to stop this—avalanche?"

Oddly surprised, the A'lan looked at her map, as if she had not seen it before and repeated blankly, "Avalanche?" Tomorrow, or the day after tomorrow, there would not be enough room on the map for the red flags. What would the A'lan do then, to salve her tender conscience—redesignate the flags to represent ten incidents of violence, or a hundred?

"What would you want me to do?" asked the A'lan. So far, she had done nothing except study her maps and read her books, and yet she looked exhausted.

"If you just write on a paper and post it that you changed your mind—the Aeyries are our friends after all—what impact will it have? Not much, at this point. But for the A'lan to come in person, to visit each township and stand with an Aeyrie at her side. . . ."

"Oh, Bet." She leaned heavily on the table. "If I could."

Bet wanted to shake her: Why can't you, then? Are you afraid of dying? Do you believe in anything more than you believe in your own security? But she held her tongue.

The servants brought in trays: beautiful, delicate porcelain plates and bowls, silver spoons and priceless serving dishes. But the supper itself Bet recognized from her farm days: festival stew and hard-crusted bread, with sweet kipsbutter and honey, followed by a tray of chilled sliced melon, the last of the season. In the Walker community of Ranor, melons had always been served on festival night, because of their egg shape, to ensure a rich harvest of children in the spring. The sweet, musky taste reminded Bet of costumes constructed of bits and pieces rounded out of storage trunks, the smell of crisp honey cakes coming out of the oven, the sweet sound of farm musicians tuning their instruments, the festival ribbons braided through everyone's hair, the masked strangers announcing their arrival with ringing bells.

"The storm is clearing," announced a servant with a smile. Bright ribbons cascaded to her shoulders.

The A'lan waved her out the door. "Go to the masque, my dear. Tell the others to go as well. The dishes can wait until morning."

"Are you going?" Ellin asked his lady, but she just laughed at him. "No one would recognize you," he pointed out. "Even if you didn't have a mask—no one knows your face. . . ."

She settled into an armchair under a bright lamp, and opened a book on her knee. "I have been a recluse too long."

Neither surprised nor disappointed, Ellin turned to Bet and held out his hand. "I have my costume. What will you wear?"

"I have no—"

"You must!" Ellin caught the servant by the hand as she went out the door. "Anni, I know you and the others have been searching through the closets for days now. Don't you have something for Bet to wear? Something outrageous."

"I will not!"

"Now, Bet, you are always too serious."

She could summon up no objection severe enough to dissuade him, and soon found herself in a dressing room crowded with the other female servants, wearing a carnelian tunic with skin-tight, topaz trousers, her hips wrapped with scarves of emerald and amethyst, being examined critically by a woman dressed in a shaggy coat of vivid rag strips, while another, bare breasts painted with ornate swirls of color, braided a few ribbons into Bet's cropped hair. "So conservative. At least undo some buttons—this is festival night. I thought you were a farm girl."

"That was a long time ago," Bet said with a sigh. But she unbuttoned some buttons, and tied the mask they handed her onto her face. She could always slip away and return alone to the Forbidden Palace. But a throbbing began in her body when she spotted herself in the mirror: a slender, muscular, exotic stranger, with a face of feathers and flowers, astil clinging to thighs sculpted by all those long climbs up the Ula stairs. Of their own will, her hands undid another button. Aeyries thought that clothing was like fur, just to keep one warm. . . .

The bare-breasted woman viewed Bet with unabashed admiration. Festival night, when there are no rules.

"Ready?" In a hullabaloo of whoops and whistles, the door was opened, to reveal the menservants, transformed beyond recognition, waiting out in the hallway. Outside, the clouds had pulled away from the stars, and two full moons poured a largesse of silver light onto the white courtyard. The guards, reminding them to keep hold of their passes, opened the gate and let them out. . . .

Into a transformed city, where each individual could have been a member of a separate exotic species. A richness of color revealed under the white globes of the paper lanterns; musicians positioned on platforms at every junction, playing enthusiastically, dancing, juggling bright balls. A stage magician producing from under a scarf bouquets of flowers, wriggling waterwyths which glowed in the half-darkness, jewel-winged insects, a plate of sweets. Vendors with dozens of colorful scarves tied to their arms, balancing on their heads huge trays of breads and candies, stuffed buns and cakes. Vendors with huge skins of wine slung over their shoulders, with which they filled the revelers' outstretched cups. Vendors of toys and late-season flowers, vendors of love charms and trinkets and shell bracelets from across the sea. Lawns crowded with dancers, graceful or stumbling, marching out the figures of a formal minuet or rushing to exchange partners in a disorganized circle dance.

Bet had no money, but somehow the silver pannikin ribboned to her waist was filled with wine, and a paper-wrapped sweet was put into her hand. She slipped her arm around the waists of people she did not know, and laughed at jokes she could not hear, and tried on trinkets she could not buy. The moons poured down their light, filling the cupped walls of the Inner City until they glowed with silver fire. Bet took someone's hands into hers, and danced the dances of her childhood: the Triple-Ring and the Tapped Wonder and the Circle of Sheaves. The sky cast down a few playful handfuls of rain, like condensed starlight.

Her dance partner bought them each a frosted cake, with a gilded festival ring embedded in the frosting. They put them on their fingers, still sugar sticky, and washed down their cakes with more sweet wine. Her dance partner wore a beaked mask with glittering bead eyes and gold-dusted, swooping fronds for a headpiece. He strutted and laughed, Aeyrie-slender, Aeyrie-bright, with a dozen red ribbons knotted through his thick, black hair. They put their hands on each other's waists to dance the Sharantish, and his thighs brushed against hers.

Then he was gone, and the woman with the painted breasts, with a face like a red-lipped half moon gave her a swallow of wine from the cup at her waist, and asked her to dance. They kissed in the shelter of an overhanging tree, and Bet came away with the last of her buttons undone and paint on her hands. Her knees wobbled under her. A hundred alien faces, the colors too bright, the edges too sharp, the stars swirling in the sky.

She felt enslaved to the night, a puppet on strings of starlight. The servants from the Forbidden Palace had all disappeared. Alone on the crowded walkways, she wandered. The bells were ringing. There was screaming in the laughter that only she could hear. In each person's heart Bet saw explosive rage, just waiting for the detonation. The end of my people, she thought, and though she felt terror, somehow she could not feel regret.

Waist-deep in flowers, a group of three twined together in the darkness, coming together and separating in a slow, sweet dance. Bet walked on, through dances and revels, past a woman, barefoot and barefaced, weaving unsteadily across a lawn. Down a grassy slope, a half-dozen people rolled like children. The long-legged creatures of the lake looked on in sleepy astonishment.

Then Bet had walked completely around the Forbidden Palace, and found herself at the gate, feet aching, showing her pass. The gate creaked open and then closed behind her. In the courtyard, she studied the silver-etched facade of the palace: the statuary and pillars and buttresses and many arched windows. She turned aside, to follow an overgrown path into the garden.

It was quiet here. The sounds of music and revelry seemed far away, muffled by the high stone walls. In the recesses of the palace, a single light burned—the A'lan, still studying her dusty tomes. The lush scent of the garden filled Bet's nostrils. She picked a blossom and tucked it into her buttonhole. She walked slowly among the dying blossoms of autumn, until at last she came to the bench in the bower. Here she sat, and shut her eyes. Perhaps she slept, but in her dreams she remained in the quiet garden, thinking nothing, feeling nothing, empty as a dry well.

When she opened her eyes, the man with the beaked mask and the glittering, swooping plumes stood before her, his beaded eyes glittering in the starlight. "I thought I'd find you here."

He took her paint-smeared hand in his, and brought her fingers to his beaked lips. "One last dance?"

Through the tangled branches and along the overgrown pathways they danced. No tumbled wallstones could trip them, no gnarled root grab at their feet as they passed. Their feet were light as clouds, light as wind. The moons shivered in the sky, the stars bloomed with light. They leapt, they laughed, they turned; slower and slower they turned, until they were scarcely dancing at all, but only standing; and their masks fell off of their faces and their hands began to shake as they kissed, and kissed again, drinking the heat and the cold of the night, the lust and the fear, the hope and the hopelessness, all mixed together in a drink that burned and hurt and scoured them through until there was nothing left but the wingless passion, and the chaotic silence.

They had already made love out in the garden when

Bet, with a kind of coldness in her heart, took Ellin by the hand and led him to her room, where they made love again. It was sweet, and good, and utterly marvelous. But the delicious passion was shot through with bitterness and sadness, and when at last Ellin slept, Bet lay awake in the fragrant blankets, her eyes aching with unshed tears. She was not young. She knew too much.

Chapter 17

Autumn, Day 22

By flying as high as the wind will support, and avoiding the larger Walker settlements, we have had an uneventful day's journey. I am writing these words by the light of the setting sun. To make us less noticeable, we are traveling without a baggage kite, so we have no lantern, and our supply of water and food is very limited. I am regretting my decision to bring this journal with me, but I cannot unmake it.

My breasts began to ache today, giving the answer to my uncertainty over whether or not this is to be an egg year for me. The last thing I want to carry, in this uncertain world, is the burden of a fertile egg, so my season's loving must come (so soon!) to an end. This is Delan's fertile year as well, as it is Eia's, though id's laying years may now be past. If I read the signs right, Delan and I both will be too egg-heavy to fly within another seven-day.

I would give everything I own (pathetically little, I admit) to be safe in an Ula right now. I can't imagine a worse time to be grounded.

Autumn, Day 23

Is'isre Inlet in sight. Delan's visions and nightmares drive idre beyond the limits of reason. We flew too far today. Id would not rest until nearly sunset. I, still not fully recovered from my illness, must struggle to keep pace. And Delan looks like a burnt-out coal. I am truly

*worried that id will fall ill—and what will I do then,
grounded with a sick companion in hostile land?*

Autumn, Day 24

We flew all day with the Is'isre Inlet at our right. At
first, boats filled its shallow water and Walker settlements lined its edges. As the day passed, glass began
to break through the soil, and the mountains drew
close. The illusion of safety, those mountains. True, no
Walker can capture us there, but neither can we find
any food to eat, or water to drink.

Delan had hoped to reach our goal today, the haven
of the Asasaran and her acolytes, but as the day grew
old and we had not yet seen the first of the landmarks
we were told to watch for, I convinced Delan to stop
early and rest. I did not tell Delan my secret fear, that
the directions given to us by the Walker sorcerer were
purposefully wrong. How amusing it would be, to con-
demn a rival mage to starvation or worse by simply
giving idre fictional directions.

Autumn, Day 25

All morning we flew over a desolate wilderness of
shattered glass, broken loose from the mountains by
some cataclysm, and dumped in tumbled piles into the
Is'isre chasm. The inlet itself, dammed by the debris
into a series of stagnant pools, is an impassable wasteland of foul water choked with vivid algaes. The smell
reminds me, a little too vividly, of the smell of the dead
ocean near Ara's Field, where the fire people spill their
poisonous wastes into the sea.

The morning passed without us ever sighting the
landmarks we seek. I could hide my concerns from
Delan, but from Ara I can hide nothing.

At high noon I spotted—not our long-sought landmark—but a distant flyer, who released a brilliant flare
to attract our attention.

We did not ask ourselves whether this flyer were
friend or foe. Even an isolate or rebel Aeyrie would be
a friend in such a lonely wilderness, in the midst of a
war. But as we drew closer to the unknown flyer, Delan

gestured to me that id knew the other person. Once we had drawn close enough to see each other clearly, I could not have mistaken the other flyer for anything other than a relative of Delan's. The silver coloring is so rare among my people that it only occurs anymore by conscious design. So I knew, even before we had flown close enough for recognition, that this had to be Ishta Laril, taiseoch t'Cwa, Delan's begotten child, given to Delan's own egg-parent Ishta in a hearth adoption.

I am less than a ten-year Laril's senior, and left t'Cwa to begin my travels only a few years before ids winging. Since even an Aeyrie of my age is still considered too immature and unsettled to manage a position of great responsibility, the naming of Laril to be taiseoch was a controversial event for all the Ulas. Laril's reputation for flightiness and unreliability, at least in ids younger days, and ids choice of a Walker for a lover did not help, of course. But tradition won out over common sense: as far back as history records, the taiseoch t'Cwa's has been a white-winged silver. And the Aeyries call the Walkers arbitrary because they choose their A'lan by lot!

Today Laril proved idreself to be neither flighty nor unreliable. Having arrived at the haven the evening before, all day Laril had been searching for us, weighed down by a burden of extra food and water in case we were in need of it. It turned out that the landmark we sought, a spur of glass with blue and orange streaks in its coloring, was unmistakable to any Walker on the ground, but from the air its unusual coloring was all but invisible. Since our directions were given to us by Walkers . . . well, we flew over it sometime yesterday, and could have searched the rest of our lives, and never seen it, nor the little-used, overgrown path which led through the wilderness to the sorcerer's haven.

We lightened Laril's load of water considerably, and followed idre deep into the barrens. Whatever ancient cataclysm reamed the inlet so deep into the landscape had left its mark here as well. The mountainsides are riven through with a thousand winding cracks, as thin as a hair or wide enough to require, here and there, a rickety bridge to transport the rare visitor from one edge to the other. The mountains themselves, rather than being of one piece, are crushed and crumbled into huge boulders. It is treacherous ground—too rugged even for the sucker plants to thrive.

It took the rest of the day for us to come into sight of our goal at last: a dusty, sun-baked cluster of squat houses, their walls constructed of gathered glass wedges cemented together with mortar. (The mortar itself must have been imported here, carried on the backs of the acolytes—those bridges are too rickety to support the weight of a draf.) A thin stream, dammed off to make an irregular pool in which to wash and bathe, trickled through the community's center. Here also had been built, one pole at a time, a scaffolding to provide shade from the blasting summer sun. It was hot, even so late in the season. As we landed, I saw that a dozen well-cherished potted plants were growing in the shade. How desperate the inhabitants must have become for the sight of greenery, to have gone through such trouble for it!

The other Aeyries' mages, whom Laril had transported through the Void, came out from the shaded area to meet us as we landed. A few Walkers also appeared from within the squat buildings: a rugged bunch, craggy and sculpted as the land in which they live, shading their expressionless faces with their hands, as the three of us landed.

Altogether, there are seven Aeyries—six mages, and myself. These are all the mages who live in the world: Delan of Triad, Laril, Marisel, Alis and Imaso of t'Cwa, and S'lin and Ilina, of t'Fon and t'Han respectively. Laril is the youngest. Ilina is, I think, younger than I, but all the rest are clearly older. Myself they examined with undisguised surprise. Of course they know who I am, for I have spent my share of time at each of their towns, but why I am here, I doubt they can imagine. I catch them looking at my repaired wings, too, in horror, or speculation, or curiosity. Like

*the Walker children of Ara's Field, they want to ask
me if it hurts for my bones to be bolted together like
this; but, unlike the Walker children, they are too polite
to ask.*

*They greeted us, they laughed with relief when Delan
explained why we had been delayed, they listened somberly as Delan told about the desperate situation in
Triad.*

*Finally, the Asasaran came out of one of the build-
ings to greet us. She is no taller than an Aeyrie, and
just as lightly built. She is not old, either, though I
expected her to be so, nor scholarly, nor particularly
reclusive in her personality. Instead, she has a certain
bluntness; a way of saying much in few words; an air
of calm expectation. Her arms were floured to the
elbows—she had been kneading bread. She did not say
much, but later we ate the bread she had baked, and
cheese from the tough little herd of kips that they are
able to keep here. In the whole community there are
less than ten residents, plus another two Walker sorcerers whom the Asasaran convinced to make the journey
here. Those two seem little inclined to even speak to the
Aeyries. I must say, I have little hope for any significant
results from this convocation.*

Autumn, Day 26

*Three more Walker sorcerers, accompanied by vari-
ous apprentices and servants, arrived during the night.
The two who arrived earlier, a male and a female, are
simple fishers who live together near the mouth of the
inlet, frequent visitors to this community and friends of
the Asasaran. These other three are what the Walkers
would consider to be true sorcerers: emotionally
remote, scholarly people with the air of bearing mysterious, heavy burdens. They traveled here from as far
away as the Is'antul harbor, first by wagon, then by
drafback, and last of all on foot. They are cranky and
full of complaints this morning, running their poor servants ragged with their impossible demands. The Asasaran will not give up her only stove and limited fuel*

*to heat water for their morning ablutions, and they had
to make do with cold, like everyone else.*

Later

   *I have done what I came here to do. I wish I could
go home now—not that I have a home to go to.*
   *I think that Delan has set idreself an impossible task.
Never, in the history of the world, have Aeyrie mages
and Walker sorcerers even spoken to each other. Now,
because the world happens to be in a state of crisis,
hundred of years of distrust, animosity, and enmity are
to be simply forgotten? Well, they may be mages and
sorcerers; they may be, (as at least the mages are)
frightened for their lives. But they are still people, and
people will be petty.*
   *The Walker sorcerers (the three city sorcerers) so far
have accused me of lying about my experience with the
fire people (I made up the story to take the heat off the
Aeyries for having murdered the Lans). They accused
Laril of lying about the other two taiseochs being murdered. They accused Delan of using desperation tactics
to try to avert the war which the Aeyries themselves
started. And when Delan told them that the Walkers
were in far greater danger than the Aeyries, they
laughed, loud and long and rudely.*
   *Delan does not anger easily. But now id rose and
said to them, very coldly, "I asked you to come here
for your benefit, not for mine. As far as the Aeyrie
people are concerned, it would be to our advantage to
stand by silently, and allow the Walkers to wipe themselves off the face of the earth, as once we did to ourselves. But I am here, not because I am an Aeyrie, but
because I am a Walker's kin. I am here because it was
a Walker's breast which gave me suck, and it is Walker's hands which raise my food, and it is Walker hearts
which hold me dear and call me friend. My lover and
my children and my dearest friends are hostage to this
war. Some of them are Aeyries, and some of them are
not. My heart will ache no less for the loss of a Walker
friend than it will for the loss of an Aeyrie. That is why*

I am here. Now why don't you tell me why you are here; because so far your words give me no clue."

I walked off to be by myself. Ara is quiescent in my mind now, a silent presence, floating in her warm pool as the tide rises, drops, and rises once again. From where I sit, I can see the Inlet gashing through the mountains. I see the glimmer of water, and clouds rising like bread dough beyond the edge of a mountain. It is a spectacular view: stark, harsh, austere. Between these unforgiving mountains, which stretch westward farther than anyone has ever been able to explore, and the desert of the sea, lies that thin strip of land where there is soil—two, three, even four feet deep.

It is this miserly geography which has determined our history, which has enforced our enmity with the Walkers, and which has all but required the Aeyries to become what we are: idea merchants, restless explorers, communalists. A society of adults, afraid of the hungry mouths and hearts of the children we hatch. A dying people, who love, dearly and desperately, the land which is killing us. And if we did leave, if we did journey in search of a new home, a new land, what would become of us? We would become something else entirely—perhaps like the fire people, amoral vampires, incapable of perceiving a Universe other than our own. And without our mountains, what use could we possibly have for our wings?

Later

I returned to the settlement, to find that the debate was still continuing. But Delan had abandoned it, to sit in the kitchen with the Asasaran, who apparently had also reached her limit of tolerance.

The Asasaran (which is to say, "the old mountain woman") was, like our Bet, tortured by her magical talents in her youth. Proscribing for herself the traditional studies and apprenticeship of the sorcerer, she came instead to this barren land and asked the earth itself to teach her what she needed to know. Far from the influence of culture and commerce, surviving on *stream water and the limited food she could harvest from the Inlet, her talents grew, untrained and unhindered. Now she is a reknowned magician, and as she will accept no payment for her services, some of the most powerful people of the Walker world are deeply in her debt. She would not discuss, even with Delan, what she does, or how. But she won Delan's respect with her very deliberateness: sometimes she may consider an action for a year or more before she does it.*

"I have no talent for this," said Delan gloomily. "At Triad, these debates are finished, the weapons long since thrown into the sea. Two generations, it took, for us to truly learn to live at peace with each other. And these people think they can do the same in an evening. They insist upon it. They will not talk about anything except politics and dead history. Who did what to whom, and why. Old grudges, old stereotypes, old resentments."

"Well, what did you think would happen?" I asked, equally grumpily.

"I don't know. I guess I expected more reason, more compassion. More vision. Less self-interest."

The Asasaran spoke, surprising me since she usually is silent. "None of these things are possible where there is no trust. So that is what we must discuss first: how do we trust each other? Especially now that we are at war. And why must we trust each other, at a time when we are supposed to be enemies?"

Delan dipped a hand through empty air, as if seeking to grasp hold of something ephemeral, invisible, inconceivably ellusive. "The situation was bad enough, before the A'lan declared war. Now it is impossible. By the mountains—" Id looked blankly at us: hollow, haunted eyes. How long id has stood, a solitary pillar holding back the nightmare. "I am afraid," Delan said. "I am so afraid."

For some time we stared at each other, and I remember thinking, with a terrible hopelessness, of ways that I at least could escape the holocaust. I have six days in which to get myself to safety—I could reach t'Han, or even t'Cwa, if the winds are friendly. The Walkers will massacre themselves and what few Aeyries they can find, the fire people will be sated and go away, and in the spring the Aeyries will emerge to find that, for the second time in remembered history, we are the over-lords of a charnel house.

Then Ara bestirred herself and spoke within my mind: a liquid voice, salted with the ancient memories of her people. Hers was the voice of a hundred Mers, each of whom remembered different memories from a different herd, the memories of their own non-Mer partner, the memories and experiences of everyone the non-Mer partners had ever met, hated, loved, lost. And all of these memories spoke within me with one voice, one consensus.

I could not argue. I could not even speak when Delan and the Asasaran both looked at me sharply, sensing, as mages must be able to do, the motion of the forces of the Universe. The tide had risen within my heart; it flooded me, it carried me. A small part of me which remained myself stood back, shocked, I think, by the simple, reasonable, even obvious solution which was proposed to me by that massive consensus of history and experience. I opened my mouth and said, "I must go to Is'antul."

I have only six days; there is no time to lose. I am leaving at once.

Chapter 18

The wind carried to the A'lan's garden the rich, fermented smell of the sea, and coated Bet's lips with a fine layer of salt. That day, she felt the walls of the Forbidden Palace closing in on her like a fist clenching over a leaf. If a section of the earth had split off from the rest and gone flying off into space with her on board, she could not have felt more isolated from the rest of the world. Digging away at weeds which had rooted in the loose stones of a wall, Bet uncovered the hiding place of a furry singer, which blinked at her groggily, its pupils closing to slits in the bright light. Its fur was the softest thing she had ever touched.

Carried on the current of a wind, clouds scudded across the sky. Bet sat back on her heels and watched them, until it began to seem to her that the clouds were standing still and it was the earth which was moving. Dizzy, she gathered up a few weeds and stood up. Loam patched her knees with brown circles against the white cloth. She turned and saw Ellin coming across the garden.

"You're back so soon," she said. She could not be glad, for his early return outside the walls could only mean bad news.

Gray dust and wormweb patched his rumpled clothes. He paused on the walkstones that Bet had only just cleared that day, and said in disbelief, "You mean you don't know?"

"This is the Forbidden Palace. How could I know anything?"

His hands clenched and unclenched in the untucked cloth of his shirt. "Come with me to the A'lan."

Bet dropped her handful of weeds, thinking vaguely that she could always pick them up later. She brushed at the mud on her knees to no effect, then, with a shrug, wiped her hands on her smock. It would do the A'lan good to see a little dirt.

On the map in the A'lan's study, the red markers spread like a swath of blood across all three lowland regions. In every city and in many of the country communities as well, there had been violence: Walker against Walker. Buildings had burned, shops had been looted, people had been beaten, stoned, and killed. At more than one town, the festival celebration of life, love, and new life had become a grim massacre.

Lately, the A'lan spent every moment of her day with her back turned to the map. Her back stooped; her hair grayed. Her strong, piercing voice became muted. She did not like to see Bet; and Bet, feeling every bit as helpless as she, obliged her by staying away. In the garden, at least, she could find a modicum of peace. In the garden, she could control a small corner of the world.

Today, the A'lan's magnificent, studious solitude had already been violated. A babble of excited voices spilled out through the door, which hung ajar, and into the hallway. A half-dozen of the Forbidden Palace's servants crowded around her, all of them talking at once. Her face drawn with strain and agitation, the A'lan listened first to one, and then to another. She herself seemed to be all but speechless.

"My lady."

The servants all fell abruptly silent at Ellin's entrance. The A'lan sighed. "Ellin, you don't know how glad I am to see you."

"Tell me what has happened."

"The guards will not allow us to enter and exit the palace anymore. Not even the servants, to get food and supplies. Orders of the Lan of Peace, they say. For the protection of the A'lan.''

Ellin sank into a soft chair, put a hand to his face, and shut his eyes. One of the servants began to speak, but held his tongue. Bet wished, passionately, that she had not left her garden. "One of your Hand has been killed. Perhaps more than one. Tor Kates has discovered the existence of your information network. I think I was only allowed to enter the city because he wanted you to hear this news. But I doubt I will be free to exit the city again.''

White faced, the A'lan stared at him. With one hand she brushed at a loose strand of hair which had fallen over her eyes. At last she spoke, her voice small and tired. "Which one is dead?''

Ellin told her, a name which meant nothing to Bet. The A'lan groped for the edge of her desk and sat on it, knocking down a bottle of ink to stain the priceless carpet. "Leave me," she said.

When the servants, Ellin, and Bet all stared at her blankly, she raised her voice to a hoarse cry. "Am I not even mistress in my own house? Leave me!''

Confused, asking each other the questions they could not ask the A'lan—when they would see their families again, where they would stay in the palace, what they would eat—the servants exited the library to cluster into a whispering huddle in the hall. But Ellin did not move from his chair, and Bet hesitated uncertainly near the doorway. She did not love the A'lan like the others, though she had come to accord her a reluctant, if critical, respect. It was for Ellin that she hesitated.

As he brought in the bits and pieces of information to his lady, and as they fit them together like pieces of a puzzle, even as each piece confirmed again what Eia and Bet had told them, thirteen days ago now, still both of them had somehow managed to maintain their disbelief. "You never actually saw the fire people," Ellin was fond of pointing out to Bet. "You believe in them because you believe in the integrity of the people who are giving you the information. But my people, in whom I believe, have brought me nothing—no hint that there might be another power loose in the world, no suggestion that Tor Kates is acting under their influence. I can't believe something so far out of my experience without proof."

She doubted that he believed it yet. But one thing had become all too believable today: that the times had changed. The implicit imprisonment of the A'lan had become explicit. Her expensive, private information network, the only thing she had accomplished in her lifetime, was being shut down. Her servants, who had always been free to come and go as they liked, now were confined to the palace. And that included Bet herself, she realized, with a belated shock of anger.

"Leave me," the A'lan said again. Then, as Ellin rose up from his chair, she spoke again, through stiff lips in a face as white and expressionless as a corpse. "For your own safety, you must leave the city, one last time. But this time you must not return. I am releasing you."

"Lady—" he began.

"Go!"

It was to Bet that he turned, when they had left the library and closed the door on the A'lan. She took his hand in hers, distressed by the deep lines riven into his skin and the hollow grief staring out of his eyes. "Where am I to go?" he said to her. "Where, in all the world, am I to go?"

It rained that afternoon but cleared by nightfall. The true heavy rains of late autumn would not begin for a thirty-day or even longer. There was a whole world of disaster that could occur between now and then, thought Bet, as she lay awake in her narrow bed, with Ellin huddled up against her. She stroked his smooth skin as he slept; the muscles of his shoulders which quivered under her touch, the coarse black fall of his hair. How could he sleep? she wondered.

The building was silent: the silence of thick walls of cut stone, and thick carpets, three or four layers deep. The silence of emptiness, and self-deception, the silence of a meaningless life turning in upon itself like a flower after its bloom is over. In an Aeyrie Ula, it was never silent. Even in the dead of night like this, one could hear the water rushing in the walls, being pumped by the wind to the storage tanks at the peak of the mountain. The wooden walls conducted every sound: an infant's wail, a dreamer's mutters, the quarrels or passion of lovers. The wind made the entire suspended community creak, sometimes, as if it were a ship at sea. On bad nights, Bet used to lie awake and wonder if the entire rickety town were about to slide down the mountainside and join the rubble below.

Tonight she was wondering something similar. And did the A'lan sleep, in her plush woolen bed, with a friendly fire flickering and a cup of wine on the bedside table? Or did the memory of the declaration of war, signed and sealed with her own hand, haunt her in her dreams?

Bet felt the walls closing around her: the walls of her room, of the building, the walls which surrounded the palace, the walls which separated Is'antul from the rest of the world. They closed around her, until she felt she could not move or breathe under the weight of cold stone. The howling wind was better than this cold, dead silence.

She did not realize that she had been asleep, until she awoke with a start. The fire had gone out, leaving the room in frigid darkness. Shivering, she wrestled with Ellin for a corner of the quilt, then gave up and fumbled along the edge of the bed for one of the blankets that they had knocked off the bed earlier in the night. She wrapped herself in it, teeth chattering with more than the cold.

Tap-tap-tap, a crisp, ringing sound in the cold room. Had that sound awakened her, she wondered, rather than the cold? She crawled out of bed, considered awakening Ellin, and decided not to. She drew the curtain to a blaze of starlight and a hunched, hooded, no, winged silhouette out in the garden.

In that moment, something happened to her: the

thing that she had been waiting for, the lack of which
had held her immobilized for thirteen days while the
world around her deteriorated toward a holocaust.
There was a great, massive, weighty shifting within
her heart. For now, Bet thought, I will choose to
believe in something. It may be true, or it may be
false, it may betray my trust or it may enlighten my
life. I do not know, and I cannot know. But I will
believe, nevertheless, and if there are consequences,
I will endure them without complaint. I will believe
that the death of the Walkers and the Walker civilization is not inevitable. I will believe that the fire people
can be stopped. Above all, I will believe—in the asser-
tions of my own heart.

The window latch squawled under her fingers, and
Ellin stirred, muttering, in the bed. Bet leaned out
and whispered in h'ldat, "Come in the window,
quickly."

"Bet?" said Ellin behind her. "Bet, what is it?"

She reached out the window for a warm, fur-backed
hand that grasped hers, a frail-boned, slender figure,
all wings and tangled mane, that she lifted, one
handed, to the windowsill. The Aeyrie came through
and dropped, gasping, to a crouch on the floor. Light
struck and shimmered in ids golden fur: Ellin, the
tinderstick with which he had lit the air lamp still in
his hand, scrambled for his trousers, cursing. Bet knelt
on the floor, stroking her hand disbelievingly through
the soft, thick fur. "Tsal?"

"A moment," gasped the Aeyrie.

"Are you injured?"

"Just tapped out—hard flight—"

She fetched a cup of water, colliding with Ellin who
hissed, "For land's sake, Bet, put on some clothes—"

She ignored his horror, though it vaguely amused
her. Tsal sipped water between gasps of air. She
watched with wonder the bellows of ids great chest,
the quiver of overextended flight muscles, the flicker
of the nictitating membrane over ids bright golden
eyes. Breasts beginning to swell, she noticed, the first
signs of pregnancy. No wonder it had been such a

hard flight. "We have some food in here, don't we?
A box of sweets or something—"

Ellin found the box. Between the two of them they
lifted the Aeyrie into a stool, and fed idre pieces of
nut candy until the box was empty. By then id had
ceased to tremble and begun to breathe normally, and
Ellin had brought clothing to Bet and convinced her
to put it on. She felt much warmer then, and thanked
him. "Now," she said.

Tsal spoke in the Walker tongue, out of courtesy to
Ellin, perhaps, whom id did not know to be conver-
sant in h'ldat. "I need to see the A'lan."

"All right. Can you walk yet? Hush," she said, to
Ellin's shocked protest. "The A'lan is a grown woman.
What do you want to protect her from?"

"Whatever the Aeyrie has to say to her, at least it
can wait until a decent hour—"

"Don't be an idiot, Ellin! Tsal has to be gone again
before daybreak!"

Ellin lapsed into silence, but Bet did not need to be
told what troubled him. Why tell the A'lan more; why
torture her further?

Because, Bet answered him, coldly, in her heart.
Because this is what she was chosen for.

At the closed door to the A'lan's bedroom suite,
Ellin gripped Bet by the arm. "Wait out here. I will
awaken her." Bet stood in the hallway, with Tsal leaning heavily into her shoulder, listening to the faint
murmur of surprised voices, and watching light appear
under the doorway. "Did Ara survive?" she finally
asked Tsal.

"She survived."

When the door opened once again, the A'lan's secretary, wrapped in a nightrobe, her face white with
sleeplessness and strain, let them in. Her eyes followed the golden Aeyrie's every movement as Bet
helped idre into the entry, and from there into the
sitting room where the A'lan was enthroned in a plush
chair, wrapped in soft wool, her feet in slippers. Ellin
stood behind her chair, rumpled and solemn.

The A'lan sent a groggy maid to fetch refreshments for her guest. Tsal approached the A'lan unsteadily on ids own two feet and bowed, palms crossed over ids swelling breasts. "Madam, I am Arman Orshil Tsal, originally of Ula t'Cwa. My egg-parent, Arman, is a respected inventor in t'Cwa; my heart-parent, Orshil, is windmaster at t'Fon. I am an explorer and mapmaker; I have no home."

This brief biography charmed the A'lan into a reluctant smile, though it could not erase the lines of care and weariness from her face. "I am the A'lan, chosen by lot when I was sixteen years old, to protect the welfare of the Walker people. Come and sit beside me. Ysbet?" With a gesture she directed Bet to pull up a stool for Tsal and take a seat where the dull warmth of the fire could do her some good.

Tsal crouched on the stool and leaned forward intently. The exhaustion of ids body had not yet touched ids eyes, which burned brightly in the light of the fire. How beautiful id was; a being of sunlight and flame, with the air lamps illuminating the translucent membranes of ids folded wings. Even the metal patches in ids shattered bones, the thin white scars in ids wing membranes, and the deeply cut scars in ids head, face, shoulder and hip where the harsh glass had gashed; even these were beautiful. Bet wondered if the A'lan recognized the meaning of the scars, or could appreciate the immense courage with which Tsal had taken up ids shattered life once again.

Tsal held out ids hands, as if challenging the A'lan to take hold of them, to listen with not only her ears but her entire being. "I have come to tell you my story, but it is not my story alone. I am Merfriend to a female whom I call Ara, because we met each other in Ara's Field. The wild Merherds remember everything which has happened in the experience of the herd. Everything—as far back as can be imagined. So when I tell you what I know, and what Ara knows, I am speaking of the memories of Mers who lived and died hundreds, thousands of years ago. I am speaking of the memory of the sea, of the ancient, first people who were born on its tides and flow on its currents. For the Mers are the oldest people, and the sea is the place where all life began.

"This is what the Mers remember."

So Tsal told the tale of the poisoned water and the Forgotten Times, and of how Ara had gone out to seek the answer to the ancient mystery, and of how Tsal had helped her and what had happened to idre. Bet, though she had heard this tale before, indeed had heard some of it from Tsal's own mouth, and had taken her own part in the rest of it, nonetheless found herself riveted: sweating as Tsal spoke of ids harrying rescue, blinking back tears as id described Ara's near death and slow, painful recovry. Tsal spoke with power, holding the A'lan riveted with ids bright, passionate eyes.

Now id spoke of the things Bet did not know: of Delan's tortured vigil over ids imprisoned lover and sleeping children, of the flight of the Triad-re to the caves at the edge of the sea, of the convocation of mages in the barren wilderness east and north of the I'sisre Inlet, where nothing was accomplished because the old distrust and hatreds could not be forgotten.

"So I have come to you," said Tsal, "as Speaker for the mage Delan who is also taiseoch of Triad, as Speaker for the Mer Ara and all the other Triad Mers and all the Mers who have ever lived, and as Speaker for myself, who want nothing more than a world at peace, where I can explore without fear. We have done all we can. We have tapped out all our resources. You must take action, or the Walker people will not survive."

Tsal had finished. The maid, who had come in unnoticed with a tray of tea and bread, set the tray down by the fire. The A'lan, still held riveted in Tsal's bright gaze, opened her mouth as if to speak, then shut it again. "Do not ask me to change the world!" she wanted to say; Bet could see it in her eyes. "The position of the A'lan is nothing but a cruel joke. I have no power; I am just a symbol, a prisoner, a slave to tradition. There is nothing I can do."

But she did not say it. The fire crackled in the fireplace. Outside the curtained windows, the wind began to blow. Standing at the A'lan's shoulder, Ellin stood very still, his thick hair in a tangle on his shoulders, his mouth a thin line and his eyes narrowed. But between his slitted eyelids, firelight glittered. The A'lan's secretary also stood very still, with one hand pressed to her cheek as if to comfort herself, and in her face an expression of stunned shock. How easy it was to dismiss the Aeyrie people as self-indulgent, eccentric aliens. How hard to dismiss them when one sat before you.

The A'lan took hold of Tsal's hand, just for a moment, no longer. Then she rose sharply to her feet. "I need paper and pen," she said. "And bring the meal. Ellin—" But he already stood at her side, a quicksilver male with a solemn mouth and bright, laughing eyes. "Do you know the mages of whom Tsal spoke?"

"Yes, lady, they live in adjoining towns perhaps a day's journey from here."

"You must go to them, if you can get out of the city."

"Bet will get me out."

The A'lan gave Bet a startled glance, though surely Ellin had told her of Bet's unique talents. Bet stood up and poured a cup of tea, and dropped into it three spoonfuls of amber honey. She brought the cup to Tsal, along with a plate of honey cakes. Tsal took the plate with a shaking hand. "How long before daybreak?" she asked idre.

"Not long enough." Tsal sipped the tea, wrinkling ids nose with disgust at the sweetness. "Ara can keep me from being seen, if daylight comes too soon. But I can't delay too long. The Mers found the Triad ship. It's within flying distance now, but I have to catch it before the morning winds pick up, or I'll never make it. I'm too tired." Tsal took a deep breath. "You don't know, do you, that the hiding place of the Triad-re was discovered two days ago. They are surrounded by soldiers on the cliff overhead and the sand below."

"Great Mountains. Where is Delan?"

"Id is in transit, and should arrive there today or tomorrow, I think."

The thought of the quiet mage flying, unwarned, into the arms of the Walker army, galvanized Bet. "I'm coming with you. I have my Wing here."

"We can't leave the A'lan without the protection of a mage. You have to stay."

The A'lan's secretary reappeared, bearing paper and ink and the A'lan's seal, which she set ceremoniously onto a desk. Tsal's passion had affected her as well, it seemed. With great solemnity, she set up her tools and began to write as the A'lan dictated. Bet stood over Tsal, keeping idre supplied with tea and bread, until id lay down on a couch to sleep for a few brief hours. Before daybreak, id was gone. Soon after, Bet escorted Ellin through the guarded gates into the Outer City. But she returned, alone, to the guarded palace and the A'lan's luxurious apartments, to stand witness as the A'lan's seal was carefully affixed to a warrant for the arrest of Tor Kates, the Lan of Peace.

Chapter 19

The sunlight, burning through clear water and captured and magnified by opaque glass, kept Ara warm. Her protected pool sustained the illusion of summer, though her skin and her blood told her it was autumn: time for migration, time for the breeding of next year's cubs; time for lazy meandering through the shallow southern ocean and the exciting, unsettling contact of other Mer herds.

Every day, the females of the Triad herd came to Ara's pool, bringing food for her to eat, and news such as only the Mers know: of the season and the tides, of the people of Triad squeezing restlessly and irritably past each other within their cramped caves, of the motion of anger and fear and hatred and distrust, rushing across the lowlands like fire in time of drought. Ara slipped out of her pool and swam with them; every day a little farther. Then she returned, exhausted, to float in her sun-warm water and once again send out her attention to the energetic, bright spirit of the Aeyrie Tsal.

The green bloom of algae faded from the water. The sun climbed wearily across the sky, each day giving up the struggle a little sooner. The cleata lizards sprawled across the salt-frosted glass, clinging with six clawed feet and flickering their tongues skyward. The minds were small, simple things; their thoughts were flashes of forked lightning. Sometimes they came up to Ara and examined her. Their eyes were like polished stones, but they did not truly see her, for they did not truly see themselves.

The other Mers patrolled the shoreline. Often Ara sensed their presence, passing by beyond the breakers. The Aeyrie Gein, a being with no edges, for whom all pain was ids pain, all joy ids joy, visited her. Id smiled worriedly at her, and pronounced her well on the way to recovery, and urged her to continue to rest as much as she could.

Then, another presence, that of a stranger, appeared at the edge of her awareness, and Ara slipped out of her pool into the safety of the breakers.

She knew the feel of a Walker mind. This one was searching for something for which he would be well rewarded. Greed sustained him. Soon Ara sensed two others who accompanied him, though they traveled at a distance from each other. In time, she saw the first with her own eyes, as he traveled down the shoreline from the north, dragging himself heavily over the obstacles of stone and water. He wore red and black; his uniform drooping in the damp salt air. He carried a pack on his back. When he looked in Ara's direction, she slipped under the surface of the water and hid herself in the turmoil of the breakers.

Her warning swam out to the other Mers, but they already knew of him, and of his two companions who traveled parallel to him, farther inland. He continued on down the shore, out of Ara's sight, and she never saw him again. But, later that day, the other Mers told her he had found the sea caves, and had guessed what might be hidden within. The Orchths converged on him that night, as he tried to climb the cliff to join his companions and tell them that he had found what they sought. They took him prisoner, and returned with him to the sea caves.

A day passed, and another. Tsal winged ids weary way across Walker lands, flying by night and hiding by day. The Mers brought Ara ragged armloads of greenleaf, which had begun to brown and shrivel in

the chilling water. They told her that something had
happened.

This is what they showed her: the sea cliff, smooth
as glass, punctured with dark cave entrances. From
one of those dark holes issued the fretful wailing of a
child. Across the boulder-strewn shore came the
Walkers, dressed in red and black. Along the edge of
the cliff gathered more, with their draf-drawn wagons
and their bright penants. Within the cave mouth, the
child wailed and would not be hushed.

No, said Tsal in Ara's thoughts. No, no, no—

But from the wagons were lowered supplies and
timbers, and, on the rocky shore, the Walkers began
building towers with which to enter the caves.

Ara ate all the food the other Mers had brought
her, and then she swam out with them, through the
breakers and into the open sea. This time she did not
return.

*Tsal plummeted out from among the stars. The Uni-
verse burned at ids back, wide as thought, deep as
passion, bright with the light of a thousand unknown
worlds. Before idre writhed the velvet black surface of
the sea where somewhere a small ship nestled among
the waves.*

*Somewhere, id thought as id fell out of the depth of
sky. Somewhere.*

Here, answered the Mers.

And then id saw it, the faint gleam of white sails.

"How did you get in here?"

More curious than alarmed, the captain of the Peace
Guard leaned against the doorsill, folding his arms
across his chest. He wore a leather overtunic, scarred
and worn by long hours in the practice ring. His sword
hung in an oiled and polished scabbard. The skirt of his
tunic was edged with delicate piecework embroidery.

Bet had been sitting in the room's only chair, waiting for his return. She stood up now, holding her face
rigidly expressionless, so that he would not be able to
guess at the fear thundering in her throat. What kind

of man was he? The cruelty with which he had tortured Eia had merely been businesslike: the cruelty of one who does as he is expected. Any future ambitions he may have entertained certainly had been hopelessly compromised by Eia's escape. Tor Kates, Bet had heard, applied blame indiscriminately and would carry his grudges to the grave.

In her hand Bet held a folded paper, sealed with scarlet and gold. "Do you recognize this seal?"

He gazed at her, one eyebrow raised sardonically. He must have followed a harsh road to have brought him here. How many acts of violence had he orchestrated, how many young people had he re-formed to fit his new mold? And did he ever think beyond his own self-interest? He glanced at the paper in Bet's hand. Only the existence of the paper itself surprised him. He looked back at Bet, with realization dawning in his face. What the paper had to say, he could predict. He could not have climbed so far, had he been a fool.

Which was stronger, his loyalty to the Lan of Peace, or to himself? If he were, after all, a person of honor, where would his honor lead him? Bet waited. She had assured the A'lan that she could escape, if he decided to turn against her. But all her assurances had been lies. When it came to death, Bet would die just as easily as anyone else, and all the magic of the Universe would not help her.

Slowly, his hand lifted and then, with a sharp gesture, he snatched the paper from her hand. He smiled a horrible smile; the smile of one who had walked his whole lifetime down only one road, and now finds that he must turn back. He broke the seal, and read the warrant.

"I know what you are asking yourself," said Bet. "If the A'lan is strong enough to do this. To ally yourself with her . . . well, it could be a very good position for an ambitious man to put himself into. But to take a stand against Tor Kates, and lose—"

He snorted without amusement. "No, I do not envy myself. Who are you?"

"I speak for the A'lan."

"The A'lan is a foolish old woman locked behind a gate."

"The locked gate has only been an inconvenience to her, and the A'lan has been in training for this day thirty years. No one in all the lowlands knows more about the country, its politics, or its inhabitants. Take yourself, for instance." Then she told him some things that he had thought no one else knew, things that he even denied to himself. She had no idea how Ellin had found these things out.

The captain's expression did not alter. But he muttered to himself, "I always knew. I told Tor . . . that female has been watching. It was because of me that he decided to lock her up."

"Then history will remember you as a very clever man who helped Tor Kates engineer his own downfall. For if the A'lan's gates had not been locked, perhaps she would never have decided to do this."

"Who are you?" he asked again, helplessly. His informants certainly told him everything about everyone that they deemed important in the known world. But Bet was just some crazy female who lived with the Aeyries. No doubt he had never heard of her.

"What are you going to do?" she said.

"Of course, I will arrest him." The captain tossed the paper onto his desktop. "You understand, I cannot refuse an order of the A'lan."

It was not true at all. Never, in hundreds of years, had an A'lan ever issued an order over her own signature. But the captain stated what all the commonfolk of the lowlands would perceive to be true: that if the A'lan could overrule the dictates of the nine Lans, then she could also rule them.

"And what do I do next?" he asked Bet. "How long do you think Tor Kates will remain secure under the custody of his own Peace Guard?"

"I think you can find a way to assure yourself of the loyalty of the Guard. The A'lan will issue a statement declaring you to be the acting Lan of Peace—of course, only your constituents can make the appointment permanent. It is up to you to consolidate your control. The A'lan will help you any way she can."

"So long as I do what she wishes."

Bet shrugged, as if to say: of course. Loyalty is repaid by loyalty.

"And the other Lans?"

"The Lan of Invisible Wealth, Samil Infatil, is visiting with the A'lan right now. As for the others—" Bet dismissed them with a gesture.

"They will turn whichever direction the wind blows," said the captain, disgusted. Of course, he was turning with the wind as well, but Bet saw no advantage in pointing this out to him. "I would like to meet with the A'lan, as soon as this order has been carried out. This evening, perhaps."

"The A'lan will receive you."

"I will send a guard to escort you out," began the captain.

But Bet was already gone. Now, she thought to herself, as she slipped out the way she had come. Now the battle truly begins.

Autumn, Day 33

It is nearly sunset. The ship's captain had absolutely forbidden the use of any light or flame, so I am writing these words sitting on the quarterdeck steps, using the flaming red sun to light my page. Standing above me on the quarterdeck, Delan leans against the rail, ids wings spreading and closing in time with the rhythmic swaying of the ship. Id is conversing in a low voice with the ship's captain. I hear only an occasional word; the rest is carried off by the wind. But each time Delan says "Triad," I cannot help but turn my head at the sound; there is so much pain, so much anguish, so much self-doubt in Delan's voice.

Delan and I have not yet had a chance to speak. Id fell out of the sky earlier this afternoon, in a landing as uncontrolled as mine three days ago. Even now, after a substantial meal and several hours of sleep, Delan seems on the verge of exhausted collapse. I have not spoken directly with idre, but I know that id must have overflown the siege of Triad. I can only imagine ids thoughts as id circled, far overhead, examining the hundreds of soldiers who hold hostage everything that id lives for.

The Mers surround the ship. If I lean over the rail, I can see them, slipping along the surface of the restless water, turning from front to back as they swim, gazing with black, liquid eyes at the deckrail. It is difficult for me to distinguish Ara from among them. Her lingering weakness has not entirely dissipated, and, more so than the others, she suffers in the increasing chill of the water. The young calves, who will be most vulnerable to the cold, have abandoned this shore along with their dams, and are riding the current southward to the warm-water wintering grounds. Ara should have gone, too, but she opted to remain. When I questioned her on this, she seemed astounded that it even occurred to me that she would leave with the others.

Her herd gave her a mission, and she must see it through to the end.

I suppose I had forgotten. Since that day in midsummer when Ara's herd first encountered the poison water, everything has changed. And yet she, though her entire understanding of the Universe has been turned upside-down, has not lost her sense of continuity between then and now. She loves me; and I love her. It is a complex thing, this love: a mystery, a young infant. It terrifies me and it absorbs me. I lie awake at night asking myself questions about it; questions that I answer "yes," and then answer "no." But for her there are no questions to answer. She loves me, but she is not bound to me. Her first obligation is still, and will always be, to the herd which first sent her out alone.

I must tell myself this, over and over again, so that if we do somehow survive this awful autumn, I will not be surprised when she leaves; I will not be surprised when I never see her again.

Tonight, with all five moons full, will be the highest tide of the year. It was to catch this tide that the ship's captain sailed so cleverly and brutally down the coast.

The crew, which includes two young Orchths and a flightless Aeyrie, a nest of seagoing onfrits, and a dozen Walkers, spends every winter at Triad. They have lovers and children there: Triad is not merely their employer, it is their home. Tonight's tide is their only chance at saving their lovers and children and beloved friends. For this, the crew has spent every spare moment on the sails, dying them black. For this, the Mers have gathered: not just the Triad Mers, but Mers from wild herds as well, herds who remember that dark time which we Aeyries have willfully forgotten. For this, the captain and Delan lean together on the rail, speechless, watching the last sliver of the sun sink into the ocean.

In the brightly lit library, the A'lan brooded over her map. The air lamps' white light blazed in the braided crown of her white hair. Shc hovered over the lowlands like a parent over a child's sickbed: solemn, frightened, determined to never admit defeat. Bet, whose feeling for the A'lan had fluctuated between pity, scorn, and reluctant respect, watched her covertly, asking herself the same question that she had answered for the Peace Captain earlier that day: Does she have the power? Does she have the knowledge? Can she do it?

It had been a cold day, and Bet huddled close to the flickering fire. She felt drained and empty. Her body sank into the soft chair, heavy and enervated. She wondered if Tsal had made it safely to the decks of the Triad ship. She pondered how frightening it must be to be grounded by fertility, so far from a safe home, with the land poised on the edge of violence. She wondered if Tsal would be seeing Laril, and what id would tell idre. Would id mention that Bet had a Walker lover? Would Laril be brokenhearted, or unsurprised? Would id someday become able to understand?

The lights seemed to dim. Heavy and exhausted in her chair, Bet could scarcely force herself to move. What does it matter? she asked herself wearily. Why does anything matter? The walls of the library seemed to recede, leaving her sitting isolated in a dim, vague cave. Even the A'lan seemed to recede, though Bet could see her raising her head slowly, as if aware that something was wrong. Bet felt the charge in the atmosphere of the disjoined room: a prickling on her skin, an ominous tension. Just like it had been in the Lan of Trade's salon that awful day. . . .

She felt embedded in her chair. Her muscles could not lift her up. She struggled weakly, writhing in the embrace of the soft cushions. The A'lan gazed at her. I understand, she seemed to say, that you cannot help me. I do not blame you for your helplessness. I do not blame myself.

"No," Bet whispered.

Her feet were flat upon the ground. She anchored them there and raised herself up from the chair. One heavy step at a time, she crossed the distance between herself and the A'lan. It seemed like forever before she held up her hand and touched the A'lan's shoulder.

And then a blindingly bright thread of light pierced through the ceiling and darted across the room toward the A'lan. Bet watched herself move—oh, so slowly— her hand dropping down and then lifting up to cup under and intercept that dynamic sliver of spun lightning. It pierced her, and she heard herself screaming as it spun through her body, down her arm, her shoulder, her backbone, her legs and feet, and then into the deep, solid, immutable earth.

She sucked the life out of them, those distant, heartless, manipulative aliens. She reeled the thread of power in, and discarded it into the great energy sink of the earth. She sensed in those attackers a startled panic, a shock greater than the shock of surprise, the shock of a world turning over. Then the thread was gone, and Bet's feet could no longer support her. She fell to her knees, ears roaring, as the A'lan called imperiously for help.

*   *   *

"What does this mean?" the A'lan asked later, when both of them had calmed themselves with sweet tea slopping over the edges of cups held in shaking hands.

"It must mean that Tor Kates was just arrested, and the fire people have just realized that when they were killing everyone who could possibly defy them, they overlooked you."

"They overlooked you as well," said the A'lan.

Soon, with the announcement that the Peace Captain was at the gates of the Forbidden Palace, Bet's guess that Tor Kates had been arrested was found to be accurate. But the arrest of the Lan of Peace seemed a minor event now. Her own reaction to the attack, in which she judged she could take some pride, she also discarded as unimportant. As she stood at the A'lan's shoulder, enduring the Peace Captain's fascinated, almost fearful stare, what she thought about was the fire people: about that moment of stunned shock when, for all their strangeness, they revealed themselves to be . . . like her.

Chapter 20

Autumn, Day 34

Under five full moons, on the black wings of our sails, riding on the soft night wind, we slipped up the coast and then waited offshore, hidden by the moving black water and the uncertain, unsteady light. From the decks of our ship we could see the watchfires of the Walker army, glowing along the edge of the seacliff, and marching down the shore by the water's edge. Delan and I and the ship's captain stood together on the deck. The ship rose and fell under our feet. The captain, who earlier had spoken of her lover and children who are imprisoned in those caves, spoke her orders in a whisper, which the members of the crew repeated from ear to ear. No sound could be heard except the slapping of the water on the wooden hull, and the padding of bare feet along the hollow deck, and the faint groaning of timbers. The crew furled the sails and dropped anchor, lowered the scull and tethered it to the side of the ship, then one by one settled onto their heels to wait.

The watchfires on the shore disappeared, one by one, as the water rose to the high tide line, and kept rising.

"They did not know to expect this unusual tide," Delan murmured.

The captain's broad, wind-gnarled hands gripped the deckrail. "Then they have no seafolk in their ranks. Probably, few of them will be able to swim, either."

It was past midnight when the people of Triad began throwing their children into the sea. Soon, the first Mer swam up to the scull, carrying an astoundingly quiet Walker infant in her arms. Only when the crewmembers took the infant from her grasp did the child utter a sharp, startled wail, quickly muffled in a blanket. The infant was handed from hand to hand, across the scull, up the rope ladder, across the deck where I stood next to one of the Orchths, and into the cabins below deck, where more Walkers waited to dry, warm, and try to soothe the fears of the children.

Wailing Walker infants, stunned, sodden Aeyrie infants, wiggling, friendly Orchth pups, each of these I held in my arms briefly, before passing them on to the Walker at my left. Then the toddlers, hysterical with shock and fear, struggling in the grip of strangers, or limp and heavy with exhaustion. Farther down the line, I saw Delan gather up a sobbing Aeyrie child and hold idre as if all the powers of the Universe could not make idre let go again. Now, the older children, shivering and solemn, walking on their own feet, holding each other's hands for comfort: an Orchth and an Aeyrie, hands clutched in each other's fur, two Walker children, so like each other that they must have hatched together from a single egg, one of them clinging in fear to the other, who stared in wide-eyed curiosity at the ship and the passing faces.

I could hear no sound from the distant shore, no shouts or cries. I could only hope that the voices of the children crying as we lifted them into the ship had not carried to the ears of the guards at the cliff's edge. With luck, the unexpected tide would have thrown all the watchers into confusion, and they did not yet realize that their hostages were escaping.

Ara, I said, projecting my silent voice into the sweet depth of water, into the inner ear of my friend who swam there. As I entered into her mind, I felt my own thoughts expand, like a flower blooming. I felt the cold water, buoying my body through the waves. I heard the crash of the breakers, and felt their pulsing power under my finned hands and feet. I saw the stars overhead, and the bright moons, clustered together in a slow, graceful dance. The tide swelled beneath me,

*frightening in its energy, and lifted me firmly toward
the cliffs, where water sprayed, white and silver in the
moonlight. On the side of the cliff I spotted several
small silhouettes: children climbing bravely down the
ladder toward the crash and spray of the waves. And
at the opening of the caves their parents anxiously
watched, waving encouragingly.*

Ara spread her mind like a hunterworm web. Within
that net, I sensed the terror and resolve of the children,
and I recognized how the Mers were holding the children's panic at bay for them. It is unimaginable to me
that an Aeyrie child, with ids inherent horror of water,
could climb alone into that dark maelstrom of stone
and sea; but with the help of the Mers they were doing
it. The adults still in the caves huddled together, their
fear and anxiety shooting out from their spirits like
lightning in a storm. Eia moved among them, a blanket
of calm following behind idre. The Merfriends spoke
out loud the names of the children as they reached the
safety of the ship. On the cliff's edge, the Walkers kept
watch. In the full light of five moons, they should have
been able to see the children suspended from the ladders below, but they saw nothing. The Mers had taken
their senses prisoner, and they saw only what the Mers
wanted them to see.

Ara dove into a twisting agitation of swirling water
and air, singing into the spindle of the crashing wave
and avoiding the tumbled rocks of the shore by the
sound of her echo. I saw through her eyes a thin and
naked child, clinging desperately to the ropes of the
ladder, with the fierce, frigid ocean dragging at his legs.
Out of the writhing water Ara grasped the child, not
just with her hands but with her mind as well, and
simultaneously she let go of me.

I stood on the deck of the ship once again, with an
Orchth shaking me by the shoulder. "More children,"
she growled at me. I do not know how long she had
been trying to get my attention. Hastily I resumed my
place in line, but all the children crossed the deck on
their own two feet, shivering with cold, water pouring
from their bare or furred skin. We held out our hands

to them, holding them briefly as they passed, soothing them with our voices. One of them smiled at me, a sprightly, lively Walker child, already reclaiming its sense of adventure from the confusion of desperate fear. It was the same child whom I had seen Ara about to take into her arms.

Ara said to me, Send the boat now: the Aeyries who cannot fly and the elderly people are next.

I leaned over the deck railing and hissed to get the attention of the Walkers in the boat, who had taken advantage of the hiatus to bail some of the water out of the scull's bottom. "You need to go closer to shore to collect the Aeyries. The Mers don't think they can carry them all the way to the ship."

The crewmembers below signaled that they had heard, and soon the scull had been detached from the side of the ship. They rowed into the darkness, escorted by a dozen Mers.

I found Delan, and we stood together, shivering in the cold wind. The fur of my breast and my arms was soaking wet from all the children I had carried. From the cabins below I could hear, from time to time, a weary wail. We had fretted, earlier that day, about the limited fuel we had for the stove. Every blanket on board the ship had been gathered up for use this night, but we knew it would not be enough for everybody.

Out of the writhing darkness, the scull reappeared. The Walkers, vague, bent shapes in the darkness, leaned into their oars. The scull dragged heavily through the water, with a half-dozen adult Aeyries clinging to its sides. Sodden, weighed down by their wings, they dragged themselves up the side of the ship one by one. One fell and disappeared beneath the surface of the water, only to reappear once again, coughing and choking, buoyed up by the hovering Mers. They all huddled together at last, on the leeward deck, a shivering mass of Aeyrie misery, leaking great puddles of water from their fur. We could not spare them any blankets or towels, but as soon as they had ceased to drip we urged them belowdecks, where at least a warm fire was burning. Some of them went below, and some *of them, worried about others who had not yet reached safety, remained, shivering, at the rail.*

The scull disappeared once again, and as we waited for it to reappear, I overheard some of the stories, of the process by which the people of Triad had decided in what order they would escape the caves, of the grim horror of the first parents to throw their naked infants into the sea, of the murmuring reassurances of the Merfriends; of Feili, and Orgulanthgrnm, and Eia, traveling through the mazes from cave opening to cave opening, encouraging the fearful, and sometimes harshly commanding the reluctant.

When the scull returned with the elderly people and the last of the earthbound Aeyries, Eia was not among them. I turned to Delan, who had been joined at the rail by ids eldest child, Nasha, a quiet thirteen-year-old with the ancient gaze of a Merfriend. "I guess this is not an egg year for Eia," I said.

But Delan shook ids tangled mane and replied in a voice hoarse with exhaustion, "It means nothing. Eia will be the last to leave, fertile or not."

How can I describe that long, nightmarish wait? Hours must have passed as, one by one, the members of Triad found their way to the ship. Many of the Walkers and all of the Orchths, who are strong swimmers, came through the frigid waves on their own power, though the Mers escorted and supported them when they began to tire. When an Orchth grabbed hold of the ladder to climb aboard, the entire ship would tip sideways. I wondered how could the Walker soldiers not have yet realized what was happening right under their noses? Even the Mers have limits on how far they can alter another's perception of reality.

Ara, I said to my friend, Do not get too tired: it is a long night.

She welcomed me once again into her thoughts. She waited now just beyond the breakers, watching the cliff. The siege towers which the Walker soldiers had labored to build for so many days had fallen over and were being crushed to bits by the waves. The moons had begun to sink toward the west, casting the cliffside into shadow. Through this deeper darkness, small bundles were ejected from the caves into the water below, where they floated, buoyed up by chunks of firewood to which they were tied. Clothes for the Walkers, all of whom had made the transit naked, and hopefully some bedding as well. The Mers gathered up the bundles to take them to the ship, but Ara remained in the calmer water, resting. I felt her weariness, and I felt her triumph. It was a night where each one of us had been a hero, but without the Mers it would not have been possible. What an effect Ara's memories of the night would have upon her herd, when she poured herself once again into the common pool of their shared mind! The entire herd would have to change, as she had changed.

I kept my sadness hidden from her. Through her eyes I watched the dark cliff, until at last I saw wings opening in the darkness, as the first flight of Aeyries flung themselves out over the water. And, now, the long feared shout of warning rang out across the water. Perhaps a Walker, wakening suddenly out of sleep, had evaded the control of the Mers. A second flight of Aeyries; and now the twang and whirr of crossbow bolts. Shouting warnings to each other, the Aeyries struggled skyward, their wings beating against the wind. The massive shape of a last Orchth leapt magnificently beyond the crashing spray of the breakers, and hurtled into the water. Two last Aeyries dove together into the darkness. One sprang like an arrow shot at the moons, but the other struggled heavily, a dark shadow dragged down by the hold of the earth.

Eia, heavy with fertility, gambling that ids athletic prowess would keep idre in the air . . . and indeed id would have made it safely to the ship, if not for the bowmen on the cliff, who by now had recovered from their surprise and could take the time to aim carefully in the darkness.

I think I must have made a sound as Eia fell. When I opened my eyes, Delan was looking at me. Ids eyes had a blackness in them so deep that no star could ever have burned there. I did not need to say it; all of the

Merfriends on board that ship must have gasped Eia's name simultaneously.

Ara, I called desperately, *but she did not respond. The scull had already started across the water again, all but dancing across its surface as the oars bit into the waves. The healers, most of whom had been preoccupied with the welfare of the children, began to gather on the deck. Nasha, shoulder-high under Delan's embrace, began to cry against ids fur. But Delan only raised ids gaze to watch as the first of the Aeyries came into sight overhead, graceful, swift shapes in the darkness. And at last some lamps were lit, to guide them to a safe landing.*

They landed to muted greetings and silence, and joined the others at the deckrail. The captain shouted orders, and the crew leapt into action, climbing the rigging, hauling at the anchor chain. But everyone else stood absolutely still, staring in to shore, where the scull had gone. I learned from the Merfriends' whispers that the Mers had searched a long time before finding Eia under the water. They had dragged idre, a limp, dead weight, to the surface. An arrow had pierced ids chest. Id did not seem to be breathing.

From Ara, I heard only preoccupied silence. She was one of those frantically carrying Eia through the thick water toward the scull; she had no attention to spare. I heard the sound of someone sobbing, and realized that it was myself. I wept, not for the person Eia, whom in fact I scarcely know, but for myself, for the Aeyrie people, whose greatest hope for survival in a world shared with the Walkers had fallen, pierced through with a crossbow bolt, into the cold water of the sea.

The ship creaked with the turning tide. The moons sank rapidly toward the horizon. Soon, day would dawn. Suddenly, Ara filled my thoughts. She rode the tide, heaving burning air in and out through her nostrils, watching the scull skud away across the swells. Is Eia dead? I asked her, *but she did not know the answer. The Walker healer on board the scull had leaned over its edge to clip the bolt and slipped it out of Eia's flesh while id still lay half in the water. There*

*had been blood, Ara told me, a lot of it. I felt such
horror that I do not know how long it took me to
realize that Eia's wound would not have gushed blood
like that, unless ids heart was still beating.*

*So they brought id swiftly to the ship, the ambassa-
dor, the Stormtamer, the revolutionary who first envi-
sioned a way for our people to survive, and lifted idre
carefully aboard, and laid idre on the deck in the midst
of the healers. In the harsh light of an air lamp I saw
ids eyes open to Delan's touch, and, with a wry grin,
ids lips pressed briefly to Delan's fingers. Then the healers lifted id up onto a stretcher and carried id away.*

*The sun rose hours ago. I could not sleep, and have
been writing ever since first light. Sleeping people
crowd the deck. The crew must dance around their
prone bodies as they rush to tend the sails. The Triad
onfrits flutter around the masts and crowd the rigging;
where waterstained clothing and blankets flap like laundry in the wind. The Orchths, below deck to protect
their sensitive eyes, are piled with children like so many
fur beds.*

*"Where are we going?" I asked Delan a while ago,
when id briefly left Eia's side to come above deck and
check on Nasha, who sleeps near me.*

*"There is only one place we can go," Delan said.
"Ara's Field."*

Autumn, Day 35

*Feili, Eia, and Orgulanthgrnm were the last three to
exit the caves. Feili's considerable energy now keeps us
organized and out of the way of the ship's crew, a role
which Orgulanthgrnm takes over at night. This is the
way things have always been arranged at Triad. Delan
is a leader of spirit, a keeper of the vision; but when
it comes to everyday matters of sleeping and eating and
getting the chores done, someone else solves the problem. Sometimes, in fact, Delan seems surprisingly isolated in this chaos: a mage, with a mage's ways,
preoccupied by visions, all but overwhelmed by the
vastness of Possibility.*

Orgulanthgrnm was the last to actually climb aboard the ship the night before last. Through the sea he had carried, strapped to his back, the ancient scrying crystal which the mage Pehtal, one of the founders of Triad, first brought to the community fifty years ago. Together, he and Eia had decided that it would be better for the crystal to sleep in the bottom of the sea than to end up in the hands of the army, but it had turned out that Orgulanthgrnm, who like all Orchths seems to only grow stronger with age, could sustain its weight on his back even during that desperate swim.

Now the crystal is safely ensconced in the captain's cabin, where Eia also lies. The healers went into Eia's chest with their knives and their thread, for the bolt had pierced ids lung and ids life was in danger. No one will say yet that Eia will survive: there are a thousand things which can go wrong. But id is still vigorous and hungry for life; I think it will take more than an arrow to kill idre. Sitting at Eia's side as id sleeps, watched over by healers, Delan scries the stone.

Most of us must sleep on deck, where it is too cold to sleep at night. To add to our misery, there is not enough food to go around, and many of the Walkers are seasick.

Autumn, Day 36

In the heat of the afternoon, we sprawl on the bare deck, dozing in the sun as the coastline, nearly out of sight on the horizon, sweeps past us. The wind is friendly, firm and dependable. My wind-crafter friend and I discuss the weather exhaustively. I also have made friends with the ship's navigator, and we spend many happy hours with chart and compass, teaching each other everything we know.

At night, when it is too cold to sleep, I look at the stars. I know them like old friends. I know their light, I know their dance. Through many long nights their beauty has filled my soul and eased my loneliness. It has been too long since I last rode my way alone on the wind, with only these stars to guide me! Will I ever take such a journey again?

Chapter 21

The old sorcerer bowed stiffly at the door of the A'lan's private sitting room. The A'lan waved him in and returned her attention to her morning sweet roll and the book of political philosophy that lay on her knee. Bet got up stiffly from the chair in which she curled, too sleepy after the long night's vigil to read any more of the book she had studied all night, as in the next room, with the door open, the A'lan slept.

"It was a quiet night," she said.

M'bala a'Sal nodded gravely, his hands clasped across his belly. "And do you find the book enlightening?"

"It's interesting. But I don't agree with the basic premise that sorcery, because it is so difficult and frightening a study, ultimately attracts practitioners of the highest moral caliber. Isn't it just as likely to attract people who seek power above all else and are willing to conquer any obstacle to get it?"

"People like me, you mean," said the sorcerer, but he was not offended. "And people like you, of course, have a higher goal. You pursue power to save the world from itself, perhaps."

It had been Bet who first brought up with M'bala the subject of some of the more appalling practices of sorcery. She had been surprised to learn that Walker sorcery had been undergoing a quiet reform over the last twenty years. Lately, their ongoing discussion had taken a more philosophical turn. M'bala brought books for her to read. The wily old sorcerer, Bet realized belatedly, was treating her like a student. And she actually liked him.

"The truth," he prompted her, grinning at her reluctance.

"I think that what I wanted, what I always wanted and what I still want, is self-determination. Just like everybody else in the world."

"So you do seek power above all else."

"Not power over others. Just power over myself."

"M'bala bowed sardonically in her direction. "Then why are you not living, like the Asasaran, in the wilderness?"

Bet bowed in return. "Good morning, sir. And thank you for the loan of the book."

The sorcerer sat in his own accustomed chair. At night, when the fire people had proved themselves more likely to attack, Bet kept guard. By day, M'bala would accompany the A'lan as she held court and conducted business, and delicately reined in the contentious Lans like a herd of half-trained spring drafs. He, too, had deterred his share of the fire people's attacks. But for now, he was reading a book also, which he had borrowed from the A'lan's library: *L'shile Caih: The Novices of Peace*, Eia's first book. "Until tonight," he said.

"Sleep well, Bet," said the A'lan.

Bet marched down the hallway among the scurrying servants, and into the kitchen, where the cook, oblivious to rank, shooed her into the servant's dining room. Breads, cheeses, fruit pies, and pots of tea ranged along the sideboard, but the only other person in the room, a black-dressed female like herself, sat alone at the end of a table cluttered with dirty dishes, picking at a slice of pie.

"When did you arrive?" said Bet.

Peline glanced up, unsurprised to see her there, though at their last parting neither one of them could have imagined that their next meeting would be in the Forbidden Palace, with both of them wearing the A'lan's insignia pinned to their shoulders. Peline examined Bet now with a certain skepticism. "Yesterday afternoon. She sent for me at your recommendation, I hear."

"I told her that you make it your business to know everything, and the intricacies of Walker politics has been your lifetime obsession. I told her that you have been effectively advising Eia for ten years—certainly, the A'lan's position is no less tricky. Of course I recommended you."

"There are a hundred as good as I."

"Well, tell the A'lan who they are. You are the only one I know."

"You did not trust me that night."

Bet finished transfering a slice of pie to a plate, and sat down opposite Peline, helping herself to her pot of tea. She had expected Peline to hold a grudge against her for deciding that her help would only be a hindrance, and rescuing Eia alone. The situation called for tact now, but Bet could only offer brutal honesty. She sipped her tea, which was too strong and not hot enough, and asked, "Do you even trust yourself, when it comes to Eia?"

"What, because I am in love with idre? You, of all people should know what that is like!"

"I do know what it is like to love an Aeyrie. So I know why it is making you crazy."

"What?" asked Peline irritably.

"They seem so fickle to us, but to them it is just flexibility. They come, and they go. They are forever changing their minds. Commitment makes them uneasy; they love for the moment and never say the word 'forever.' They are changeable as the wind . . . and if you can't love that in them, then you can't love them at all. Instead, you will go mad with trying to control them."

Peline clanked her spoon noisily onto the saucer. "So you are having an affair with a Walker male. Are you trying to be as fickle as an Aeyrie, or to find a lover you can control?"

"Great Winds! A lover I can control! Ellin is as fey as. . . ."

Peline, preoccupied with her own obsession, did not notice or care that Bet never finished her sentence. "Besides," Peline said, "it's none of your damn business."

"You brought it up."

"Because I want you to stop meddling with my life! First you prevent me from rescuing Eia, and now you've done everything you can to make sure I never work with idre again."

"Do you really believe that?" Bet took a mouthful of pie, but her appetite had disappeared, and the pie seemed tasteless. "Do you really think I'm spending my precious resources on trying to keep you and Eia apart? Use your common sense, Peline. Why should I even care?"

"Why? Because you're Delan's friend, that's why."

"And why should Delan care?"

This question stopped Peline in her tracks. "What?" The crust of her pie was a crumbled mess, but, like Bet, she had not eaten much of it.

"What do you think I've been telling you? Aeyries don't mate for life. In h'ldat there is not even one word for 'family.' The only relationship which they expect to last a lifetime is the relationship between parents and children."

"But they've been together for twenty years."

"And in those twenty years they've left each other a hundred times. They just keep coming back to each other."

Peline's hair was drawn back tightly in a severe, businesslike bun. Had she ever bared her breasts on festival night and danced drunkenly under the stars? Had she and Eia maybe lain down together on such a night?

Bet said, "If you want to return to Eia, if any of us even survive this disaster, I am certain the A'lan will not keep you here against your wishes." Bet's body felt heavy and earthbound. She had to struggle out of the chair, her swollen belly scraping on the table's edge. She leaned over Peline, who stared up at her, stark-eyed. "But learn to love the wind. And if you can't, then turn your back and walk away."

She had crossed half the distance to her room, which was now in the same wing as the A'lan's suite, when she heard heavy, quick footsteps behind her. It was Peline, as ungainly as all females in this season, running awkwardly toward her. "I heard a voice," she gasped.

"Careful, Peline. I would hate for you to fall."

"I heard a voice. It said—'Tell Bet to go out into the courtyard.' "

"I'll go at once. Are you coming?"

The irony of Delan having to communicate with her through Peline was only one of many ironies in Bet's life. But she found it to be a particularly delicious one, and she grinned to herself as she and Peline waddled back to the entrance hall, and out into the magnificent courtyard of the Forbidden Palace, where the gates stood open now, though still watched over by armed Peace Guards. They saluted as she approached, having been thoroughly instructed in the new order of things. Tipping herself backward to counterbalance the weight of the developing egg within her abdomen, Bet wished passionately for the arrival of Egg Day, when, after a few hours of effort, she could rid herself of the weight and walk gracefully once again.

"Something strange is about to happen," she told the guards.

They eyed her nervously. The A'lan's insignia separated her from people in a way that would have been unimaginable within an Ula, and somehow her sorcerous talent had become known as well. "Something strange? Like what?"

"I'm not sure. Just don't assume prematurely that we're under attack."

The guards saluted once again, but at least one of them also made a superstitious gesture behind his back, a vain effort to ward off a sorcerer's influence. Bet started toward Peline, who had taken a seat on a stone bench in the shade. She felt groggy and stupid with fatigue. Usually, she would be lying in her bed by now, with the heavy drapes drawn across the windows.

Peline seemed very far away. Each time Bet set her feet down, her balance seemed farther out of kilter. Or was the earth itself shifting beneath her feet? The hairs rose on the nape of her neck. She tried to walk more swiftly, but the distance kept seeming to change. She heard a faint screaming, like a wild hellwind slicing itself across the mountains' knife edges. The cobblestones seemed to flow under her feet, appearing and disappearing, now close to her, now far away. She was caught in a current, a torrent of time flowing back into the sea. She could not break free of it. Then the fabric of reality ripped open in front of her, and the screaming winds of the Void shocked across her eardrums. The earth tore open under her feet, and she hung suspended over the endless, mysterious, gaping emptiness of the Void. Scrabbling helplessly for the balance which had now completely abandoned her, she began to fall.

A hand caught her arm. A voice murmured in sweet h'ldat, "Steady, love."

A thunderclap shattered through the silent courtyard. Within the palace, a startled servant gave a shriek, and there was the sound of glass breaking. The winds of the Void fell abruptly silent, the shifting of time and space ceased, and Bet looked once again at only the formal courtyard, the pruned plants dropping their leaves, the paving stones white with a recent scrubbing. She turned, and looked into Laril's face. There were others with idre, but for that moment she could see only the dark eyes still wild from riding the winds of the Void, shielded by an unkempt mane, wings still spread to counterbalance them both against the forces of the Universe.

She turned again and shouted sharply to the guards, "It's all right!"

Frightened faces appeared at the windows. Bet waved reassuringly. "Now that was a sloppy landing," she muttered to Laril.

"If you hadn't been standing in the way . . ."

"Who are these people?"

Laril's bright eyes sparked. Was it hurt Bet saw there, or just the Quai-du dancer, rising joyfully to the challenge? "Your fellow mages and sorcerers, as summoned by the A'lan." One of the Walkers, a male brightly dressed in red and gold astil, stepped forward deferentially, holding out a much-creased paper, with the broken seal of the A'lan still attached.

Bet knew what the letter said. After all, she had helped write it. "She did not summon all of you," she began helplessly.

Peline had arrived by then, and for once Bet did not mind having her take charge. Imperiously, she summoned servants, commandeered a waiting room, arranged refreshments, and sailed off to inform the A'lan of her guests' arrival. "Great Winds," muttered Laril, obviously intimidated, "Who is she?"

The dozen mages and sorcerers filled the waiting room, the wings of the restless Aeyries offering the servants, with their trays of tea and cakes, a nearly impassable obstacle. The dazed sorcerers sat on the ornate, uncomfortable furniture and accepted cups of tea, all except one short, older female dressed in plain peasant's clothing, who examined the priceless woodwork with an air of astonished skepticism. The Aeyries had the look of travelers who had been flying stormwinds for too long. They milled, uncomfortable in a room which did not even have a chair on which they could sit, and did not even try to converse with each other.

Bet took Laril by the arm and dragged idre out into the hall. Id was dressed for war, in quilted cleata-skin and metal vambraces, Quai-du knife tied securely into its scabbard and strapped to Laril's thigh. A scrying glass hung by a cord around ids neck. "What's going on?"

"You tell me, love."

"I mean with—" she gestured helplessly. "The world."

"Ah. Delan and the people of Triad are safely, if you can call it that, aboard the Triad ship, sailing north toward Ara's Field. We intend to join idre to plan our confrontation with the fire people. But three of the sorcerers, when we arrived to collect them (without much hope, I will say, of success), insisted that they had been summoned by the A'lan, and could not go. Delan thought that it would be best to bring them here, and so here we all are. Bet—" Laril grasped her by the arm, and the surprising heat of ids flesh burned through the cloth of her shirt. "Are you going to her? Tell her to put on a show. Some of the Walkers are . . . reluctant to take responsibility for the welfare of the world."

"She's already planning to wear her mask."

"Her mask? What does that mean?"

"The A'lan is masked because she is not acting as an individual. She is a symbol of the land itself, and of all its inhabitants. She speaks for all of them."

Laril's dark, intense gaze held hers. And then it was idre who looked away. "You actually believe that."

"I know more than anyone that she's just an ordinary scholarly woman, reclusive, maybe something of a coward. But when she puts on the mask . . . well, you will see."

"I will never understand Walkers," said Laril wearily.

"Certainly not if you don't try."

Those dark eyes sparked again. Laril leaned closer to her. She could smell ids herb-scented fur, and feel the heat of ids fiercely hot life fire. The tangled, charcoal mane strayed wildly out from ids triangular, sharp-boned face. Id spoke a few husky words, so softly she could scarcely hear them. "Perhaps I just haven't tried enough."

Bet had to lean against the wall for support. "I was up all night with the A'lan," she said, to explain the weakness in her knees.

"Ah," said Laril. But id knew, and ids bright eyes laughed at her, or at idreself, remorseless in their humor and in their frank anguish. "Not with your lover?"

Had someone told idre? Or had id just guessed?

"Ellin is tracking the plague of violence southward, with the others of the A'lan's Hand, trying to get ahead of it, block its spread somehow. I haven't seen him in seven days."

"I wish him well," said Laril sincerely.

Bet felt nasty, incapable of even pretending to be polite. "What about your lover?"

Mildly, Laril replied, "Which one?" Id took hold of Bet's arm once again. She could not bring herself to pull away. "Just tell me, Bet. Are we friends, or are we enemies? It's hard to tell."

She lifted a hand then, to push idre away, and instead found herself paralyzed, with that soft, fragrant fur under her fingers. Laril cautiously put ids arm around her, and then, somehow, she was holding ids slender frame, all muscle and bone, in both of her arms. "Friends," she admitted after a while.

Ids voice as soft as the fur under Bet's fingers, Laril murmured, "Is your egg fertile, Bet?"

"Probably."

"What are you going to do?"

"I don't know. What are you going to do?"

"Whatever I have to do to stay your friend."

"Well—" she lifted her face from ids narrow, bony shoulder. "You, at least, are doing a fine job."

Laril's mouth smiled, but not ids eyes. "A little too late, maybe." Ids gaze shifted to look over Bet's shoulder. "Here comes that frightening female."

"She loves an Aeyrie, too."

"How you must pity her."

Trapped by this truth, Bet could not speak. Laril let go of her. "Whatever I have to do," id said again. But the tone of ids voice said good-bye.

Chapter 22

Later

At midday, Delan came out of the captain's cabin. The sight of idre, simply standing there, doing nothing, was so disconcerting that I rushed over to idre, prepared to hear the worst. But Delan's face, so often drawn with weariness and worry, contained for once a certain calm.

"How is Bet doing?" I asked, guessing that id had been scrying the glass again. I always ask: something about the Walker Bet twitches at my heart, and it is not just that she went out of her way to save my life.

Delan surprised me with a laugh. "She is having quite an interesting day. So," id added, "are we."

And at that moment, the air before us . . . split open. And through that opening walked the five Walker sorcerers who had come, with varying degrees of skepticism, to the convocation. Behind them, the Asasaran herself, and the Aeyrie mages from the three Ulas, with Laril last of all.

I suppose it is a measure of my own peculiar desperation that I was relieved to see them only because each one of them was struggling under the heavy burden of a bag of food.

Autumn, Day 37

"So this is war," Laril said to me.

Id had come up to stand beside me where I leaned

249

at the rail, watching the tangle of Mers swimming in our wake. I turned and looked where idre gazed, across the deck, where Aeyries and Walkers lay or sat, digesting their first real meal in two days. Even those who have been miserably sick for these two days could not resist the smell of that stew.

All of us have the look of refugees. A blank, burned out look in the eyes, a weariness which goes beyond the mere discomfort in which we must travel. Even I, who had no home to lose, must have that look. Certainly I feel it in my soul, a kind of hopeless, weary disdain for the illusions of purpose and meaning with which we usually sustain our lives.

"Yes, this is war," I said. So far, Eia is the only Aeyrie physically injured in the war. But I cannot imagine how our lives will ever again be the same.

Laril grasped the railing. Painfully young, id seemed, bearing too early the burden of knowledge: how fragile we are, how fragile our lives, how fragile our spirits. "The A'lan gives you greeting," id said. "She thanks you again for making that journey. It was not in vain. She asked me to tell you that."

I know this; and yet I do not know it. It is possible that my few words, spoken so passionately to that aging stranger, have changed the course of Walker history. I know this, and yet I shrug dispassionately. What good does it do me, to have changed history? I am still a refugee.

Laril seemed suffused with sadness. Yet id had the good grace not to burden me with whatever lover's pangs id suffers. "We had quite a discussion. Bet had some ideas about the fire people . . . she spoke to me very strongly. We were in agreement, but I never had the chance to tell her so."

"In agreement on what?" I asked.

"Well, it is so easy for us to gather here and talk among ourselves of how we are going to use magic to entrap and destroy them. The Walker sorcerers are great weatherworkers; we are thinking of blocking the fire people into their haven with snow—I can prevent them from escaping through the Void—and starving

*them to death. It may take a while, but eventually the
fire people will die. We know this from what you have
told us."*

*"Yes," I agreed. I felt—I do not know what. Oddly,
I have never felt rage or fear at the fire people and
what they did to me. I suppose it is pity. They have so
much power, and yet they are blind. They are no more
cruel and heartless than children who simply cannot
comprehend the damage they cause. They have been
corrupted by circumstance; they are doomed, ultimately, to death. And even if it were not for this plan
of Laril's, I think that the end would come relatively
soon for them. Though not soon enough, I fear, to
save this world from their meddling.*

*"Bet warned me against the mistake of reducing the
fire people in my mind in the same way they have
reduced us in theirs. They are not just balls of fire or
bolts of lightning: they have an intelligence, a history,
a purpose, a tragic folly. If we are to destroy them, for
our own survival, then we must accept their deaths onto
our conscience. We are destroying a people, a race, to
serve our own ends; just as we are trying to prevent
them from doing. Do not make the mistake, Bet said,
of thinking that our cause is just, and theirs is not."*

"We will destroy them in the end, just the same."

*"Well, there is always a choice. But I, for one, have
no intention of dying so that the fire people can live."
Id gazed once more at the refugees. In ids face I saw
a struggle, but its content the young taiseoch never
revealed to me. Instead, id sighed and said to me, "But
there is a price we must pay for destroying them, and
perhaps in the end it will destroy us as well. Who can
predict what this kind of meddling with the weather will
do to our world?"*

*We stood a long time in silence. All things are inter-
connected, the weathermasters say: rain in one country
means drought in the next; a warming in the south
means disastrous storms in the north. What, indeed,
would it do to us to make a change like this, with so
little forethought, against the inclination of the season
and the region? Would circumstance force us into mak-*

ing a horrendous mistake, blindly, because we are afraid, and desperate, and worried for the welfare of our children?

Laril lifted up ids wings, spreading them slightly to the wind, as if id were testing the air in preparation for taking off. "I must go."

Where are you going? I wanted to ask, for there was something in ids manner and voice which suggested the beginning of a long, hard, dangerous journey. But Laril turned back to me and added, with a quirk of the mouth that communicated to me that id knew perfectly well how ridiculous this would sound, on this day, in this place. "Arman would never ask you, you know that. But you should come back to t'Cwa . . . maybe spend the winter there. We will outfit you for your spring journey, whatever you need."

"Now," I said kindly. "You sound like a taiseoch. My parent must be feeling ids age; and of course you are concerned because ids continuing productivity means continued income for the Ula. So you think that a visit from ids long absent child—"

With an embarrassed grin, Laril turned away, and stepped through an opening in the air, and disappeared.

Autumn, Day 38

Even traveling day and night, we are still five or six days' journey out of Ara's Field, assuming that the weather holds. The mages and sorcerers confer separately, then come together to confer again. The Triad weathermaster laughs at their attempts to predict what the long-term results of their weather meddling will be. "They cannot possibly know," id says simply, and when they come to idre for advice id will not give them any, refusing to contribute to the illusion that they can predict the unpredictable.

They brought Eia out to sleep in the sunshine this afternoon. How white ids hair has become!

We are all going mad with boredom. The children are uncontrollable, and more than one loving relationship has fallen on the rocks. I spend many long hours *in communion with Ara. I keep telling myself that she will never be completely gone from my life, so long as I have so much to remember. But I cannot fool myself into forgetting that for a while I hoped that my days of journeying alone were over.*

Autumn, Day 43

The malaise which overlays this ship took hold of my heart as well, and for five days I have not written in this journal at all. Truth be told, nothing has happened that seemed worth writing about: only the endless petty disputes, emotional catastrophes, and minor tragedies with which we all are miserably harrassed. This is the stuff no historian will record: social upheaval at its worst. Three peoples, of all ages (too many of them children), crammed together into a tiny ship with no privacy; not enough food, clothes, or bedding; and nothing to do. Add into that the spice of sexual frustration, simply because this is that time of year, and the Walkers, whose egg day is far earlier than that of the Aeyries, getting cranky with pregnancy. I suppose it is surprising that we have not all killed each other.

But this morning, at last, there was a change. The navigator and I completed our morning's calculations, located ourselves on the chart, and then both turned simultaneously to peer at the distant shore. When we went below to fetch the captain's spyglass, she and Delan both came up with us, and we took turns examining the rugged, barren coastline of Ara's Field. We have arrived.

Autumn, Day 44

I am writing these words by the light of a flickering air lamp which we could not get calibrated to work properly in the damp. Thirteen people and a half-dozen onfrits are crammed beneath a tarp shelter, which sags wearily under the weight of the pouring rain. Twice already, one or another of us has gone out in a futile effort to tighten the stretching ropes. In the center of our cramped circle, the air lamp flickers spasmodically. All of us are wet, and weary, and chilled to the bone.

We have no fuel with which to build a fire, and we are too cold to sleep.

The storm (a natural storm, not one called forth by magic) blew in during the night, and by daybreak the first drops of rain had begun to fall. We disembarked in a squall, and stood in a miserable huddle on that isolated shore, watching our ship sail away to seek shelter of that southern farming community who lent me the use of their barn roof this summer (we can only hope that the war has not yet reached this far south). Perhaps everyone in the landing party felt the same hopeless disbelief. I do not fear the wilderness, but I have never been so foolish as to venture into it completely unprepared, as we are now, on the edge of winter, and unable to fly. We can easily be completely crushed by these forces which tug at our shelter now.

The Walker sorcerers have surprised me: not the Asasaran, whose stony strength reminds me of Ysbet, or the two fishers, who give every appearance of having endured worse than this, but the others, who seemed at the first convocation to be so engrossed in ensuring their own comfort, and so distracted by petty concerns that the urgency of our situation completely missed their notice. I wondered then why the Asasaran, whose judgment seemed sound enough, had called these spiritual weaklings to so important a meeting. Now something, perhaps the meeting with the A'lan, has summoned forth their true colors: not just a surprising ability for stoic endurance, but persistence, and courage, and even something like integrity.

Laril was expected to reappear some days ago, but there is not yet any sign of idre. I am afraid to ask Delan where id has gone. Ids appearance of strong, implacable resolve is wearing thin, and I think if Delan appeared to weaken, every last one of us would collapse and dissolve, like crackers tossed into a puddle.

Autumn, Day 45

Rain continues. Tonight we are too tired to even argue with each other.

Autumn, Day 47

Yesterday was much like the day before, except that for a few hours in the afternoon the rain stopped falling, only to resume once again by nightfall. With no soil to absorb the rain, the entire countryside has become one vast, shallow river pouring into the sea. Exhausted, we waded wearily upstream, burdened by our sodden bodies. We stumbled and fell on uncertain ground. One of our number injured an ankle and could no longer walk at all. The Orchths, besides all of our gear, now carry idre as well.

This afternoon we at last stood at the edge of the chasm which gives entry into the fire people's haven. The chasm is full of water now. The crack through which I first entered the fire people's abode is invisible behind a whirlpool. With some hunting, we discovered that other opening I remember, the gaping crack in the ceiling of their vast chamber above the river. Half laying in a pool of water, with others holding onto my legs, I hung my upper body into the opening and glimpsed the flooded river in the shadows below. The fire people are almost invisible along the upper rim, faintly glowing patches which seemed to fade even as I gazed at them.

By evening, the rain had let up once again. I followed Delan out from our makeshift camp, and sat with idre on the coarse edge of a cracked stone. "Maybe the elements are already doing the job for us," I said. "Maybe we have mustered enough of a resistance to their manipulations that we already are starving them, to the point that they will not be able to continue their attack. Maybe their numbers are so depleted from the last time they were here that they aren't really able to create a bitter war out of thin air anymore."

"Maybe," Delan said. "But can we afford to be wrong?"

"Can we afford to do what we are contemplating doing?"

"Great Winds—tell me the alternative!"

So I was sorry then, that I had followed idre out like this, because I had exposed ids anguish; layers and

*layers of it, saved up over the many long, terrible days
of this summer and autumn. Worried that I had started
the inevitable crumbling of Delan's facade, I took ids
hand in mine, and we talked—about Ara leaving me,
and Delan's young children's nightmares, about
Delan's fear for Eia, about my fear that I will die with
so much of the world unexplored.*

"Where did Laril go?" I finally asked.

*"Laril is in the Void," said Delan, ids face flat with
weariness.*

*Even the mages themselves are fearful of the Void.
They speak of it hesitantly, struggling with their words.
The Void is an unpredictable mystery, an unexplored
and incomprehensible Universe, where the laws of time
and space are mutable, and nothing can be predicted.
All magic taps into the Void, for magic is nothing more
than a complex, creative manipulation of these laws.
There are some who say that the crystal core of our
world is in some mystical way rooted in the Void,
which is why we Aeyries see visions of the Void in the
depth of the Glass Mountains.*

*Laril, it seems, is an explorer like myself: but the
wilderness which forever draws at ids heart is this ulti-
mate wilderness, the unknown and unknowable country
of the Void. And, as with any other wilderness, those
who venture in do so with full knowledge that they may
never come out again.*

"What does id seek there?" I asked.

*Delan brushed irritably at a stray tangle of ids wet
mane, which persisted in falling forward into ids face.
Though the clouds hung low and threatening, they still
had not begun to drip rain again. In the interim, our
fur had begun to dry, and for the first time in several
days I felt reasonably warm. Delan's own fluffing fur
masked ids gauntness somewhat, though nothing could
disguise the hollowness of ids face. "What does Laril
seek?" id repeated, as if in bewilderment. "Id is young;
id persists in hope when older hearts fail. Perhaps you
have heard some of the stories about the Void—how
people have entered it one day, and exited two days, a
week, a year earlier than they went in. How some say*

they have come out in other worlds, or in worlds so like this one, that they are peopled by the same friends and relatives that the traveler left behind, only in some small or major way it turns out . . . that it is not their home world at all."

Fascinated, I could only listen.

"Laril is looking in the Void for our future. Id hopes to find there the answers to all the questions we could not resolve. What will happen to us if we do nothing? What will happen to us if we alter the weather patterns of the world? These questions which you, too, have been asking yourself."

"If Laril can do such a thing . . ." I could not even complete my sentence, I was so astounded by the possibilities.

"I have a small heart, Tsal," said Delan wearily. *"I just want to see idre alive again."*

Later

It is quite a challenge to continue writing this narrative under these circumstances. I remember that the journals I used to keep, before my accident, were concise, dry things, little more than logs in which I recorded my location and the sites I had measured. I never intended for this one to become such a history, but on the other hand I never expected to end up at the center of this maelstrom either.

Now I find myself nearing the end of my supply of bound paper. Earlier today, as I looked at the few pages which are left, I thought to myself, "Well, this whole business must be over soon, for I am running out of paper on which to record events." Then I laughed at myself; for whether I have enough paper or not, the events themselves will continue.

But now I know that I myself am unlikely to be here to record them.

It has begun to rain again. I am oddly isolated in our shivering huddle of people under the leaking tarp. They gave me the air lamp for my exclusive use, and now no one speaks as I write. They understand that I must be alone . . . I, and Ara, who will not speak to me.

Earlier today, as the members of our party shared our meager supper and watched what we could see of the sunset, the Void suddenly spewed Laril out and closed with a thunderclap behind idre. Id tumbled almost to Delan's feet and huddled there, wings askew, staring up at ids parent's face in amazed disbelief. In ids arm id nestled, tenderly as a new-hatched child, a book.

"This is the right place," said Delan. Only I, who have seen the depth of ids love and worry for this, the child id never raised, knew with what effort Delan remained so calm. We helped Laril to ids feet, and fed idre every last trace of our carefully rationed out meal.

Delan's face became very still as id examined the cover of the book Laril gave idre. "A history of the Aeyrie people," id read out loud, "written by Asil Atal Amil, in the year 1052."

This, of course, is the 526th year after the Forgotten Times. Was this a book written five hundred years in our future? The prospect of reading it only inspired in me a kind of horror. Why would anyone want to know what such a book contained? And how could we refuse to open it, now that it was in our hands?

As one, we turned our baffled faces to Laril. The food seemed to have anchored idre more firmly to this moment's reality. Id said, "The last visitation of the fire people began in the year 1053."

So then we understood. The book contained, not our future, but our precious, insanely destroyed, hopelessly unrecoverable past.

Others must recount what Laril had to say to us then, for I am too tired to record word for word the extraordinary story Laril told us. It is a matter for mages and scholars. No doubt Laril idreself will have to write a book about it. Suffice to say (since my supply of paper, as I have noted, is running out), that Laril traveled both to the past and to the future. Id got lost, and, with help from a distant mage in a distant time, *found ids way home again. I ached with envy, hearing this tale. Id learned and saw more things than a single person should know and see. Ids eyes were wild with knowledge; I can see how one might go mad with it.*

But this is the knowledge which we need now, which Laril delivered to us as coherently as id was able, given ids starved, exhausted, and overwrought state. First, id spoke of our land and our world, with all of our precious soil washed away by torrential rains, and only bare crystal remaining, a world inhabited only by Mers. Is this what will happen to us if we meddle with the weather? Laril shrugged maddeningly. "It is what I saw," id said. Second, id spoke of a world empty of Walkers, dominated by Aeyries. Will we be any better caretakers than the Walkers have been? Laril refused to make that judgment, but I guess by ids silence that the answer to that question is not what one might hope.

Was there a world in which the Aeyrie and Walker population was in balance, and all the peoples of our world lived in peace? There are secrets in that young Aeyrie's eyes: id has decided that there is much that id must keep forever a secret.

"I found something else," id added after a moment. "I found a hellish, horrible world, a world of fire."

We are all stupid with weariness. Laril actually had to explain to us what this discovery meant: A home for the fire people, a place where they can end their hopeless wandering. Laril can take them there, if they will agree to go with idre. If we can somehow communicate with them. If we can make them see us as people, if we can give them reason to trust us.

There is nothing to discuss. It is obvious to everyone that it is I, and Ara, who must approach them. But she will not speak to me.

Chapter 23

The Triad Mers were calling her name. Ara, they sang. Ararararara. . . .

The rains of winter fell, tiny darts of light and air piercing through the surface of the cold winter sea. Below, the plants had folded up their fronds and laid them aside; the small scuttling things which occupy the sea floor had gone into their cottages of sand and shut the doors behind them. The south moving current tugged in Ara's blood. Far, far away her herd had swum by now; chasing the fey sun over the edge of the earth, into that shallow sea where the water slips through castles of coral and polishes the sea plants like jewels.

Oh, she sighed for that warm sea, for the crisp crunch of the salty lettuce in her mouth, for the finely ground sand sifting over her hands, for the tangle of her herd and the slow, sleepy days that rise and fall with the tides. She sighed to be lost once again in the ageless, unforgetting consciousness of her herd: comfortable and painless, fearlessly suspended in the current of time. Oh, she longed to no longer be afraid of that sneaking stranger, death.

Ararararara, sang the Mers.

Oh, Tsal, she sighed. Oh, Tsal must you stand again in the hellwind? Every moment I love you, I also fear for you. I cannot bear the fear any longer.

Tsal: *I cannot do it without you.*

* * *

At the first pale, weary light of the winter sun, Tsal began ids descent. Spinning slowly, suspended like a hunterworm from its thread, id was lowered on a rope into the dark crevice where the river roared. The inner wall of the crevice belled out into a polished curve of white stone. This gray morning's weak sunlight glittered on the reflective stone, stirring the torpid fire people to a faint, nearly invisible shimmer.

Ara saw them through Tsal's eyes. Expecting a feast, they came to this land, but instead they found only more hunger. They are old, but in their age they have left wisdom behind. Traveling through the millennia, they lost their very selves. Everything they once were is lost and forgotten, except for their hunger, and their will to survive. And even that is weak and weary; worn out by the knowledge that they have nothing to survive for. Without passion, they are lost. They have been lost for many long ages. Pointlessly they wander, seeking sustenance in places they have already plundered. Their original purpose they long ago abandoned. They have forgotten who they are.

Ara felt the ropes digging into Tsal's thighs. She felt ids hands gripping the thin rope. She felt the thunder of fear in ids throat. Below, the water plunged through its narrow channel, shoving wildly at the rocks, heaving and struggling within its confines. Its frustrated roar reverberated through the cavern, pressing and releasing against Tsal's ears. Slowly id spun on ids rope, viewing, again and again, the curved, damp walls of the cavern, the fire people shimmering in the faint light of dawn, the struggling river below.

The fire people were hungry. The weak sunlight only whet their appetite. They began to stir and then—

Ara and Tsal were noticed. She felt their attention, like the painful piercing of light through darkness. She laid a single image out onto the doorstep of the mind where she and Tsal resided together: an image of a fiery paradise. Behind the closed door the two of them waited, huddled together for comfort, like children holding each others' hands. Outside, the fire people examined the gift.

They withdrew. They returned. They withdrew again. They returned. They knocked at the door.

We remember you.

Ara said: *There is much we could have taught you, but you never listened.*

We are listening now.

So they listened, and Ara told them: she told of the world they tried to plunder, and why they failed. She told them about the stubborn hearts of the Orchths, and the clever hands of the Walkers, and the inventive minds of the Aeyries, and the ancient memories of the Mers. She told them how hard it was for the world's four peoples to begin to understand each other, and how enlightened they had become in the struggle. She told them the truth about what could be done to destroy them, and why the mages and sorcerers could not bring themselves to do it.

And then, once again, she offered them the gift: Laril's memory of the world id saw, which Ara lifted intact from ids mind. The fire people had experienced enough of Aeyrie minds to know the authenticity of that memory. But would they trust Laril to take them there?

Why have you come back to us, after we would have destroyed you?

So you would believe in our sincerity.

A moment passed, as long as a lifetime.

Then, *We must believe you,* they said.

This was one journey Bet could not take by air. From the beginning, she traveled the hard way: overland, since the ships were at their winter anchor, and the ships' crews had all gone home to sleep the winter through. During the first leg of the journey she had a companion, one of the A'lan's white-dressed servants, who complained of the loneliness and the hoarfrost. This was the first time the servant had tricked her body with lights and stimulants, so that she did not feel compelled to hibernate. But she could not see the wonder of the bitter winter. When Bet reached the Is'isre inlet, she sent her companion away, along with the A'lan's fine, carved and painted carriage and the dancing-hooved young drafs which drew it so lightly.

She rowed herself across the inlet in a boat she rented with a coin laid inside the fisher's door; for everyone was asleep, and the ferry floated at dock, firmly secured to ride out the tides and storms which were yet to come. From the south shore of the inlet she walked, day after day, down the lonely cliff's edge, with the gray ocean at one side and the gray land at the other, with the cold wind blowing through her many-layered clothes, utterly alone, until one night, as she lay sleeping, Orgulanthgrnm's touch awakened her.

"Ysbet," he rumbled. "I thought it was you I smelled on the wind. Let me carry you home."

He played his nishi flute as he carried her through the frosty night, past the boarded up farmhouses and the sleeping draf herds set loose to survive on the dry grass of winter. The stars swept past overhead: a million worlds, a million possibilities, a million dreams. So she came to Triad with her body filled with starlight, and ate her breakfast in a sweet crowd of friends, Aeyrie and Walker, not one of whom had chosen to sleep through the winter with their children. There were pictures to paint, books to write, print, and read; there was love to make, the luxury of childlessness to enjoy, the spring planting to plan.

Among them she found Tsal, bright as a flame among ids maps and charts. The winter winds blew, and the snow fell. They sat together by a warm stove, and they talked about the journeys they would make, the changes they would see. Delan would not leave ids studio in the attic, but Eia left the writing of ids memoirs to join Tsal and Bet for a while, and Bet asked idre to accompany the A'lan in the spring, when she intended to visit every single town in all three of the lowlands.

Eia leaned back in ids stool and laughed. A deep scar still dimpled ids black chest, not yet overgrown by thick, silken winter fur. "Oh, my dear, you do not know what you ask! Two eggs incubate on my hearth. If I come, Delan must come with me, and the two hatchlings, and the Orchth females who have offered to help us nurse the hatchlings, and their young cubs, and our other two children as well. Is the A'lan ready for this?"

"You know Peline can arrange anything. Two eggs!" said Bet in astonishment. It was the rare Aeyrie parent who willingly raised more than two children. To raise four—and two of them hatching at once—was unheard of.

Eia said gravely, "There is a time to be cautious, and there is a time to throw caution to the winds."

"Have you not heard?" said Tsal. "This is the year of the Peace Children."

Bet wrapped her arms around her body, where a soft, heavy bundle was strapped, farmer-style, between her breasts. "I had not heard."

"The Aeyries are going to start rebuilding one of the abandoned Ulas, because so many eggs are expected to hatch this spring. We are naming it Ula t'Caih, the Nest of Peace, in honor of Eia. So this spring's hatchlings are the Peace Children."

When Bet left Triad to continue her journey, now on draf-back, Tsal offered to come with her. So they crossed the gray winter landscape together, cooked journeycakes on hot stones together, and shared body heat together beneath the frosty sky. A strange, peaceful journey it was, though each of them carried their private burdens of sadness and uncertainty. Tsal, who ached with loneliness, missing the Mer who had left idre to return to her herd, and Bet . . . ah Bet, who once and for all had chosen her alliance, only to wonder if she still had a choice to make.

In the middle of a howling snowstorm, they arrived at t'Cwa. They did not need to stand out in the storm to wait for someone to open the lower door, for the door was already unlocked, and a huddle of older l'shans, who had been playing cards and stones by lamplight, hastened to take charge of the drafs. Tsal glanced at Bet with a raised eyebrow, as they started the long, weary climb up the stairs. "I guess we are expected."

"The A'lan sent a letter by onfrit, asking Laril to receive me. I am an ambassador now."

"You always were an ambassador."

"'She did not want to let me go," said Bet. But she could not begin to explain how torn she had become, those last few days, with Ellin and the A'lan both clamoring like children for her to stay.

At the top of the stairs, Laril was waiting. White and silver in the warm light of the common room's fire, id stood silently at the doorway. Worlds and more worlds lay behind ids eyes, the shadows of the Void. Bet took ids hand in hers. There was nothing she could bring herself to say. Id let go of her to greet Tsal, but her fingers still tingled. There was so much she did not know.

"How many books have you brought now?" asked Tsal.

"Ten," said Laril. "The scholars fight over them. The inventors are ecstatic."

"How many more will you bring?"

"I don't know. Sometimes I wonder if I have already brought too many."

"That knowledge is our birthright!"

"Yes. But it is the knowledge of another world—a world where there was no magic, and the Aeyries had not even an inkling that Walkers, Orchths, or Mers even existed. This is our world now—this. And every moment, we make a new decision which alters the future. I am concerned that we will forget that it is this moment which matters."

With a few whispered words, Laril sent several l'shans scuttling on errands. "Come with me," id said, "You must be cold." As the two of them followed Laril down the hallway, many came out to greet Tsal with the whoops and whistles of a hero's welcome. Tsal, who had never ceased to insist that it had been Ara alone who convinced the fire people to leave, hung ids head in embarrassment. As for Bet, many kissed their palms and clasped her hands between them, greeting her as they would one of their own who had been on a long journey.

Bet watched the bright wings and slender, muscular thighs of Laril as id walked ahead of her. Id wore only the thick, deep fur of winter. Ids mane flowed loose except for a single silver braid with a few beads and a colored thread braided into it. At the leading edge of ids wing, the fine sensing hairs caught the light of a passing lamp: filaments of light in winter's gloom.

She had heard that the many long, strange journeys through the Void had changed idre. Id had greeted her formally, had in fact scarcely spoken to her. The long winter lay before them: the wait for spring and the hatching of the Peace Children. After Bet told idre why she had come back, id would have plenty of time to ponder.

At the doorway of a bedroom suite on the third level of the Ula, several sh'mans and a healer had gathered, Arman among them. Within, a banked fire smoldered, and a steaming tray of food sat on the table. The woven kipswool coverlet on the bed was new: Walker work, purchased with trade credits. On the wall hung the portrait Delan had painted of Bet and Laril, leaning heavily on each other, illuminated by light spilling through an open door, framed in a dark hallway where stars could be seen through a distant window. So Delan had first seen them together six years ago now, and that very night had begun painting this portrait. Both of them looked very young.

With all of ids counselors surrounding idre, Laril turned to Bet at last. "I wrote back to the A'lan that we are more than willing to shelter an ambassador at t'Cwa. Will she send other Walkers to the other Ulas?"

"I think so, when she finds the right people. Her government is very young."

"You plan to spend part of the year here, and part of the year in the lowlands."

"Yes."

"And your child?"

It was like a taiseoch, to fill the room with counselors, and then ask a question which cut to the heart like this. For the taiseochs, there are no private choices.

Bet touched the ornately embroidered, delicately quilted case, a gift of the A'lan, in which her egg had traveled, no light burden, strapped against her breasts. She could not even be certain that the egg had survived the winter cold. Normally, one would have waited for the hatching before embarking on a journey.

"I want my child to be hatched and raised here at t'Cwa. I am asking you, Laril—to be the child's hearth-parent."

"What about the child's other parent?" Laril asked softly.

"He has released all his claims. Laril, of course I don't expect you to decide right now."

Laril glanced at ids counselors, but none of them spoke. The healer stepped forward and helped Bet to unbuckle the straps of the case. Beside the warm fire they unpacked the egg from its layered wrappings. Holding it in both ids hands, the healer lifted the egg to the light of the fire. Through the translucent sheath the firelight shone, red and gold. And there, within a tiny Universe of thick fluid, nourished by a rich deposit of yolk, a red heart beat.

Id gave the egg to Bet and she huddled her body over it to keep it warm while the healer built a little cairn of eggstones, which moderate a fire's heat to the proper temperature, on the hearth. But it was Laril who took the wrappings and made a soft nest within the stones, and took the egg out of Bet's lap, and laid it there.

"Hear me," said Laril. "With my own hands I have laid this egg upon the hearth. The child who hatches will be my own child, and I will nurse it at my own breasts, and I will love and raise it to its wingday—" Here Laril faltered, glancing at Bet, with a spark of humor piercing through ids solemnity. Walker or no, perhaps the child would indeed fly. "—when I will release the child to the wind."

Suave and urbane, Laril accepted congratulations, doled out refreshments, and planned the announcement that id would need to make in a few hours at the common meal. Arman and Tsal left in search of a map, without which Tsal did not seem able to carry on a conversation of any length. The counselors soon followed after them. Laril closed the door on the last of them, and leaned on it, heaving a sigh of relief.

"You must have known," Bet said accusingly.

"The A'lan wrote me a very frank letter. I gather she cares for you a great deal. But there was nothing to consider. I told you I would do whatever it takes, Bet. So did you think I would refuse to raise a Peace Child?"

Lithe and slender, Laril paced to the table to fiddle with the remains of the food. Bet's wet cloak and boots already stood by the fire, now she removed another layer of damp clothes, and hung them up as well.

"Why did you decide to come back?" Laril asked.

Bet remembered: the excitement and terror of those critical days as the pace of violence across the lowlands slowed, and finally ceased. Ellin, returning to the Forbidden Palace, happy as a Quai-du dancer on a dangerous wind. Then the settling down, the wheels of state beginning to grind, the sycophants coming to call. The lowering clouds of late autumn, the garden falling dormant, Egg Day, Bet awakening suddenly in a bedroom nearly as plush as the A'lan's, with an aching longing in her heart.

"I wanted to hear the wind," she said.

"Careful. You're starting to sound like an Aeyrie."

"I realized that I love the Walker people only so far as they ally themselves with the Aeyries. I even love Ellin only so far as he reminds me of an Aeyrie. But most of all, I love the wind."

"You sound like an Aeyrie," said Laril after a moment, "Because you practically are one."

"I grew wings, didn't I? All I need now is extra eyelids, hollow bones, fur. . . ."

"Oh, no." Laril held the back of a high stool as if for support. "Not fur," id said.

Bet had to sit down on the edge of the bed. Only passion can cross the gulf, she thought. Only passion.

"Are you having trouble with these buttons?"

Laril stood over her. Those soft, sensitive hairs at the edge of ids wings tickled Bet's fingers. Laril's wings trembled, and she heard the breath begin to rasp in ids throat. Ids fingers fumbled with the damp buttonholes. She touched ids wings again, soft as astil, warm as milk . . . Laril began to collapse against her, and they were falling together, falling into a depth of sky. And then the wind caught them, and carried them.

Spring, Day 15

Winter's grip is easing here in the south, and I arrived at the farming community at the edge of Ara's Field to find that several Triad farmers, who have come by ship to help put in the first crop, are here before me.

I am eager for this journey. But I don't know how I'm going to endure the loneliness.

Spring, Day 16

An astonishing thing. I could not believe my eyes; I had to land to get a closer look. In scattered patches across the wasteland, there is greenery. Tiny, tough threads of bright green grass, rooting in a layer of dust as thin as my fingernail. Brief little lives these tiny plants must lead, over almost as soon as they have begun—already, many of them are beginning to give off spores. I pressed some samples to bring back to the botanists. Such hope they give me.

Spring, Day 17

When I awoke in the morning, I heard her voice in the sea.

Ara.

*She pierced me with her joy. I knew, she said, that
I would find you here.*

*I actually waded out into the waves to hold her in
my arms. Now that I have been half Mer, I forget how
easily water can kill me.*

*She found her herd, and gave up all her memories
to them, and lost herself in them, as she had to do.
But when the currents turned toward spring, they gave
the memories all back to her, and separated her from
the herd once again. "It is clear to us that the world is
changing," the herd said. "It is clear that you have a
new current to swim."*

*Now she is swimming to Triad to join the herd there.
But she is not gone. No, she is not gone. I feel her
here, bright and liquid, gentle and rich as the sea.*

We have a whole world to explore, she and I.

DAW

Laurie J. Marks

THE CHILDREN OF TRIAD

☐ **DELAN THE MISLAID: Book 1**   (UE2325—$3.95)

A misfit among a people not its own, Delan willingly goes away with the Walker Teksan to the Lowlands. But there, the Walker turns out to be a cruel master, a sorcerer who practices dark magic to keep Delan his slave—and who has diabolical plans to enslave Delan's people, the winged Aeyrie. And unless Delan can free itself from Teksan's spell, it may become the key to the ruin of its entire race.

☐ **THE MOONBANE MAGE: Book 2**   (UE2415—$3.95)

Here is the story of Delan's child Laril, heir to the leadership of the winged Aeyrie race, but exiled because of an illegal duel. Falling under the power of an evil Mage, Laril must tap reserves both personal and magical to save the Aeyrie people from the Mage's deadly plans for conquest—plans which if successful, would set race against race in a devastating war of destruction.

☐ **ARA'S FIELD: Book 3**   (UE2479—$4.50)

For many years, members of the Community of Triad have been striving to make it possible for the four primary species of their world to coexist. Now, the sudden, ugly murders of many high-ranked Walker and Aeyrie officials have shattered all hope of peace. Caught in the chaos of imminent war, the children of Triad must discover who is playing this deadly game of death and somehow force them to stop—before their world erupts in a genocidal war of species against species.
